"I want to love somebody, Lib."

He smiled as charmingly as ever, but his eyes remained solemn.

"What if this woman you care about doesn't want kids?" What if this woman he "cared about" was like Libby? But she wasn't going to think about that.

"I don't know. I don't have all the answers. You asked me what my wish was, and that was it." His voice was as chilly as the air over the frozen six hundred acres of Lake Miniagua.

Tucker had been her friend her whole life. When no one had asked her to dance in the seventh grade, he had—and seen to it his friends followed suit. When her mother died when she was fifteen, and her father committed suicide a few years later, he'd supported her through all the stages of grief until she could bear it. He'd bought her the telescope that time. "See the stars?" he'd said. "They're still there. Wish on them if you want."

Sixteen years later, she still wished on stars, and counted on him to be there if she needed him. The least she could do was try to make this one wish come true for him.

"I'll help."

Dear Reader,

The Happiness Pact wasn't the book I intended to write when I first presented the idea to my editor. It was meant to be a funny and gentle journey through the courtship of friends. Then clinical depression inserted itself into the story and it became much more. While the humor and gentleness stayed because they were inherent parts of Libby and Tucker, their journey had some unanticipated twists and turns.

Authors aren't supposed to have favorites—I think it's one of those unwritten rules. But from Libby's messy braid to Tucker's klutziness, as their story led me to those places I never intended, I fell in love with the book, the people, and—once again—Lake Miniagua. I hope you do, too.

Liz Flaherty

HEARTWARMING

The Happiness Pact

—

Liz Flaherty

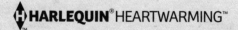
HARLEQUIN® HEARTWARMING™

Recycling programs
for this product may
not exist in your area.

ISBN-13: 978-0-373-36866-2

The Happiness Pact

Printed in U.S.A.

Liz Flaherty retired from the post office and promised to spend at least fifteen minutes a day on housework. Not wanting to overdo things, she's since pared that down to ten. She spends nonwriting time sewing, quilting and doing whatever else she wants to. She and Duane, her husband of...oh, quite a while...are the parents of three and grandparents of the Magnificent Seven. They live in the old farmhouse in Indiana they moved to in 1977. They've talked about moving, but really...forty years' worth of stuff? It's not happening!

She'd love to hear from you at lizkflaherty@gmail.com.

Books by Liz Flaherty

Harlequin Heartwarming

Back to McGuffey's
Every Time We Say Goodbye
The Happiness Pact

Harlequin Special Edition

The Debutante's Second Chance

My heartfelt gratitude goes to Danna Bonfiglio, who introduced me to Venus and inspired me to make it Libby's guardian planet in a way I never could have imagined on my own. Danna's commitment to the high school students she teaches is an even greater inspiration.

Thanks also to author Jim Cangany, whose wholehearted sharing of his knowledge of clinical depression made *The Happiness Pact* a better book. I couldn't have written it without his answers to my shamelessly intrusive questions.

In nearly every town there is a building full of books, CDs and DVDs, there for the education, enlightenment and pleasure of all who enter. I work in one, have had cards in others and appreciate every one of them, so it is to libraries—and to their tireless librarians, boards and Friends—that this book is dedicated.

CHAPTER ONE

LIBBY WORTH TAUGHT the primary class at St. Paul's when Mrs. Miller wasn't there, tended bar at Anything Goes Grill when Mollie needed a night off and quilted with friends on Sunday afternoons. She made pastries for Anything Goes and the Silver Moon Café because she loved to bake and because sometimes she needed the money. She owned, operated and loved the Seven Pillars Tearoom and lived in a spacious apartment above it with her Maine coon cat, Elijah.

Her very favorite thing was to stand in her backyard and peer into the eyepiece of her telescope. Her knee-trembling, heart-pounding fear of thunderstorms was no match for her fascination with the light show offered by the sky. Besides, Venus was her guardian planet. Other people had guardian angels, she was fond of saying, but her mother made sure she had a whole planet.

She liked country music, high school football and reading travel brochures. She never went anywhere—she'd only been in the states whose borders kissed Indiana's—but someday she was going to visit all those places. Someday.

Seventeen and a half years ago, on prom night, she'd been in an automobile accident that killed three people and forever changed the lives of the other nine in the church van they'd used for transport. The losses had caused ripples in the small community of Lake Miniagua that could still be felt all this time later. The wreck had come almost exactly a year after Libby's mother's death from cancer, and a year before her father's suicide.

Everything had changed with that painful string of events, naturally enough, but she'd made a life for herself in its aftermath. Although that life was mostly uneventful, she never lost the feeling that any minute now, the other shoe would drop.

Today was New Year's Eve. It was also the day she turned thirty-four. Looking into the mirror in the corner of the tearoom kitchen that morning, she'd been pretty sure her jaw was softening and the double chin she'd always had a touch of was generating a third tier.

"Yo, Lib."

The shout from the front foyer of the big old Victorian on Main Street startled her before she could get good and depressed about the life she had a feeling she'd slept through. She looked up at the schoolhouse clock on the wall and flinched when she saw that it was nearly a quarter past eleven. The tearoom had opened for business ten minutes ago and here she was standing in the kitchen with an unbaked quiche in her hands.

She slipped it into the empty oven. "Be right there!" She stopped in front of the mirror again to tuck her brown hair behind her ears—she'd forgotten to put it in its customary braid that morning—and frowned at her round face with its freckled nose and slate-gray eyes. She pushed her wide mouth into a smile, tucking in the corners with her fingertips the way her mother had when she was a child. The memory made the smile genuine, and she stepped through the door.

Tucker Llewellyn, the best guy friend a girl ever had, was at the antique buffet that she really needed to move. While there was enough space for the swinging door to clear the piece of furniture, there wasn't enough room to keep her from walking smack into him.

He caught her before they both fell, pulling her clear of both the buffet and the door. He gave her a quick hug and kissed her forehead in the process. "We have to quit meeting like this. You know the lake grapevine. We'll be having kids by sunset."

She laughed, shaking her head and pushing away from him. "We've had that talk. I don't want kids. I want excitement. Adventure."

"Hey, look at my nephew, Charlie. Believe me, that kid's absolutely an exciting adventure."

"You're right about that." Libby handed Tucker his regular to-go cup of coffee. "You want an early lunch?"

"I do, but I can't. Jack and I are working this morning to keep the office from being such a crazy place when the plant opens back up after New Year's. I came by to remind you about the party at Anything Goes. Want me to pick you up?"

She quirked an eyebrow at him. "So I can drive us both home?"

"Probably." His grin was not only infectious, it was gorgeous. As were his corn-flower-blue eyes, streaky blond hair and the way he tilted his head to one side when you talked to him. It was a pity the man she'd known ever since he was born the New Year's baby when she was twenty-seven minutes old had absolutely no romantic effect on her. He might be her favorite man in the world—she was closer to him than to her brother—but he was just Tuck.

And he invariably drank too much at their shared birthday party. When it came to liquor, he was a complete lightweight. He probably was about other things, too, but she loved him anyway.

"We're thirty-four, although you are a day older than I am," he said, reminding her of what she'd been perfectly content not think-ing about. "You've been driving me home from birthday parties ever since high school. It's my turn."

"At least. The way I figure it, you need to drive *me* home until we're in our fifties." She waved when the front door opened, admitting Marie Williams and her daughter, Kendall. Marie had been in their high school class, and Libby thought resentfully that she still looked seventeen. She could probably still do the splits and be the top tier in a cheerleader pyramid if she was so inclined. "Do you want to take Jack some coffee?"

But Tucker didn't answer her. His attention had already strayed. He went to greet Marie with a hug, seeming not to be in a hurry anymore. Libby shook her head, ignoring a ribbon of sadness the couple's seemingly mutual attraction created at the back of her mind. She liked being single, always had, but sometimes it would be nice if someone looked at her the way Tuck was looking at Marie.

"Hey, Kendall." Libby plastered on a smile for the twelve-year-old who'd gone to stand in front of the shelves holding the tearoom's collection of cups and saucers. "Choose your cup and we'll fill it with whatever you want to drink."

"Can I drink soda out of these cups?" The adolescent reminded Libby of herself at that age. She was a little overweight and awkward in the bargain, and Libby sometimes had the impression she was a disappointment to her busy beautiful-people parents.

"You sure can. I drink water out of them all day long. Help yourself to whatever you want and give Elijah a good rub—I tossed him on the floor this morning when I got out of bed, and he's feeling neglected. You want quiche when it comes out of the oven? It's your favorite kind today."

"Yes, please."

"Hey, Lib, can I get Jack a cup, too?" Tucker stood near the coffee urn. Marie went to join her daughter at a corner table.

"It's been a whole three minutes since I asked you if you wanted some for him." Libby moved to fill a cup for Tucker's brother. "You picking me up at seven?" She smiled sweetly and tipped her head in Marie's direction. "Or do you have another date by now?"

"Be nice." He took the cup from her. "I'll see you tonight." He bent his head to peck her cheek as he always did, but she was turning to look at the door at the same time and the kiss landed on her mouth.

It wasn't a peck, exactly. And Libby felt a little ripple along her spine.

Obviously she needed some caffeine to clear her head.

OTHER THAN AN addiction to coffee and tea, Libby wasn't much of a drinker, but she loved the bourbon-laced hot chocolate that was a specialty of Anything Goes Grill. She usually had just one, and even then only on special occasions. Like when the Miniagua High School Lakers had won the football sectional in November or when the tearoom had ended the previous year not only in the black, but in the *very* black.

Even more occasionally, if she was out with friends and one of the others was driving, she'd have two mugs of the delicious concoction. They always sat at the bar and begged Mollie for the recipe, but she never gave it. Libby tried to duplicate it every time she filled in for the bartender but hadn't yet mastered it. She had never had more than two hot chocolates from the Grill.

Until now.

All the presents—mostly gag gifts but some not—had been opened. Midnight, complete with many champagne toasts and a cacophonous rendering of "Auld Lang Syne" and the birthday song as a medley, had come and gone. Jack's fiancée, Arlie, who was the resident designated driver, had confiscated Tucker's keys.

The Grill emptied quickly. By twelve

thirty, there were fewer than a dozen people at the tables, four or five more at the bar.

"You know—" Libby spoke softly, because the sound of her own voice was intolerably loud in her ears "—my real wish now that I'm thirty-four is for a little adventure. Nothing big like a trip to Europe or Hawaii, just something more exciting than deciding which quiche and which tea are the specials of the day."

Tucker blinked owlishly. "Huh?"

She'd forgotten the hearing loss that made him tilt his head. It made him seem exceedingly adorable, especially after she'd partaken of three mugs of the Grill's chocolate.

Rather than raise her voice, she moved to sit beside Tucker in the chair her brother, Jesse, had vacated when he'd left a few minutes past midnight. Libby repeated her birthday wish.

He blinked again. "You have very pretty eyes. Did you know that?"

She rolled them. At least, she was fairly certain she did. They didn't seem to be stopping quite where she wanted them to. "They're battleship gray."

"No." He leaned closer to stare into them.

"They have little blue sparkles around the edges of—what is it you call the colored part?"

"I call it Iris in my right eye and Georgina in my left. And there isn't any blue there, unless bourbon and Mollie's secret ingredient interfere with your vision. Which could well be," she conceded and peered into their mugs. "These are empty."

Mollie brought clean cups. "Chocolate's all gone, but the coffee's fresh and free. Enjoy."

"So, about this adventure. What would you like to do?" Tucker sipped his coffee, then gave it a suspicious look. "This might keep me awake."

Libby gave the question some thought. "I'd like to go skiing. I've never done that. I mean—it *is* winter."

"I noticed that. The snow was a dead give-away." He nodded, his lips pursed as if he were in deep thought. "What else?"

"Parasailing. Zip-lining. Niagara Falls. Go to a casino with a whole two hundred dollars I don't mind losing. Can you imagine that? I've whined over a twenty before." She leaned in close again and whispered into his good ear. "Skinny-dipping. Of course, I'd wear a swimsuit, because I wouldn't want to scare the fish or anything."

He squinted at her. "It's not skinny-dipping if you wear a swimsuit."

She straightened, offended. "It is if I say it is."

He started to answer but must have thought better of it and nodded.

"What's *your* birthday wish?" She took a drink of coffee, reflecting that it tasted better than the chocolate had. Maybe she wasn't meant to drink alcohol. Although that buzz—which was already settling down into a quiet little hum—was kind of fun.

"You won't believe me."

"Try me."

He shrugged. "Okay. But I've never told anyone this." He raised a peremptory finger. "Don't laugh, either. You know how easily I cry."

She snorted. She could count on one hand the times she'd seen him cry, not counting when they were in the same room in nearby Sawyer Hospital's newborn nursery—and anything she said about that would be pure conjecture. The last time had been at Arlie and Jack's impromptu engagement party only a few days before. Libby had been the one who brought him to tears, and she'd loved it. "Let's hear it, big boy. Your secret will be safe with me."

After clearing his throat, finishing his coffee and clearing his throat again, he said, "I want to get married. I want to have a kid. I want to buy a house that's just a house—you know, four bedrooms, two baths and a basketball hoop in the driveway. With a garage that's too full of sports equipment and garden tools to get the cars in it."

She stared at him, aghast. "You have the Alba…the Hall. It's a mansion. Why do you want a house?"

"You can call it the Albatross—Jack and I do. We both hate it, but I'm the one stuck living in it since Grandmother died in the spring. We're thinking about selling the whole estate. That's what I wanted to talk to Marie about this morning—she's a Realtor."

"Oh." Libby was a little pleased by that, although she couldn't have said why. "So, why don't you do all that? You're rich. You always have a beautiful girlfriend. Or more than one." She grinned at him. "You know where babies come from."

"No." His voice was quiet suddenly. Serious. "I want to love somebody, Lib. I don't have to be completely over-the-top about it, but I want to care about someone and have a family with her. I want her to care about me and having kids and maybe planting flowers. Someone's gotta use those garden tools in the garage." He smiled as widely and charmingly as ever, but his eyes remained solemn. "I'm thirty-four—no one knows that any better than you, since you're even older than I am— and if I'm going to umpire my kids' baseball games, I need to do it before my knees give out. I don't want to wait on the kid thing."

"What if this woman you care about has a career? What then?"

He put an arm around her shoulders and spoke patiently, just as though she were a small and not-too-bright child. "I do believe two-career families flourish all over the world, even on the shores of Lake Miniagua, Indiana."

"What if she doesn't want kids?" What if this woman he cared about was like Libby? She wasn't going to think about that. Not on her birthday. Or his. For this day, her secret would just stay in the dark place she kept it.

He hesitated, and she sensed his withdrawal. It was as if a cold breeze shot between them, leaving gooseflesh on her arm.

When he spoke, his voice was stiff, as chilly as the air outside the windows that looked out over the six hundred frozen acres of Lake Miniagua. "I don't know. I don't have all the answers. You asked me what my wish was, and that was it."

He had been her friend her whole life. When no one asked her to dance in the seventh grade, he had—and he'd seen to it his friends followed suit. When she'd had her appendix removed during freshman year, he'd brought her homework and helped her do it. Her mother died when she was fifteen, and he'd supported her through all the stages of grief—over and over again—until she could bear it. Her father's suicide a few years later had thrown her right back into the maelstrom of mourning, and Tucker had been there for her again even though life had dealt him some hurts of his own.

He'd bought her the telescope that time. "See the stars?" he'd said. "They're still there. Wish on them if you want, but they're their own reward. No matter what happens, the stars will guide you to a safe place. You'll be able to see Venus up close and talk to her whenever you like." He'd never laughed at her assertion that Venus was indeed her guardian planet—and feminine in the bargain.

Seventeen years later, most of which he'd lived in Tennessee, she still wished on stars, talked to Venus and counted on Tucker to be there if she needed him. The least she could do was try to make this one wish come true for him.

"I'll help." She nodded and smiled thanks at Mollie when the bartender topped off their cups. "I'll introduce you to women. I know you better than most anyone, and I see people every day. What are your specs?"

"My what?" The coolness was gone, but now he looked befuddled.

"You know, specifications. Blonde? Brunette? How old?"

He shrugged, and she knew the I-don't-care gesture was legitimate. While Tucker had dated a lot of beautiful women, he'd dated even more who weren't.

"You know me as well as I know myself," he said. "If you want to play matchmaker, I'll go along for…oh, say six months. Provided."

She raised an eyebrow. "Provided?"

"Provided we use the same six months for me to grant your wish. You introduce me to prospective wives and mothers to my children and I'll introduce you to adventure. What do you say?"

She arrowed a look at him. "I say you had one too many of those hot chocolates."

"Hey, if I know anything, it's adventure. That's why when Jack and I divided up the CEO job at Llewellyn's Lures, I got all the travel parts. Even when I headquartered at the Tennessee plant, I traveled to Michigan at least a half dozen times a year. That meant I stopped at all points in between just in case I'd missed something along the way."

"I can't travel. I can't afford it, for one thing, and I have the tearoom, for another—which I'm going to enlarge this year by making the carriage house into a smallish event center. I need my adventures to be of the cheap, two-hour variety."

"You have Sundays and Mondays off and an assistant manager who'd love to have some time in there without her micromanaging boss."

As much as Libby hated to admit it, that

part was probably true. Neely Warren had owned her own tearoom in Michigan before retiring to the lake with her husband a few years before. She'd been one of Libby's most loyal customers, and when her husband asked for a divorce, Neely asked Libby for a job. Libby had agreed hesitantly, but it had been one of the best decisions she'd ever made.

"All right," Libby said cautiously. "Let's try it. You need to come to my church tomorrow. There's someone there I want you to ask out. She's a single mom, and she's really nice. She has a beautiful garden, so I'm sure she likes planting flowers, too. I've never been to her house, but if it doesn't have the four-and-two combination, you can buy a new one."

"Tomorrow is New Year's Day. It's my birthday." He looked at the clock behind the bar. "Well, actually, it's already my birthday. I think people should sing to me again."

"It's also Sunday. St. Paul's has never yet closed due to hangovers within its congregation. And you don't need to be sung to anymore."

He sighed so deeply she felt its vibration in the arm that lay alongside hers. She got gooseflesh again. "Okay. Fine. Ten o'clock service?"

"Yes." She got to her feet. The Grill would close soon, and Jack and Arlie already had their coats on.

"I'll be there." Tuck finished his coffee and stood, holding her coat for her to slide her arms into. "Ground rules. I won't hold you responsible if you introduce me to entirely unsuitable women—"

She planted her hands on her hips, her coat hanging loose from one shoulder. "I would never—"

He talked right over her, tucking her arm into the empty sleeve. "—and you won't screech and get all girly when I choose adventures. Shall we shake on it?"

She extended her hand, then snatched it back. "I never screech." Except for that time there had been bats in the attic of the tearoom and Tuck and Jesse had come to get them out. She'd cowered under a table in one of the dining rooms. Screeching the whole time.

"Then you won't have a problem agreeing not to." Tuck grinned at her, and she knew he was remembering the bat incident. The fact that he didn't mention it was only one of the things that endeared him to her.

"Okay." She slipped her hand into his, her breath catching a little at the warmth of his touch. They might have been just friends forever, but he was still an attractive guy and she was a girl who hadn't had a boyfriend for a while. She withdrew her hand, pulling on her gloves. "I'll see you in the morning."

"Right."

"Actually, you'll see each other in the car. Arlie's the designated driver, remember?" Jack, a bearded, glasses-wearing replica of his ten-months-younger brother, grasped Tuck's scarf and towed him along, gesturing for Libby to precede them toward the door.

When they reached Seven Pillars, Tucker walked Libby to the back door. "Happy birthday, older-than-me." He scrubbed a hand through her hair, which she'd worn down for the occasion. The friction created sparks.

"Happy birthday, sweet young thing."

He hugged her, then kissed her cheek. She thought she felt a few more sparks, but that must have been leftover effects of the hot chocolate. Had to have been.

"Tomorrow, after church and once I meet

your friend, you and I are taking off." He smiled cheerfully. "You'll want to dress warm and bring an overnight bag."

Libby's mouth dropped open, although she didn't realize it until his tap on her chin prompted her to close it. "Overnight bag?"

"Yup." He winked. "The adventure begins."

CHAPTER TWO

"CHEMISTRY? HOW CAN you possibly know there was no chemistry? You talked for all of two minutes in the fellowship room." Libby sat sideways in the passenger seat of Tucker's Camaro, her hands lifted in supplication. "It was barely long enough to exchange phone numbers." And how could anyone female possibly be with Tucker and not feel chemistry? Other than herself, of course. She never felt anything—the sparks the day before had been purely imaginary. Even if they hadn't been, the knowledge that he wanted kids and that he would drive her insane within minutes was enough to put out any fires.

"Which we did not do, because her kid bit me." Tuck held out his hand to show Libby the barely visible teeth marks. For the third time. "Fasten your seat belt."

"It is fastened. He probably felt threatened."

"After he bit me, he called me something I'd have gotten my mouth washed out for saying when I was in *high school*, for heaven's sake. Then he threw his cookie on the floor and stomped on it. Calling me a name is one thing, but wasting one of Gianna Gallagher's cookies is just ridiculous. I'm pretty sure I saw Father Doherty cross himself."

Libby rolled her eyes. "He's a priest. That's his job."

Tuck snorted. "He did it to keep himself from hiding the rest of the cookies."

"What did Allison do?"

"Nothing. She said it was nice to meet me but that it probably wasn't a good idea right now. I agreed. We smiled pleasantly and I ate another cookie. I must admit your church has excellent cookies and coffee."

"Doesn't yours?" She knew it did—she'd been there with him.

"I don't know. When I do make it there, I'm usually late. I sort of slip in after everyone's done shaking hands and sit in the back pew."

"Where are we going?" She frowned when he turned onto the highway heading south.

"You'll see."

"You do realize I'm hungry, right? Do I get lunch on this adventure?"

"How long do you think you can wait before you expire from hunger?"

"Probably about ten minutes." She gave him a pointed look. "If there'd been any cookies left by the time I finished applying first aid salve to your hand, I probably wouldn't be that hungry."

"Think so, huh? Well, then." He turned the car sharply so that her shoulder bounced against his.

"What are we doing here?" She frowned at the Hall as he drove around to the back of it. She could count on one hand the number of times she'd been in the Llewellyn mansion, although she probably knew every inch of its grounds. Tucker and Jack's grandmother had never welcomed their friends inside.

"Having lunch."

"You're cooking?" As far as she knew, Tucker's culinary skills started and ended with microwave popcorn and takeout menus.

"No. Even my sense of adventure has limits."

By the time she had her seat belt unfastened, Tucker was opening her door for her.

She stared at him. "What's this? The last time you opened a door for me was when I fell out of a tree and broke my arm."

"I had to then. It was our tree and I felt guilty because I might have pushed you a little. Now I'm doing it because it's part of the adventure." He led the way to the back door of the huge house and opened it for her, too. "Don't get used to it."

The kitchen of the Hall was outdated and gloomy, even more than the one at Seven Pillars had been before Libby gutted it. Frowning at the worn linoleum, she was glad she didn't have to cook here. "I thought you had the Hall remodeled last year."

"We did, but we left the kitchen so that whoever ended up buying the hall could oversee its design." He pushed open a door to their left. "This is the breakfast room, but the dining room is a nightmare in formality, so we're eating here."

"Oh." The space was charming, with yellow walls, white-painted trim and a hardwood floor. A small round table sat in front of the large mullioned window, dressed in white linen and set with what Libby was certain was Royal Copenhagen china and sterling silver flatware. Not that she had anything like it at the tearoom.

"Have a seat." Tucker pulled out a chair for her, then sat across the table. "Colby, one of the college kids who works summers and vacations at the plant, is studying culinary arts, and this semester is French cuisine. I think today we are his term paper. He was hiding in the pantry when we came in and will be serving any minute now. Wine?" He held up the bottle at his elbow. "It's not French. I hope that's not a problem."

"Not at all." Libby recognized the label from Sycamore Hill, the local winery. She served their wine at private parties in the tearoom, but beyond the specifications of red and white, she didn't know one from another. "Actually."

He raised an eyebrow. "Actually?"

"I'd rather have ice water. With lemon."

His eyes lit, and his smile broadened. "I thought maybe. Wait here."

He was back in a couple of minutes, carrying two glasses and a pitcher of ice water garnished with lemon slices. "Colby assured me that drinking *l'eau glacée avec citron* with our meal wouldn't lower his grade."

"Well, I'm impressed. The only French I know is *merci beaucoup*, which I only know because the French teacher at the high school comes to the tearoom for lunch every Saturday and she says that. *Quiche* is a French word, too, and I say that a lot. Every now and then someone will say 'kwitchee,' and I'll have to stop myself from doing that the rest of the day."

"Don't be *too* impressed. Colby had to say it to me three times before I got it even close to right—he kept flinching at my pronunciation—and I couldn't repeat it now. 'Kwitchee' works well for me."

The food and presentation were excellent. The student was earnest in his descriptions of the appetizer, the soup, the main course and the dessert. His service was impeccable. Although he was respectful, he wasn't obsequious. The experience made Libby wish aloud that she'd taken classes instead of poring over cookbooks and using her friends as guinea pigs when she developed Seven Pillars's menu.

Tucker stayed her hands when she started to stack dishes. "Leave them. You're the guest today, and it may be the last time—surely to heaven someone will buy the Albatross soon. Let's get going on our first adventure."

Back in the car after heaping praise and a substantial tip on Colby, Tucker headed north and east. "Why didn't you take classes?" He frowned at the hovering clouds.

She shrugged, thinking back to those putting-one-foot-in-front-of-the-other days. "Jess was out of the navy, but still in vet school. We'd just sold part of the farm's acreage to the Grangers for the winery and were finally out from under the threat of foreclosure. I was still living on the farm and managing the dairy, but I hated every minute of it. I only intended to stay until he finished school and came back there to live, but one weekend when he was home, he found the realty poster for the house on Main Street. It wasn't a tearoom then, just a grand old lady who needed some new clothes, but I had all the plans written out for making it one." She laughed, remembering. "I had a business plan, too, written in longhand in a spiral-bound notebook, and even paint chips for the outside and the trim. I'd never even been inside the house, but it was my dream and Jesse knew that. He suggested we sell the cows and invest the profit in Seven Pillars. Inside of a week, that's what we'd done. I suppose I should have given things more time and more thought, but it had been rough since my mother died. I couldn't wait to start a new life."

She stopped. "Why did I just tell you that? You were there for the worst of it." Tuck had been there with her the whole way, flying home from wherever he was at the time on weekends to scrape and steam wallpaper until he swore he'd never get either the paste or the moisture-induced curl out of his hair.

"I was," he agreed. "But you never let anyone see how bad things were. You just kept laughing."

"That was how I kept going. Jesse just clammed up. I couldn't do that—I'd have gone out of my mind—so I stayed social and laughed a lot." She smiled at him. "It's a tactic you recognize."

She didn't have to say more. Of course he recognized it. It was a coping mechanism they shared. There was more to her story, too—things Tucker didn't know. And she wanted to keep it that way.

"Where are we going?" Libby loved farm-

land, but she saw it every day—Lake Miniagua sat smack in the middle of it. Driving
through it wasn't all that adventurous.

He reached to place his hand over her eyes.
"I'll wake you when we get there."

"I never fall asleep in the daytime," she
said scornfully. And promptly did just that.

TUCKER LOVED DRIVING. It would be fine with
him to just keep going until they reached
Michigan's Upper Peninsula, where one of
the satellite plants of Llewellyn's Lures was.
He flew up there sometimes, if the visit was
urgent, but he preferred the drive. It would
be a great place to show Libby, even in the
dead of winter. They both had their passports
with them, so they could go on into Canada
whenever they liked. But she would panic
if they did that. She was okay with spending the night somewhere, but she needed to
be back by Tuesday morning—Seven Pillars
was as much a safe haven for her as driving
was for him.

Adventure. He'd promised her that, but he
had no idea how to deliver on the promise.
The lunch back at the Albatross had been

great, but he hadn't made up his mind where to go from there.

While Libby slept, he thought about the young woman she'd introduced him to that morning. In all fairness, Allison had been both attractive and pleasant—he'd enjoyed what little conversation they shared. He didn't mind her kid being bratty, either. In his experience, most of them were at one time or another. Charlie, Jack's precocious and hilarious twelve-year-old son, had gone AWOL from his grandparents' home a few weeks ago—during an ice storm, no less—and had the family and everyone else at the lake in an uproar. Of course, the kid was still grounded. Jack insisted puberty would be a nonissue because Charlie was going to spend the duration in his room.

But, as Tucker had told Libby, the chemistry hadn't been there with Allison. It was too bad. Really, it was. He'd meant what he said—he honestly did want a wife. A family. A home. But he wanted what Jack and Arlie had, too, that click between them that was both indefinable and undeniable.

He looked over at where Libby slept with her head tucked into the pillow he kept in the car. It would be nice if *they* could develop that chemistry, because she was pretty close to being his favorite person. But, regardless of what happened in some of the movies she'd dragged him to and he'd pretended he didn't like, he didn't believe friends necessarily made good lovers.

As he drove, the sky appeared more and more as if it was filling up with snow to dump on them. Winter had been an ongoing progression of record-breaking badness so far, each snowfall or ice storm heavier than the one before it. Buying the new *Farmer's Almanac* had done nothing to prepare him for the unpredictable weather.

It had promised a cold but clear day today, but no one who lived in the Midwest ever took promises like that seriously.

Taunting him, the clouds opened and began the process of dropping their contents. They weren't on the interstate, which made driving through the snow in a Camaro even more of a challenge than it might have been otherwise.

Two inches of snow later, the clock in the car insisted it was four, but the lowering sky indicated it was lying. The wind speed had increased at least ten miles per hour, making the thick white stuff even more impenetrable. Libby came abruptly awake. "Where are we?"

"The North Pole. I took a wrong turn."

She called him a mildly profane name in a pleasant voice, then reached back between their seats. "Coffee?"

"Please."

She found the thermos and filled their cups. "I'm sorry."

He sipped, welcoming the warmth, and arrowed her a quick glance. "For what?"

"If we weren't going on an adventure, we wouldn't be driving through a snowstorm."

He laughed, reaching over to give her hair a tug. "It's not the first one we've driven through."

"That's true." She peered through the windshield. "Are we near a town?"

He nodded. "About six more miles, I think, judging by that sign about an hour ago that said it was eleven miles away."

She punched his arm lightly. "Do we exaggerate much?"

His cell phone made a percolator sound that signaled a text. Tucker sighed. "There's my brother, telling me to get off the road. He's so predictable."

"Do you want me to check it?"

"Yeah, you'd better. The last time I drove in a storm, the plant had a fire and Charlie ran away."

"But the Colts won that day, so it wasn't a total loss." Libby tapped his phone to read the message. "You're right. It is Jack. He says if you're driving to get off the road, you—" Her eyes widened. "I don't think that was a very nice thing for him to call you."

"You're just mad because you didn't think of it first."

"There is that."

They laughed together, their timing as on as it always was. "Man," he said, "look at that truck coming. No headlights and he's flying." The other driver had no intention at all of sharing his landing strip, either. Tucker stretched his arm out in front of her. "Hang on, Lib." He edged over as far as he could, praying the right-side wheels of the Camaro wouldn't slide into the ditch.

The petition went unanswered when the car not only went into the ditch, but hit a culvert that was under an unseen driveway. The truck went on by, going fast enough the Camaro trembled—Tucker thought probably with rage—when it passed. His hand, shaking, went to her shoulder. "Are you all right?"

"I'm fine." Her fingers covered his. "Are you?"

He nodded, searching for and finding the emergency blinkers. The car wasn't going anywhere. As far as he could tell, they were mostly off the road. He squinted, peering through the driving snow at the farmhouse at the other end of the lane they were blocking. "I hope whoever lives here wants company. Why don't you stay in the car while I go for help?"

"Why don't you not be an idiot?" She shrugged into her coat and pulled on her gloves, flashing him a smile. "Quite the adventure so far, Llewellyn. I'm impressed, but I'm really scared to ask what's next."

"Good thinking. At least wait there until I come around to help you."

"Okay, my hero."

As he inched his way around the front of the car, he found a spot of ice under the snow. His feet, still clad in the slick-soled shoes he'd worn to church, went out from under him. He landed flat on his back, coming to rest jammed against the bumper of the car, which was all that kept him from sliding under the engine as if he were on a mechanic's creeper.

The passenger door opened and closed, and a few seconds later, Libby knelt beside him. *Good Lord, she's wearing a dress.* He hadn't even realized that.

"Are you okay?"

He met her eyes as her face hovered close to his. "You're laughing, aren't you?"

"Give me a little credit here. I'm trying not to."

She didn't try hard enough, and by the time she'd helped him to his feet and was brushing snow off him, they were both laughing so hard they could barely stand.

"Come on." He tucked his arm around her and they started toward the farmhouse. "If we stay in one spot too long, they'll find us frozen in place when everything thaws." He squinted into the snow. "Is anyone home? I know it's early, but it's dark enough there should be lights on and I don't see any."

She pointed. "In the barn. I'd say it was milking time, but I don't see any signs of dairy."

They plodded through the snow, growing more breathless as they discussed the combined lack of foresight that resulted in her dress and his slick shoes. When they got to the white barn, Tucker rapped sharply on the tall door before pushing it open enough for them to slip inside the hay storage area. "Hello?" he called, keeping Libby's hand in his as they moved toward the light source.

"In the stable." The voice was muffled, but they were able to follow it.

The scene they walked into was one Tucker thought he'd only seen on television. A man stood in a roomy stall with his arm around a boy who looked about eleven or twelve. A woman, visibly pregnant, was outside the stall with a little girl who was probably five beside her. The little girl was holding a cat.

The adults looked helpless. The boy was trying not to cry, leaning his head into the man's chest and wiping his nose on his sleeve.

Tucker remembered being that age, when for whatever reason it wasn't okay to cry anymore. The dog he and Jack had shared had died. His mother and Libby and the Gallagher girls had been in tears, but he and Jack and Jesse had toughed it out. They'd buried the dog under an elm tree in the woods around the Albatross without shedding a single tear.

Instead, they'd used a lot of forbidden swear words and taken the rowboat out to one of the little islands in the middle of the lake. They'd stayed out there until Jack got hungry and Tucker got leery of being on the island after dark.

He didn't think this kid had an island available to him right now, and he was losing the fight against tears. Also standing in the stall was a black-and-white cow—a Holstein like the Worths always had—who didn't appear to be enjoying herself. Unless Tucker missed his guess, she was in labor, and it wasn't going so well.

The man seemed to realize for the first time that the family was no longer alone in the barn. He shook himself a little, his hand stroking through his son's hair. "I'm sorry. May I help you?"

"We slid off the road," said Tucker. "I'm not sure you have anything to tow with, but I'm pretty sure we'd get too cold out there waiting for a truck. We've come to beg warmth."

"I'll pull you out soon. I hope you don't mind waiting." The man gestured toward the straining cow. "Joanna's having some trouble."

"Wow, she sure is." Libby took off her coat and gloves and carried them over to the little girl. "Will you and your kitty watch these for me? I'm always losing things."

The little girl nodded, her expression solemn.

"My name is Libby Worth, and my friend is Tucker Llewellyn. What's yours?" Libby was looking around, smiling when her gaze encountered anyone else's.

"I'm Mari," said the little girl. She pointed at the boy. "That's Gavin. He's my brother."

"And my name is Dan. This is my wife, Alice," the man said, finishing the introductions. "Joanna is Gavin's 4-H calf, all grown up." He shook his head. "I'm afraid being midwife to a cow is outside all our skill sets."

Libby nodded. "Do you have shoulder gloves?"

Gavin drew away from his father. "The vet gave us some, but we don't know what to do with them."

"Well, I do, and so does my friend Tucker here, although it's been long enough for him he probably doesn't remember. Do you have some chains for calving?"

"Yes. They were left here." Gavin's father

looked apologetic. "I'm afraid I don't know how to use them, either. Sometimes moving to the country from the suburbs seems to have been a mistake."

"No, it's not," his wife protested softly. "We just haven't learned everything yet. What do you need us to do, Ms. Worth?"

"It's just Libby." She smiled at the woman, who'd come to stand nearby, her hands resting on the large mound of her stomach.

Tucker thought the whole barn, even Joanna, relaxed in the glow of that smile.

"Okay. I need water, please. Warm, if you have it." Libby pulled the long glove into place and stepped behind Joanna. "Gavin, this is your cow. Are you going to help her have this baby?"

The boy's eyes were wide. Tucker thought his own probably were, too. "Yes, ma'am."

"I was about your age when my cow Arletta had her first calf, and she took her time about it, too." Libby nodded at Dan. "Will you hold her tail? If I make her mad—which I very well might—and she flips it around, she could knock me down." She aimed a smile at Tucker. "You need to get your coat off if you're going to help here."

Which he obviously was, whether he wanted to or not. Her expression told him there'd be no good in arguing that point. Tucker took off his coat, gloves and the pullover sweater he'd worn to church. The shirt he'd worn under it was fairly expendable, but the sweater was cashmere and he really liked how it felt.

"My brother is a vet," Libby explained to Gavin, "and we grew up on a dairy farm, so I really do know how to do this. Understand, I don't *like* doing it, so you'll probably have to do something wonderful for me after this, like make me some cookies or something."

Holding the calving chains until she asked for them, Tucker listened to Libby as she spoke first to the worried boy and then to the frightened cow. "My friend delivers human babies, and she's given me all kinds of new instructions I didn't know about," Libby said, her voice soothing and quiet. "You need to breathe just right, Joanna. Do the hoo-hoo, hee-hee thing like they show on television. I'll bet Alice can tell you how. That way I can put the chains around your baby's legs and help you out a little."

"That's right about the breathing, although I never considered it for a cow." Alice was at the cow's head but standing outside the stall, little Mari and her cat at her side. The woman stroked the side of Joanna's neck. "You can do this, girl." She looked over at where her husband stood holding firmly to a long and manure-encrusted tail. "*We* can do this, too, Dan Parsons."

Her husband smiled at her, reminding Tucker of how Jack and Arlie looked at each other. He wanted that. Maybe he wanted the whole over-the-top part of it, too.

He didn't think he wanted any cows, but if that came with the package, he guessed he could live with it.

He flinched as Libby slipped her arm into where it had to go, talking to the cow all the time. "Just be glad it's me instead of Tuck or my brother, Joanna. They have big hands and arms and…ouch…let me get that…no, hold still." She stopped for a moment, panting as Joanna did, biting down on her bottom lip. "Okay, let's try that again. Let's get this baby out for you so you can have a nice rest. Attagirl…oh, ouch, ouch, ouch, you're not being very grateful, are you?"

Tucker stepped forward, but she shook her head at him. "I'm okay." She smiled and patted the cow's hindquarters with her free hand. "She is, too. She's just tired."

"Do you think it's going to be all right?" Gavin's tone was solemn. "Sometimes cows die giving birth. Their calves die, too."

"You're right." Libby's expression was as serious as the boy's. "It seems as if there are risks in everything you do, but if you don't risk anything, you don't gain anything, either." She grinned suddenly, her face lighting up. "And you'll never have any adventures. Right, Tuck?"

"Right." He sounded too hearty, he knew he did, but the boy's face brightened, too, so it was okay.

"Okay, good. There we go. Tuck, you set to back me up? Dan, you want to be there to give Gavin a hand if he needs it? He probably won't, but just in case." Libby stepped away, holding the end of one of the chains and giving the other to Gavin. "Now, when she strains, we're going to pull real slow and steady, working with her contraction. Don't jerk and don't pull too hard. Think you can do that?"

"Yes, ma'am." He looked frightened, but no more so than his father.

"It scares me, too," Tucker told the boy, moving into place behind Libby, "and I've done it before. I think you're *supposed* to be worried about it."

Gavin took a deep breath. "Well, if I am, I've got that part down. Now, ma'am?"

"Now."

Rewarding the efforts of a small woman in a red dress, a determined young boy and an extremely tired Holstein, a large calf was born in a rush of fluid. Tucker stepped away from Libby in time to catch it, although he fell under its weight.

"You did it, Joanna! You did it!" Gavin dropped the chain and ran around to hug his cow's neck. "It's a...what is it, Dad?"

"A heifer," said Dan, helping to rub the calf down with straw. "A big, strong girl." He looked up at where Libby was shaking her arm to regain full feeling in it. "We can't thank you enough."

"Yes, you can," she promised. "I know you don't know us at all, but if you'll let us take a bath and change our clothes, I think we'll consider ourselves thanked."

"I'm pretty sure we can accommodate

that," said Alice, "plus there's a roast in the oven just crying out to be eaten."

Tucker exchanged glances with Libby and shrugged slightly. "Sounds great."

A few more inches of snow had fallen while they'd been in the barn. Drifts created whipped-cream mountains everywhere they looked, some of them all the way up to the eaves of the garage. "I have a tractor," said Dan. "I'll be able to get you out of the ditch, but you might want to plan on spending the night. I don't think you'll get far, especially without all-wheel drive."

"We don't want to put you out," Libby protested.

Alice and Dan laughed together. "You haven't been inside yet."

Except for its fully finished and beautiful kitchen, the old farmhouse was a construction zone. "It will be wonderful someday," said Alice.

Tucker looked around, at framework with doors but no walls, at the living room subfloor partially covered with area rugs, at the beautifully curved stairway without a rail. He saw where the children had hung their coats inside the back door in what would eventually be a mud/utility room. He watched as Dan Parsons patted his wife's stomach, high-fived his son over the birth of the calf and knelt to talk seriously to little Mari about how the new baby would be all right sleeping in the barn with her mama.

It will be wonderful someday. "No." Tucker met Libby's eyes. *This is it. This is what I want.* "It's wonderful now."

CHAPTER THREE

LIBBY SLEPT ON an inflatable mattress on the floor of Mari's room. When Stripes, the kitten, crawled into bed with her, Mari followed, bringing her own pillow. The blow-up mattress was twin-size, so it didn't leave a lot of room, but Libby slept well anyway, the little-girl scent and warmth of her roommate making for a comfortable night.

She woke before dawn, dressed in the clothes Tucker and Dan had brought in from the car last night, and plaited her hair into a messy braid. She tiptoed downstairs to the kitchen, stopping on the landing to look through the window and find Venus, clearly visible in the post-storm sky. "Hi, Mom," she whispered, and went down the rest of the stairs. She found her hostess at the table with a cozied pot of what smelled deliciously like Earl Grey. "Ah," said Libby, keeping her tone hushed, "a girl after my own heart."

Alice waved her to a chair. "And one after mine, who knows any voice over a whisper will wake my children at the crack of dawn on a snow day. We homeschool, but we adhere to the public-school schedule."

By the time she and Alice had drunk two pots of tea and told each other most of their life stories, she'd constructed a quiche guaranteed to make the kids happy. "But don't call it a quiche," Libby warned. "Call it something else so they don't know that's what they're eating. In the tearoom, we call it yellow junk with bugs in it. They all know it's not really bugs, but they do love the whole gross-out part of the story."

"Do they know it's spinach?" Alice slipped the pie plate into the oven.

Libby gave her a blank look. "Know what's spinach?"

After breakfast, Dan drove his tractor up and down the driveway, a blade on the front pushing snow out of the way. Tucker, with Gavin's help, shoveled out from under the Camaro so that the wheels had a place to go when Dan pulled it out. There was some damage done to the bumper and the spoiler, but they were repairable. More importantly, the car didn't want to pull in one direction or the other when Tucker drove it. If the roads were semi-clear, they should be able to get home without encountering any more ditches—provided they didn't meet other trucks whose drivers had homicidal tendencies.

They visited the barn, where Joanna was munching cheerfully on some hay and little Liberty was gamboling about the stall. "Do you mind?" said Gavin. "Mom said not everyone would want to have a cow named after them."

"Well, I would." Libby gave the boy a hug before he could get away and grinned at his mother. "We had a cow named Alice, too. I think she had an even dozen calves. My dad really liked her."

Alice grabbed her stomach and groaned. "Three's going to be enough for this Alice!" She hugged Libby, then reached past her to hug Tucker, too. "We'll be down to see you in spring."

"We'll be waiting," Libby promised. She knelt to smile into Mari's eyes. "Thank you for sharing Stripes with me. When you come see me, I'll introduce you to Elijah."

"Will he like me?"

"Yes, he will."

"I'll bring him a present."

"Thank you." Libby wanted to cry. She made her eyes really wide and blinked hard against the tears. They didn't come, of course. Libby often *wanted* to cry, but she never did.

Tucker was beside her then, taking her hand when she straightened. "I have to help her walk," he explained to Mari, "so she won't slip."

"You could carry her," the little girl suggested. "Daddy carries me sometimes so I won't fall."

Libby gave Tucker a none-too-gentle push with her elbow, almost knocking them both off balance. "It'll be okay. He might hurt his back."

A few minutes later, they were in the Camaro and back on the freshly plowed road headed toward Miniagua. Tucker reached to tweak her braid. "I'm sorry about the adventure."

She laughed, clasped his hand and gave it a squeeze. "I thought that was a pretty good one, myself. How do you beat making a whole family of new friends and having a calf named after you?"

"THE NEW NURSE-MIDWIFE at A Woman's Place—" Libby looked around the tearoom to be sure no one needed anything and almost flinched at the Valentine's Day decorations she thought she might have overdone. Satisfied everyone was taken care of, she took the empty chair at the table Arlie shared with her stepsister, Holly, and her stepmother, Gianna. "Is she single?"

Arlie nodded. "Divorced."

"How old is she?"

Arlie tilted her head thoughtfully. "Thirty."

"Ish," Holly added.

"Very pretty," said Gianna.

"What's her name?"

"Meredith."

"Kids?" Libby poured some tea into her cup.

"Two." Arlie set down her fork and stared fixedly at her. "One of each. Six and eight. I think maybe she's a Taurus. She puts purple highlights in her hair and it looks great—I might hate her a little for that. Anything else you want to know right off the top of your head?"

Libby thought of Allison's little boy. And of Allison. No chemistry, Tucker had said, and when Libby had urged him to at least give it a chance, he'd caved and asked Allison out to dinner. She'd gone, and they'd ended up back at Anything Goes laughing because their chemical disconnect was so complete they thought maybe they were siblings separated at birth. Tucker had introduced Allison to an engineer who worked at Llewellyn's Lures and now they were dating.

Next had been Cindy, who worked at the winery, followed by Risa, who taught algebra and coached middle school volleyball. After Risa, Libby had threatened Tucker's life if he used the word *chemistry* in her presence ever again.

"Well," Libby explained, taking in the three pairs of curious eyes at the table, "Valentine's Day is in two weeks. I thought maybe I could find Tucker a good date for the party at the clubhouse. My last day off, he took me to the casino at Rising Sun and gave me two hundred dollars. When I won two thousand and he lost five hundred, I tried to give the two hundred back, but he wouldn't take it." She was a little embarrassed. "I think I could really like gambling, so I probably don't want to go back."

"Seriously? You *won*?" Holly's eyebrows rose. "I don't think I've ever done that."

Libby nodded. "Yes. I'd won before, but to me winning just meant not losing, as in I went home with the same twenty dollars I took to gamble with. So two thousand was great."

"What did you do with it?" Arlie went back to eating.

Libby sighed blissfully. "I got a new stove. I'd been getting by on the two four-burner ones I bought used when I opened the tea-room ten years ago. They were okay for a long time, but I was down to two burners on one and three on the other, and one of the ovens wasn't working right. If I had to bake for a party or got a double order from some-one, I was in a mess." She nodded at Gianna. "You know that—I borrowed your oven often enough. You need to come into the kitchen and see it before you leave. I feel like a kid at Christmas."

All of the Gallagher women loved to cook, so they had to understand the feeling. "Well, then, you do need to find Tuck a good date. He earned at least one." Holly chuckled. "I think he's spent time with about everyone on the lake, though, except maybe Mollie and you and me. And don't even think of asking me," she warned. "That would be way too much like dating my brother."

"I get that." Libby took a moment to ponder offering her real brother up to Holly. That was a thought that deserved some serious consideration.

"I'll say something to Meredith if you like," Arlie offered. "She's mentioned dating, but only in general, not specifically, so I don't think there's anybody special."

"Thank you. Maybe you could have them for dinner at the same time? I'm always there for these introductions, and Tucker and I end up talking about high school basketball or constellations. The woman he's supposed to be entertaining…er…isn't entertained. I don't go on actual dates, thank goodness, but I'm still in the way when they meet." Libby smiled, although she didn't feel quite as happy as she had a little while ago.

Arlie nodded. "We'll do the dinner thing."

"Thank you." Libby looked around again. "I need to get back to work. Enjoy your lunch. The tea's on me since I just drank half the pot." She kissed Gianna's cheek and waved at Arlie and Holly before going to refill coffee cups and teapots.

The day was busy. Even the little gift shop in the sunroom did a booming business, a good thing for the local vendors who stocked it with their creations.

Libby was more relieved than usual when she locked the doors at four o'clock. She wondered sometimes if she should consider staying open for evening hours all the time instead of just when a party booked the tearoom. The extra income might be nice, but since she'd have to give up baking for Anything Goes and the Silver Moon, she might lose money in the long run.

If she hurried, she could get a walk in before darkness fell. She wasn't usually alone, since many of the lakers gathered to walk or ride bicycles in the evening, but she liked it best on the rare occasions that Tucker came. They didn't walk together, since the group had the usual divisions—gender, age and interests—but they usually ended the walk with a glass or cup of something at Anything Goes.

He wasn't around tonight, though. She walked half her normal route and turned to go back. "I'm just tired," she said when some of the others expressed concern.

At home, she prepared dough for the morning. She loved baking, loved kneading and forming the dough, but her fatigued muscles burned a path of protest across her shoulder blades when she was done. The long shower she took afterward was like an answer to a prayer.

Dressed in pajamas and a robe, she carried a glass of wine and a book out to the enclosed porch off her living room. She settled into the wing chair that had been her mother's and that Libby had reupholstered in soft teal corduroy. The porch was insulated and heated, with windows all around and a skylight in the ceiling. The enclosure had been a Christmas-and-birthday gift from Jesse and Tucker two years ago—the best present ever. She kept her telescope downstairs so it was easy to take outside, but she watched the sky up here, too. She was never alone as long as she could sit in a comfortable chair and see the stars and talk to Venus.

Elijah settled into her lap, bumping his head against the bottom of her book when she went too long without petting him. She relaxed, sipped her wine and thought about what a nice life she had. She had wonderful friends, a fairly successful business, a brother she loved and a nice cat. She dated sometimes when she wanted to or when the stars were aligned just so. She was happy. No, contented.

And sometimes she was lonely.

TUCKER LOVED TIME with his family. He loved coming to the Toe, Arlie's house that sat on a skinny inlet of the lake called Gallagher's Foot. However, coming here to meet a woman felt weird. And uncomfortable. Where was Libby? She was the one who'd arranged it— she should be here to pick up the pieces when it all fell apart. As it invariably did.

"Meredith is a nice girl. She has good kids and a neurotic poodle-mix puppy." Arlie didn't even look at Tucker. She was reading Charlie's journal entries for eighth-grade English class. "Did you help with this?"

"No." Tucker shot his nephew a scowl. "I offered, but he indicated he was likely better off without me."

His future sister-in-law finished reading, initialed the pages and caught Charlie in a headlock so she could kiss his cheek loudly. "Good job!"

"With the journal or because I didn't let Uncle Tuck help?"

She grinned at him. "Both, wise guy. Go tell your dad supper's ready. Tucker, Meredith is walking up to the front door. Answer it and be on your best behavior. Got it?"

Charlie moved toward the stairway, walking backward. "Do I have to stay? You're just going to talk about grown-up stuff, and Grandma Gi said I could come to her house. That way you could talk about me and it would at least be interesting."

Jack came down the stairs, catching his son before he could trip over the bottom step in his reverse progress. "The kid has a point. Not that he's interesting but, you know, we should let him go because we'd probably have more fun without him."

Tucker hiked an eyebrow at Arlie. "And you're worried about *my* behavior?" He opened the door, smiling a greeting. "You must be Meredith. Welcome to the Toe, where madness and dysfunction prevail."

Man, she was…gorgeous. As in the drop-dead variety. Her hair was short and spiky, dark with purple tips. She was wearing a slim black skirt—Libby called them pencils or stovepipes or something—and a sweater the same color as her hair.

"I realize I look ridiculous—I should be wearing a coat," she said. "February first on a lake in central Indiana calls for it, but the kids got a puppy, and she peed on it."

"Don't say you got a puppy in front of Charlie." Tucker put his hands over his nephew's ears. "He'll think it's a new trend."

The boy rolled his eyes. "It's nice to see you again," he told Meredith politely. "I'm going over to my grandma's. She needs help eating her lasagna."

"I'll pick you up at nine thirty," said Jack.

"Wear your coat," said Arlie.

When the door had closed behind Charlie, Tucker said, "I'm Tucker. It's nice to meet you." He didn't know what else to say. He'd dated beautiful women before, but he'd never gotten particularly good at just talking to them. He would never admit it to his already-too-smart nephew, but they seriously intimidated him.

"You, too." She smiled at him, but the expression faded. "I'm sorry. You're the first date I've had since…well, since I got married, I guess. I don't know how good I'm going to be at it."

Huh. She was beautiful, but she was also scared and unsure of herself. And a puppy had peed on her coat. The least he could do was be a nice guy. "My friend Libby says I'm really lousy at the whole dating thing, so you're in good company."

Jack stepped forward. "Don't listen to him, Meredith. He's never good company."

"Dinner's ready. Let's get started so that Meredith and I can talk shop about our shared profession and turn you guys green," said Arlie brightly. "I haven't had a good breech-birth conversation during the main course in a long time."

Tucker gestured for Meredith to precede him to the dining area. "That's okay. Jack and I can hold forth about fishing lures and go into graphic detail about when Paul Phillipy had to extract a hook from my leg."

The evening was okay. More than okay, really. Tucker liked Meredith. He asked her if she'd like to go into Sawyer one night to see a movie and have dinner. Her kids could come, too, if she liked. Tucker liked kids.

She said she'd like to, blushing the whole time, but that she'd get a sitter. She didn't think they were at all ready for the idea of Mom dating. She shook her head then, and Tucker thought for a minute she was going to tear up, but then she admitted, "I'm not sure Mom's ready for it, either. But I like you. I'd like to go if it's a chance you're willing to take."

Tucker thought it was.

She left at nine, anxious about the children she'd left with someone they didn't know well. Tucker refused her offer of a ride. He hadn't walked in a few days, and the weather was unseasonably mild. "Come on," said his brother. "I'll go with you as far as Gianna's. Arlie has someone on the verge of delivery, so she's not leaving her post."

They walked around the lake, and Tucker felt a familiar rush of gratitude to be so close to his Irish-twin brother again. Born ten months apart of different mothers, they'd been reared mostly together. But Jack had left Lake Miniagua the autumn after the prom-night accident, guilt driving him away from both Arlie and his younger brother. Their father, who'd been driving drunk and caused the collision, had been angry at Jack at the time. In Jack's grieving seventeen-year-old mind, he should have been able to prevent the accident and keep everyone safe. Not until their grandmother's death had he returned and made his peace with both himself and the people he loved.

When he moved back to the lake, Tucker did, too.

"You're a great dad," Tucker said as they walked toward Arlie's mother's house. "Where'd you learn that?"

Jack laughed. "From Charlie. Same place you learned to be a great uncle."

They walked on in silence. Finally, Jack said, "What's on your mind, Tuck? Why the sudden urge to jump onto the marriage and family wagon?"

Tucker grinned at him. "At the risk of sounding like the stereotypical younger brother, I want what you have. What you and Arlie have. I don't think I'm going to feel about anyone the way you do about each other—unfortunately I'm wired more like our father than my mother. The feelings just don't go that deep. But I can like somebody a lot, and she can like me and we can both love kids. There are worse reasons to be married than just wanting a family."

"There are." Jack's marriage to Tracy, Charlie's mother, had been based on friendship alone—in college, he'd wanted to help the lab partner who'd been impregnated by an abusive boyfriend. The fact that Charlie wasn't Jack's biological son had never had any bearing on anything. "Tracy and I are still close. We probably always will be." He slowed enough to capture Tucker's gaze. "But we couldn't be married. Friendship wasn't enough to base a marriage on."

"I know. If it was, I'd marry Libby." As soon as the words were out, Tucker regretted them. They sounded disrespectful, as if she would be a fallback choice. Libby Worth might not be particularly beautiful, based on society's magazine-cover criteria, and her only claim to a degree was a diploma from Miniagua High School, but she was no one's last resort.

His brother hooted laughter that rang out across the still lake. "Like she'd have you."

Tucker walked to Seven Pillars from Gianna's, suddenly anxious to talk to Libby about Meredith. He hadn't seen his best buddy since her new stove was delivered, when she'd called him to come and see what she'd done with her gambling spoils. She'd pulled a small cherry pie out of the new oven while he was there, gotten out two forks and poured two cups of coffee. They'd eaten every bit of the pie and emptied the coffeepot, laughing the whole time.

Maybe she'd be up for a cup of Mollie's hot chocolate at the Grill, although the lights on in the tearoom kitchen usually meant Libby was still baking for the next day. He tapped on the back door and pushed it open. "Lib? You still working?"

She looked up from the island Caleb Hershberger had built from scrap wood when he'd helped remodel the big Victorian that housed the tearoom. She smiled a welcome that went a long way toward warming Tucker's cold feet. "Come on in. Help Nate test the new pie recipe."

Another survivor of the accident and the owner of Feathermoor, the golf course near the lake, Nate Benteen was also a lifelong friend. He was sitting on a stool at the far end of the island with a cup and a plate in front of him. He looked comfortable there. Very comfortable.

But what was he *doing* here? He was supposed to be in North Carolina designing links-style golf courses. Even as he was shaking hands, Tucker asked the question.

"The owners of the new course are coming up for a few days in April. They want to get a look at Feathermoor now that it's been here a few years and matured, so to speak," Nate explained. "They're going to stay at Hoosier Hills—not the campground, but the cabins. I was looking for a place to have long business dinners with them without going into Sawyer or Kokomo, so I came to beg Libby to feed us."

Libby handed Tucker a cup of coffee and waved him to a seat. "Did you meet Meredith? Did you like her? More to the point, could she stand you?"

"Yes and yes, and she said she'd go out with me, so maybe. She was fun to talk to."

"Good. Are you taking her to the Valentine's party at the clubhouse?"

"On a first real date? No. Although if the first date works out well, the party would be a great second or third one. Are you going?"

"I'm going with Nate. We figure our last date was when he was a senior and I was a junior, so maybe we should try again." She beamed, but there was something a little off in the expression. What was it?

Oh.

That had been the night of the accident, when everyone's lives had changed. Nate, who'd had a golf scholarship and plans to play professionally, had ended up with pins in his hips. He'd settled for designing golf courses for a living instead, starting with Feathermoor. Back then, it had still been his parents' farm that had abutted the Worth place. Nate didn't like the term *settled*, though, and he was one of that happiest people Tucker knew.

Tucker had lost most of the hearing in his left ear that night, Holly had lost a foot, Sam Phillipy an eye, Arlie her singing voice. People had died. Libby had suffered a head injury that left her in a coma. She never talked about it, even to him, but he knew she still got headaches.

But they'd come back, except for the ones who'd been lost. And except for Cass Gentry, who'd left the lake and never been heard from again. Jack and Arlie had come full circle and were going to be married in May. Maybe Nate and Libby would, too.

Tucker couldn't come up with a single, solitary reason he hoped that wouldn't happen.

But he hoped it anyway.

CHAPTER FOUR

NATE CALLED LIBBY after church on the day
after the Valentine's Day party and asked
her if she'd like to play golf that afternoon.
Since the alternative was waxing the tearoom
floors, Libby agreed. How hard could it be to
hit a little ball around?

It was, she learned quickly, kind of hard,
but by the time they parked the cart in the
garage beside Feathermoor's clubhouse, she
thought she liked golf. She'd like it even better, Nate promised, when it was more than
forty degrees and they weren't the only people on the golf course. He mentioned that lessons would be a good idea come spring and
that it was perfectly all right to swear when
she lost her ball in the weeds—everyone did
that.

She liked Nate, too. He was tall and handsome and fun to be with, but so was the
golden retriever rescue Jesse had brought

by with the suggestion she and Elijah might like some company. Libby hadn't been sure about the addition to the family, but Elijah had given in right away, so now Pretty Boy slept on a rug in Libby's room and made the occasional appearance in the tearoom.

Nate, on the other hand, was a good conversationalist and didn't shed in the house. Elijah wasn't fond of him, but he drove a nice car and told good jokes, and the only time he kissed her she thought maybe the earth might have moved a little. It didn't—they'd looked at each other and laughed—but it had definitely been enjoyable.

That had been after the party, when she'd worn her favorite red dress and five-inch black stilettos. The shoes had necessitated rubbing Icy Hot on her calves and feet before she went to bed and wearing sneakers to church the next morning, but it had been worth it.

Tucker came after she closed for the day on Tuesday to help change lightbulbs in the chandeliers in the parlors. "The party was fun," said Libby, handing him the little flame-shaped bulbs.

"It was. Meredith had a good time."

"She's beautiful." An old and not-missed boyfriend had referred to Libby as "pretty enough"—that was as close to beautiful as she'd ever come. She couldn't quite keep the envy out of her voice.

"She is."

She cleared her throat. "Are you seeing her again?"

"We're taking her kids bowling day after tomorrow."

"That'll be nice." But would it? Didn't he always play poker on Thursday nights? Was Meredith becoming that important to him that quickly?

"You seeing Nate again?"

"He's back in North Carolina until the first of March."

"That's too bad." But Tuck didn't sound as if he thought it was too bad. He sounded kind of like a smirk looked.

"He asked me to come down there for a weekend. He has a house on Topsail Island. It won't be beachy weather, he says, but still warmer than here."

Tuck screwed in a few more lightbulbs. "Are you going to go?"

"What do you think?" She stepped from

one achy foot to the other, feeling like a ten-year-old uncertain about whether she was ready for fifth grade. "Do you think I should?"

He hesitated and didn't look at her when he answered. "I think you're an adult, Lib. I can't tell you what to do when it comes to relationships." He reached to take more bulbs from her. "Don't go this weekend, though, okay? It's time for another adventure. Can you take an extra day off?"

"Probably. Neely pushes me out the door every chance she gets." Libby put the old bulbs into a box for recycling. "Which is great for me. I'm thrilled the business can support us both. It just feels weird. I haven't taken extra time off for years, and all of a sudden I am. What should I pack?" She knew better than to ask where they were going—he never told her.

"Walking shoes."

She stifled a groan. She'd better pack the Icy Hot, too.

"FLYING? WE'RE FLYING?" Libby's gray eyes were huge. Unless Tucker missed his guess, the little blue lights in them were shooting sparks directly at him. "Tucker, I've never flown anywhere. I've barely left Indiana."

"About time then, isn't it?" He pulled into a parking lot.

"Where are we going?"

He swung into a parking place and grasped her chin gently between his thumb and fore-finger, forcing her to meet his eyes. "Trust me. Okay?"

"Why would I do that?"

It was there again, that look he couldn't quite grasp the meaning of, and he'd have said he knew all Libby's expressions. He'd seen it when they'd mentioned the night of the accident in her kitchen. She was grinning, open and challenging, but there was some-thing missing, too.

He sniffed. "You wound me with your lack of faith. I've never told anyone about you los-ing your lunch when we rode the bullet at the 4-H fair when we were in the seventh grade, but you still don't trust me?"

"Well, since I did it in front of half the county, I'm really impressed that you kept my secret. Okay, I trust you. But if I lose my lunch on this plane, you'll be sorry."

He opened his door. "Come on, Nausea

Nellie, let's go. See that shuttle coming? We're going to ride it to the terminal."

By the time they'd checked in, he'd had to tell her they were on their way to Nashville, Tennessee. To be tourists, something she'd spent precious little of her life doing, and go to the Tennessee branch of Llewellyn's Lures and his apartment in nearby Gallatin. He'd lived there until moving to Indiana to share the CEO duties with Jack at corporate headquarters. He still missed it.

He never flew first-class, considering it a waste of money, but for Libby's first flight, he'd booked two of the roomy front seats on the plane. They were still on the ground when she was holding her first cup of coffee.

"See there?" He pointed to the pocket in front of her. "That bag is for when your stomach decides you don't like flying. You did have breakfast, didn't you?"

"Just that drive-through biscuit."

"Oh, Lord." The biscuit sandwiches were good, but they also sat like lead on a normal stomach—heaven only knew how hers would react. "Read the magazine."

But she couldn't. She was too excited. When the plane taxied down the runway a little while later, her eyes widened with anticipation. "I'm not scared. I thought I'd be scared." But she grabbed Tucker and cut off all circulation to his right arm.

Other than a little gasp when the plane lifted, she did well with takeoff. "Well," he said, "that's a relief. I don't have to be embarrassed."

"Right. Like you *can* be embarrassed." She sipped the last of her coffee and set the cup aside. "So, now that I'm an expert in commercial flying, let's talk about your personal life."

He snorted. "If you want a nap, just say so. You know my personal life is boring."

"Well, sure, I know it, but I didn't know you did." She patted the hand that was only beginning to resume normal blood flow. "Tell me about Meredith. She's come into the tearoom with Arlie. She seems very nice. And beautiful."

"She is nice. And beautiful. Her kids are good, too. They miss their dad."

"That's too bad."

"It is. It's not like Jack and me—we never missed ours at all. From everything Meredith says, he's a good father. He lost his way in the marriage, though."

"Do the kids see him?"

"Yeah. He lives in Indianapolis and he comes and gets them every other weekend and drives up and has dinner with them one night during the off week. Pays support right on time, even early. But he and Meredith don't communicate at all except for texting about the kids or the very occasional phone call. When he picks them up, she sends them out to the car. When he brings them home, she stays inside and opens the door when they come onto the porch. She's never said why they broke up, but it must have been serious stuff." He hesitated. "Is that more than I should say about her?"

"I don't think so. I—" Libby stopped. "You know what? It probably is. I mean, I'm not going to repeat anything you tell me. You know that. But if I were dating someone, I wouldn't want him talking to another woman about me, even if that woman was twenty-seven minutes older than him and no competition whatsoever. I'd feel as if he owed me some loyalty, or at least confidentiality."

"You're right." She was, and it bothered him that he hadn't hesitated at all in talking about Meredith. If he *had* known truly private things about her, if they *were* having a physical relationship, he would have felt safe talking to Libby about that, too.

Sometimes he wasn't nearly as sure about his nice guy status as he wanted to be. "But, hey," he said, picking up on something she'd said, "what do you mean, *if* you were dating someone? You are. You're dating Nate." Although it didn't feel right to him, and he couldn't really figure out why. Nate was one of the good guys, too.

But maybe not good for Libby. Maybe that was what didn't feel right.

"Not really dating. I think he still looks at me only as Jess's little sister. There's someone in North Carolina, too. The more he tries not to mention her name, the more often 'Mandy' enters the conversation." She smiled, a lazy, sleepy expression, mildly regretful. "He is fun, but it's definitely a buddy thing."

The flight attendant came around, bringing more coffee and assuring them the weather in Tennessee was going to be great today. She smiled at Libby's drowsy expression and procured a blanket and pillow from the compartment above.

"Do you want something more?" Tucker

asked when the woman had moved toward the back of the plane. "More than fun, I mean."

"I do." She drank, then set her cup down on the tray table and turned her head to look out the window. "I want to be something besides good old Lib to someone."

"Oh, Rhett!" Libby fluttered her eyelashes at Tucker as they toured the gardens at the Hermitage, the home of Andrew Jackson. "How you do go on."

"You're in the wrong state, Miss Scarlett. I assume you know that?" He lifted his phone to take pictures of either her or the flowers in the beds behind her. In case it was her, she tried to straighten her hair a little and wished she'd freshened her makeup before they left the airport.

"Of course I know that. I've read *Gone with the Wind* at least once a year ever since seventh grade. But I figure this is the closest I'm going to come to Tara in this lifetime." She knelt to look at the crocuses peering out from between the tulips. The flowers were the same as the ones that grew at home, but Tennessee was well ahead of Indiana on the color scale. "It's so nice to be here. I'm ready for a glimpse of spring, aren't you?"

More than a glimpse, she realized. The depression that was nipping at her heels was becoming frightening. She needed light, lots of light, and February in the Midwest offered very little. Spring tossed other demons in her path, but at least she got to fight them with sunshine in her arsenal.

"I think the long winter is easier for me because I travel so much." Tucker's eyes were darker than usual, and he wasn't smiling. "What's wrong, Lib?"

Am I trying too hard? "Nothing." She kept her voice bright. "Except I'm hungry. You picked me up at zero dark thirty this morning and all I've had since the drive-through are those crackers on the plane, which I lost while we were landing in Detroit. I never knew Detroit was on the way to Nashville, did you?"

"You learn new geography every time you fly." He helped her straighten, then went on in a truly appalling Humphrey Bogart voice, "Stick with me, sweetheart, and you'll be throwing up all over the world."

She laughed, elbowing him, and didn't draw away when he pulled her in close and kept his arm around her as they went to the on-site restaurant for some lunch.

"Where do we go from here?" she asked after they'd ordered and she'd consumed a small pot of tea.

"Downtown."

They walked for miles, stopping to listen politely to every fresh-air musician they passed and leave generous tips in open guitar cases. They rode a tourist bus all over town, ending at the Grand Ole Opry.

"This was the only place my parents ever went on vacation," she remembered. "They never took us, but every couple of years, they'd hire someone to help with the milking and come down for a few days. Going to the Hermitage, walking around downtown and listening to the heart's echoes in the Ryman just now—it felt as if I was with my mom. She loved it here. It was where she grew up, and even though she didn't have any family other than us, she still felt at home here. Dad brought her down when she was sick. He always thought the trip shortened her life, but even if it did, it gave her joy she wouldn't have found anywhere else."

Libby didn't know how many years it had

been since she'd wept. The losses were things she kept buried in a safe place. Arlie and Holly's mother had once called that place a pocket behind her heart, because grief wasn't measured by tears. Libby remembered feeling so relieved when Gianna said that, because maybe it meant the girl who'd stood dry-eyed at her parents' funerals wasn't broken after all.

She didn't cry tonight, either, sitting beside Tucker in the Grand Ole Opry watching some of the same artists her mother had loved in addition to ones Libby listened to. But her heart ached to a depth she'd forgotten existed. It was good to feel something other than numbness, she supposed, but she hadn't thought feeling this much would be as heavy as it was. Not after all this time.

Tucker laughed beside her, drawing her attention to the performer on stage. He'd been around since her mother's time. *Oh*, her mother used to say, *he's a case, he is. He grew up on the same mountain as I did, only a little deeper in the hollers.*

And there he was, at least a decade older than Crystal Worth would have been, still singing the songs she'd sung as she cleaned the redbrick farmhouse where Jesse still lived and helped with the milking. Libby wondered if her mother had ever sat in this row when she came to the Opry. Maybe in this very seat.

"Dad used to say—" Libby spoke before she knew the words were coming, and they stuck in her throat. She had to clear it before going on, leaning to speak into Tucker's good ear under cover of the music. "He used to say Mom should have sung at the Opry, that her voice deserved a bigger audience."

Tucker took her hand. "He was probably right. Remember when all the churches had Bible school together in the clubhouse at the lake? Your mom always led the singing and she'd get us to sing, too, no matter how bad we were. I still know all the words to 'Deep and Wide.'"

Libby chuckled, the weight of old grief lifting a little. "Father Doherty said we created whitecaps on the lake when we sang. I don't think he meant it as a compliment."

Tucker laughed, leaning his head back. She looked at the line of his throat above the sweater he wore and thought how handsome he was. How much she appreciated him holding her hand. And how good that felt.

Something in the pool of too-intense emotions she was feeling right then warned her that maybe it felt a little too good. It was like sitting where her mother had been, listening to the songs her mother had heard—it was pleasure to the point of pain.

CHAPTER FIVE

"No KIDS?" INSIDE the town house in Sawyer where Meredith lived, Tucker looked around and raised his eyebrows. There were no toys in the small living area, no TV noise in the background, no sounds of sibling joy or its noisy opposite. "How did that happen?"

Meredith smiled, although her eyes looked shadowed. "Their dad got an unexpected long weekend and asked if he could have them. He picked them up from school and is taking them for pizza and the movies and then to spend two nights in a motel with an indoor pool. They told me I wasn't any fun anymore and Daddy was." The shadow came perilously close to being tears, and she turned away abruptly.

Charlie had played that con-the-parents game with Jack, telling his father that Uncle Tucker was the fun brother. Jack had called Tucker and asked if Charlie could come and live with him because being a dad wasn't fun anymore. Tucker yelled, "No way!" over the phone, and they all ended up laughing.

He didn't think Meredith would see the humor in the story, so he didn't tell it. "Let's go do something," he suggested instead, hooking her arm with a gentle hand and turning her back toward him. "Hey." He thumbed the tears from her cheeks. "They'll be home in a few days, Mer, and he's a good dad. It's not like he's going to abscond with them."

"Oh, I know." She leaned against him, and he held her, dropping a kiss on the top of her head. Her spiky hair felt odd against his lips. Not hard, exactly, but not soft and warm like Libby's, either. Meredith was taller than average, too. When they'd gone to a wine-tasting party, she'd worn skinny high heels and they'd been eye to eye. He'd liked that. She'd been fun to dance with. She was fun to *be* with, for that matter. She liked football, made really good potato soup that went well with the crusty bread he bought from the Amish bakery and had nice kids. He was attracted to her.

And yet.

It was the *and yet* that got him. It was okay

that he wasn't falling in love—other than Jack and Arlie and a few friends here and there, he'd never really observed being in love as all that healthy a part of a relationship. Plus, he and Meredith had only been seeing each other for a short while. He liked her more than anyone he'd dated in a very long time. He enjoyed the kids—he'd even taken Zack with him to play basketball with Jack and Charlie at the elementary school on open gym night. They'd played for an hour, working on Charlie's jump shot and teaching Zack how to do layups. Afterward, Tucker sat quietly with Zack at the ice cream counter in the Silver Moon and heard between the lines of the eight-year-old's conversation how much he missed his dad.

"I know he's a good dad. It was husbanding he failed at." Meredith shrugged, the movement slight against Tucker. "What would you like to do? We've already seen both the movies at the theater."

"You want to go roller-skating?"

"What?" She pulled away from him, laughing. "I'm thirty. All I do at the rink these days is tie the kids' skates and be ready with Band-Aids when they fall down."

Disappointment nudged, although he couldn't have said why. "Pool?" he suggested. "We could go to Kokomo or even back to the Hall. The table there is regulation."

She shook her head. "Can we just stay here? Maybe order pizza and stream something on TV? I'm sorry. I'm in kind of a crummy mood."

"Sure, we can do that. It's okay." It wasn't. They'd seen each other nearly every day since their first date, but they hadn't reached that stage of comfort and conversation with each other. He didn't know how either would bear up through an evening of inactivity.

At first, it *was* okay. They wrangled, laughing over what pizza to order, then again over what to watch. The movie they finally agreed on didn't hold Tucker's interest, and he had to work to stay awake. Halfway through, she said, "This is crummy, isn't it?"

At first he thought she meant the two of them trying to make a relationship out of too little substance, but it was too early in the dating game to make that assessment. At least, according to Libby it was. He still wasn't sure if she'd forgiven either him or her friend Allison for being completely unattracted to each other from the get-go.

"Crummy." He let the word percolate between them for a moment. "Why?"

"There's no plot. The only conflict is stupid stuff Shelby's first-grade class could have developed. What's her name has had so much plastic surgery she's unrecognizable."

Oh, the movie. He almost laughed, but thought once again that she wouldn't see the humor in the situation. "It's not great," he admitted. "Let's go have a drink somewhere. We shouldn't waste an evening on a movie we don't like. I'll even buy."

"Okay," Meredith said reluctantly, turning off the TV and standing up. "I don't know any place to go in Sawyer, though. If it's not kid friendly, I haven't been there."

"Sawyer has places, but we can go to the Grill. It's only five miles over to the lake." He hoped she would go for that, because he didn't want to stay here. Her sadness was heavy and all-consuming, filling the room with an unhappiness he couldn't begin to penetrate.

She nodded. "All right." She brightened. "What about darts? Do you like to play?"

He did. He and the Thursday night poker

players often played when the cards weren't
falling right. Plus, he was glad to see her be
enthusiastic—he'd have probably joined the
dominoes table in the corner of the bar if
she'd wanted to, and he didn't even remember how to play.

On the way to Anything Goes, they talked
about her job and the move from a practice in
an affluent suburb to a small-town one with
many Amish patients. She liked it, Meredith
maintained, because she loved working with
Arlie, but she wasn't completely comfortable
with the differences between the two practices.

"The rules are the same, and the laws, and
I'm glad to have people call me by my first
name and ask how my kids are doing, but it's
just so informal. I never expected to work in
a facility that had a hitching rail and a water
trough in addition to regular customer parking."

He nodded. "The Amish workers at
Llewellyn's Lures ride their bicycles to work
or ride with one of the English. Jack asked
one of the guys if we needed to add hitching rails, and Fred, who's a supervisor, said
no—they weren't going to leave their horses

standing there for eight hours. It wasn't one of my brother's brightest questions."

She laughed, the sound quiet and polite. "You don't travel much these days, do you? Do you miss it?"

"No. I still go on the road once a month or so, but I really like being settled here." Although he got lonely sometimes. He'd probably gotten lonely when he lived in Tennessee and spent half his time on the road, too, but he didn't remember it. Of course, then he hadn't been in pursuit of the whole wife, kids and four-bedroom house dream.

The dartboard was already in use in the Grill, and literally every table was occupied. Libby and Nate were sitting in one of the booths beside the windows overlooking the lake. Nate waved them over, and Tucker captured Meredith's hand as they wove between the tables. He waited until she'd slid into the booth beside Libby, then sat next to Nate. "'Sup?"

Libby pointed an accusatory finger in his direction. "You sound like Charlie."

Tucker grinned at her. "Only because Jack and I *practiced* sounding like Charlie. The kid can't start a conversation without saying that."

"So that's why Zack's been saying it." Meredith beamed over the discovery. "When I asked him to stop doing layups in the living room, he paused for the moment and said ''Sup, Mom?' and dunked the ball right into the ficus tree."

Libby and Nate laughed, and Tucker did, too, but he wondered where this cheerful woman had been when they were at her house trying to watch a boring movie she'd chosen. She'd been taciturn and moody and on the verge of tears.

They talked about spring—surely it would come eventually—and about golf and the state high school basketball tournament. Tucker asked about Libby's plans for remodeling the carriage house at Seven Pillars to be used for larger meetings than the tearoom could accommodate, and Nate promised her more business when the expansion took place. Meredith listened and contributed to the conversation and laughed as long and loud as everyone else when it was warranted. Or when it wasn't—clients in the Grill weren't picky about what they laughed at.

All four of them left at eleven, parting in the parking lot with hugs and handshakes.

"They're such nice people," Meredith said when they were in the car driving toward her house. "How long have you known them?"

"Always." His answer was immediate, but then he thought about it. "Well, Nate just from kindergarten. I've known Libby since she was twenty-seven minutes old. She was my first roommate the night we were born." He glanced at Meredith. "Do you have friends like that?"

She hesitated, not looking back at him, then said quietly, with pain adding shaky needles to her voice, "I used to. Just one."

LIBBY KISSED NATE'S cheek and grinned at him. "See you later. I'm glad you had such a great trip to North Carolina."

He winked at her and stepped across the enclosed porch that sheltered the tearoom's back door, turning back at the last second. "Don't forget, there's enough room for you and even Tuck at the beach house, so come on down for a few days. I'd like you to meet Mandy."

"I want to meet her, too, but I'm still thinking about it."

She did want to meet Nate's fiancée. His engagement to the woman from North Carolina was so new and so sudden he hadn't told anyone at the lake except Libby about it yet, but he was ecstatic. "We've all waited so long, it seems like, those of us from the accident," he'd said earlier that night, before Tucker and Meredith had joined them. "Sam's the only one who's married. Arlie and Jack didn't get engaged till this winter. You, Jess, Holly and me—we've done okay, but none of us has married or had kids. We don't know what happened to Cass, but I'll bet she hasn't, either." He'd smiled into Libby's eyes, although the sadness in his own wasn't hard to see. "It's like we're all renting our lives. I don't want to do that anymore. I want to take ownership. Mandy and I have danced around a relationship ever since we met a couple of years ago—it was time to stand still and let ourselves be caught."

When she got home, Libby changed into sweats, poured a glass of milk and sat on the upholstered window seat in her bedroom, looking out over the lake. She sipped slowly, willing her mind to become still. Her head ached, the throbbing slipping down her temple and through her cheekbone and jaw, ending with an eddy of swirling pain in her neck and shoulder.

She'd thought she was having a heart attack the first time she got a tension headache a few months after her father died. Arlie had driven out to the farm and taken her to the emergency room at Sawyer Hospital. "It feels like I'm going to die." Libby had held her head in her hands as Arlie drove too fast on Lake Road.

Arlie shook her head. "You're not going to die, no matter what. I'm in nursing school, remember? If I have to, I'll pull over right here and be heroic. I know you won't do anything to make me look bad."

"I'll do my best." But she hadn't thought she'd live long enough to make good on that. She'd given Arlie end-of-life instructions as they drove.

Several hours later, she'd been tested and questioned and her pain was assuaged by a healthy dose of a tranquilizer. She left the hospital carrying an appointment slip. "I'm supposed to see my own doctor tomorrow." She hadn't looked at Arlie, just stared through the windshield into the darkness. "They think depression is a strong possibility."

"Does that surprise you?" Arlie asked gently.

Libby hesitated. "No, but it makes me afraid. What if I do what my father did? He was depressed, too. He took pills for it all our lives, and he still hung himself in the barn because he didn't want to live without my mother."

"You're not your father, and we won't let anything happen to you."

"I don't want anyone to know. You have to promise not to tell, Arlie."

"Let me tell Gianna. She always knows what to do."

That was true. It had been Gianna's single-minded devotion and firm decisions that had held her family together after her husband died in the accident.

"Okay." Libby nodded, just slightly—it still hurt to move her head. "Just your mom, though. No one else."

"I promise. And *you* have to promise to ask for help if you need it."

Arlie had kept her vow and Libby had, too. She'd consulted a mental health specialist, who'd diagnosed both clinical depression and anxiety disorder and prescribed medication and therapy.

The anxiety attacks that accompanied the disorder had both terrified her and planted a seed of defeatism somewhere deep inside. She read everything she could about the angry spiral created by her condition and watched with resignation for all the symptoms that could insert themselves into the coil.

She did everything she could to make herself healthy in both mind and body, but sometimes she felt hopeless even with the medication on board. And so bone-deep lonely she thought she might die from it. She didn't get frightened anymore, and she couldn't have said why not, but she worried that the lack of fear had much to do with a general apathy caused by her depression.

And exhaustion. She loved being "good old Lib." She liked that her friends counted on her, that she never thought she wasn't loved, that nearly every day held a good time within its hours. But keeping the secret wore her out. Pretending she'd rather be alone when she wouldn't. Pretending the job she used to love and still liked a lot was still enough.

Pretending loving other people's kids was enough when her heart fairly screamed that she wanted to love a few of her own. Pretending she'd rather be in like than in love any old day because she wanted adventure more than steadfastness.

But she couldn't take the chance. She couldn't subject anyone else to the person she was underneath her Pollyanna exterior. What if she had a child and turned on it because she couldn't stand its crying? What if she fell in love with a man and turned on him because he couldn't love her back? How *could* he love her back, damaged as she was? And if he did…if by some unbelievable miracle he actually *did*, what if she took the path her father had and ruined other lives besides her own in the process?

It was easier to bear the headaches, the heartaches, the anxiety attacks and the regrets of secrecy than hang the millstone she carried around the neck of someone she loved.

Because what if she had a daughter who blamed herself?

It always came back to that, Libby realized as she sat unmoving in the window seat. She understood how parents felt about their children—she'd seen it in her mother, in Gianna and Dave Gallagher, in Sam and Penny Phillipy, and in Jack. She knew beyond all doubt that if she had a child she'd love it that much, and she ached right to the center of her soul to experience that love. But the monster that was depression wasn't something she could bear to pass on.

The moon shone on Lake Miniagua below her, and she fancied she could hear the slap of lapping waves on the shore. It was a comforting sound, reminding her of her mother rubbing her back and telling her boys were indeed terrible people but that they kept life interesting.

"If you're ever alone—" her mother's beautiful, musical voice had been raspy near the end "—remember that you're not really. I'm always with you. When you talk to Venus, you'll be talking to me."

Libby breathed deeply there in her safe place in the window, willing away the headache while trying to keep the memory close for just long enough to ease her heart and push back the viper. She'd even given her depression its own name with lots of imaginative synonyms. Viper. Beast. Monster.

"Please," she whispered when yet another pain snaked up her temple. She searched the sky until she found the planet that was her talisman. "Please."

Her cell phone made the popping sound that signaled a text, and she picked it up. Hope you're awake. Coming up.

Tucker knew the combination to the downstairs lock, so she wasn't surprised when he tapped lightly on the apartment door, then let himself in. "Yo, Lib."

"I'm in here." She couldn't muster the strength to get up, to smile and make cracks about him coming to her bedroom in the middle of the night. Although...what *was* he doing in her bedroom in the middle of the night? "Something wrong?"

"I don't know." He crossed the room to her, lean and loose limbed in jeans and one of the cashmere sweaters he was fond of wearing. This one was the same blue as his eyes, and if he hadn't been her best friend and if she'd felt better, she'd have gone weak in the knees. He looked that handsome.

He stroked his hand through her hair, and she flinched in spite of herself when the pain twinged along in the wake of his fingers. He went still and sat on the edge of the window seat, pushing her legs aside to make room. "I don't know," he said again. "There *is* something wrong—I can tell that just by looking at you. However, since you are a girl in spite of everything I tried to teach you while we were growing up and I am a typical male, I don't have a clue what it is."

She laughed. "I'm fine, Tuck. Really, I am. You want some hot chocolate?"

"It'd be good. Why don't I make it?"

"That would be nice." She waved him away. "I'll wash my face and meet you in the kitchen."

She went into the bathroom and splashed her face with cold water. She took a couple of pain relievers, hoping the pain would ebb, then ran a brush through her hair.

Brown. Everything was brown. Her hair, her freckles, the sweats she'd put on because they were the first ones she'd come to in the drawer. Her eyes, usually clear and dark gray, looked muddy. No wonder she was alone— she was so lacking in color she disappeared right into the woodwork.

It's like we're all renting our lives. Nate's words echoed in her mind. Haunting. Hurting.

She loved her life, her friends, the tearoom. She adored Jesse, although they didn't talk much. They never had, but that didn't make them any less cognizant that they were each other's only family.

If I were gone, who would care?

She opened the medicine cabinet to look at the row of medications on the middle shelf. Vitamins. Calcium. Capsules that were supposed to be good for her hair and nails and joints. House-brand allergy pills. At the end of the row, hidden behind the pain relievers, were the antidepressants.

God, she hated them. She'd tried to stop taking them more than once, but the headaches and hopelessness had immediately returned to being impenetrable.

"I know you don't like depending on them." Arlie had sat with her in the doctor's waiting room in October, the last time she'd tried going it alone and ended up with a panic attack and skyrocketing blood pressure. "I had to take them after the accident and I hated them, too, but Gianna said it was better that I hate pills than that I hate myself." She held Libby's gaze. "She said she'd lost Daddy, but she wasn't going to lose one of her girls. She's my stepmom, Lib. I'm no more her blood than you are. We're not losing you, either. You go right ahead hating the pills—I don't care at all—but don't you stop taking them. Hear me?"

What would happen if I took them all at once?

She closed the mirrored door and shook her head at her reflection. "I don't know what's the matter with you," she muttered, "but you need to get a grip." She clipped her hair into a messy knot at the back of her head and went into the apartment's miniature kitchen. "Are you done with that chocolate yet, Llewellyn? You are so slow."

"It's ready. Here." He handed her a cup. "Let's go do some stargazing. What do you say?"

She followed him onto the porch and they sat on the lounge, leaning back to stare up at the clear sky. "Want to go roller-skating soon? A three-hour weeknight adventure?" he asked.

"I'd love that. I can still beat you, you know, and I can get under the limbo stick a half foot lower than you can." She probably couldn't, but that was how their conversations always went, and she loved them. Loved him. She loved Jesse, too, but Tucker would have been a better brother.

Or maybe not.

He snorted. "In your dreams. How long's it been since you skated?"

"Hmm…" She sipped chocolate and gazed at the Big Dipper. "I believe it was November when Holly took all the cheerleaders—she's their coach, remember? I went along to chaperone. We raced for a prize. I came in second behind Holly."

He laughed. "Tuesday night?"

She nodded. "Good. Want me to fix us some dinner?"

"Great."

They relaxed there in her favorite place, pointing at this star and that one and delineating constellations with more energy than precision. They argued, as Midwesterners often do, about when autumn's harvest moon actually occurred until she went in and looked it up, and then they argued about the accuracy of the *Farmer's Almanac*. By the time her cup was empty, Libby wasn't sure where the pain in her head had been. She didn't care, as long as it was gone, and it hadn't left any voices behind to whisper wondering questions or worries about a rented life.

Suddenly Tucker's arm was around her shoulders, tugging her closer to him. "Over there," he said, pointing. "The brightest one. See it? Wish on it, Lib."

For just that moment, with his lean cheek brushing her temple, his heartbeat solid against her hand when she laid it on his chest and his voice her talisman against depression's threat, she felt entirely safe. Entirely happy. Entirely loved.

And she wished for always. For ownership.

CHAPTER SIX

"I TOOK ALL the skin off. That was not my intent." Tucker looked at his rink-rashed knees with minor disgust and major discomfort he was doing his best to hide. It was one thing to know your pain threshold lingered between zero and one, but quite another to admit it.

"You were showing off. I told you to wear knee pads." Still wearing protectors on both her knees and her elbows, Libby swabbed his wounds with something caustic enough that the slightest of whimpers escaped his lips. "Oh, hush, you big baby."

"You might have warned me about the whole thing with cracking the whip."

"And you might have been paying attention. It's a good thing to do in a skating rink with a bunch of fifth graders." She put large Band-Aids over the abrasions. "Do you need to lie down while I finish dinner, precious?"

"I think you're being unnecessarily mean

to me." He pulled the legs of his sweatpants down over his knees. "Can I help you with it?"

"You can cook the spaghetti while I get the garlic bread ready. Did you bring any wine?"

"I did." He got to his feet, following her to the kitchen. "If you'd been nicer to me, I'd even have brought you some. Oof!" He doubled over when she elbowed him, exaggerating to please her.

She smeared butter onto the bread while he ran water in the pasta pan. "Are we going to talk about your dates?" she asked. "It's kind of been all me lately, what with looking at the stars the other night and tonight's adventure. I'm ready to butt into your life again."

He grinned at her. "I don't need your oar in. I'm doing just fine on my own." He wasn't, but he didn't think she could do anything about whatever the problem was between Meredith and him.

"Of course you do. If it wasn't for me, you'd probably be signing up on a dating site and meeting people for coffee in remote and anonymous coffee shops halfway to Indianapolis."

She looked so serious, he was afraid she

had experience in the matter. "You haven't done that, have you?"

"What? Met someone online? I have. We exchanged bread recipes and he wanted to get together somewhere so I could share sourdough starter with him. I didn't have time that day, so I had to say no." Her eyes were wide. "His hopes were raised and swollen to twice their size, so I had to punch them down before it got out of hand."

He sighed heavily. And sighed again, thumping his forehead in feigned despair. "That's a disgusting play on words. But I'm assuming you belong to a group of bread bakers online, right?"

She laughed, clapping her hands. "Good for you, Llewellyn. You picked right up on that. And the guy who wanted to meet me is Max Harrison."

Tucker put dry spaghetti into the pan, folding it down into the boiling water. He shot her a disbelieving look. "The high school principal? The one who's been dating Gianna for the past few years?"

Libby smirked, pushing the bread into the oven. "The one you're still scared of? Yep. That's the one."

"I'm not scared." He drizzled olive oil into the water, gave the pasta strands a separating stir and set the timer. "Cautious, maybe, but not scared."

"Yeah, right." She turned on the burner under the sauce. "So, how's Meredith? The whole staff of A Woman's Place had lunch at the tearoom today." A Woman's Place was the gynecology clinic on the lake. "However, so did the English department from the high school, so I didn't get a chance to talk to anyone."

"She's okay." He gave the boiling pasta another desultory stir. "Actually, she's great."

Libby handed him the cheese grater and a chunk of parmesan. "You want to put this on the table?" She took it back. "Never mind. You pour the wine. The last time you grated cheese, I was cleaning up cheddar for a week." She took the things to the table and added, "I'm glad to hear that."

"Hear what?"

"That Meredith is great. I'd be gladder if you were more convincing."

He poured wine into the stemless glasses they'd learned the hard way were best for them to use and gave her one. "It's not something that can be forced. A relationship, I mean." They clinked glasses and sipped. "I thought we weren't going to talk about my dates."

"That's what you get for thinking." She took the bread out of the oven.

They filled their plates and sat at the round table in the dining area. "Maybe I should ask Marie Williams out," he mused. "I think she's divorced again."

"No, she's not. They may be living apart some of the time, but they're not divorced. I truly think that's a kettle of fish you might want to avoid."

"You don't like her, do you?" Which was saying something. Libby liked everybody.

Usually. "Not much."

"Why not?"

"Because she's mean to her daughter. I don't mean she hits her—I'm sure she doesn't—but she makes her feel bad because she's on the heavy side and she's probably not very pretty right now. But how's she ever going to *feel* pretty if her own mother doesn't think she is?"

A good point. There was likely something Freudian in Tucker's penchant for loving mothers, but he didn't know what it was. He would have to ask his own the next time he talked to her. She'd no doubt be entertained by the notion.

"It's moot anyway. I'm still seeing Meredith, and we all know I'm loyal as a puppy."

Pretty Boy padded into the room as if he'd been called, coming to stand beside Libby's chair and frown disapprovingly at Tucker.

"It's all right, sweetheart. Somewhere in his little bitty mind, Tucker knows he's not a puppy," Libby soothed, petting the dog's smooth golden head. She frowned across the table. "You're also not one for exclusivity in dating. Is that something new, or do you think you and Meredith might be heading toward commitment?"

He couldn't tell how Libby felt about that. She was smiling, but her eyes seemed to be devoid of expression. He wondered how she did that and realized with startling suddenness how often she did. If asked, he would have said he knew her better than nearly anyone, but there were mysteries to his best buddy that he had no clue how to solve. Especially since he was fairly certain she didn't *want* them solved.

"WE GOT AN offer on the Albatross. Can you believe it?" Tucker entered the tearoom late Friday afternoon, wearing a dress shirt and tie with black jeans—an outfit she was unaccustomed to seeing on him. "I may not have my four-bedroom house yet, but I won't have to live in the Hall, either. How about that? Why are you still open? It's after four."

Libby looked up from setting out stacks of plates and rows of forks on the dessert table. "I know, but we have a bridal shower here tonight. Neely's working it, but I'm helping with setup." She smiled at him. "Was it a good offer?"

"It wouldn't have been good enough for my grandmother, but Jack and I are pleased. We're keeping much of the grounds, including the acreage with the barn and the Dower House where Jack and Charlie live, so we'll still have plenty of frontage and room to put in another dock and maybe another house."

"Are you going to move in with Jack?" She handed him two sleeves of plastic wedding cups and pointed to the table beside the buffet.

"Until the wedding. I'm pretty sure Arlie won't want me there after that—she's already taking on Jack and Charlie. The handsome and charming brother and uncle might be a bit much."

"She might rent you the Toe after they get married."

He nodded. "It's a thought." He opened the doors beneath the buffet to get out the punch bowls. "I think I spend too much time here. I know where everything is."

Libby frowned, looking at the clock. "I thought you and Meredith were going to a play in Indy."

"That's tomorrow night. She took the kids to their dad's tonight, then she's going to her folks' for the rest of the weekend. I'll pick her up there."

"Did you get the text from Dan Parsons yesterday?"

"That's why I came by. I wondered if you wanted to go see the new baby. If we leave now, we can be up there by seven. We could take some pizza. There's no snow this time, and not likely to be any."

"That would be great. Pour us some coffee while I change clothes. You want to make sure they're up for company?"

He looked sheepish. "I already did."

Libby changed into jeans and a sweater and came back down, carrying wrapped gifts for all three Parsons children. "Don't say a word," she said. "Gavin's and Mari's are just sweatshirts with the Lake Miniagua logo on them. I thought they'd like them."

"I didn't say anything," he protested, pulling off his tie and tucking it into his jacket pocket.

Libby went into the kitchen to tell Neely she was leaving and came back out carrying a cupcake with messy icing plus a bakery box holding another dozen. She handed the loose one to Tucker. "An oops. Don't get that stuff on your shirt—it will never come out."

When they got to the car, she saw why he hadn't teased her about her gifts for the children. In addition to a gift bag with the words *It's a boy!* emblazoned on it, there were two long boxes on the back seat. "Fishing poles," Tucker said. "Promotional ones from the plant. One of them might be a little girly."

The late February air was crisp but not cold. They talked all the way to the Parsons' home. "What's it like, going back to a farm? Don't you miss it?" he asked, pointing at a herd of cows milling around behind a fence. It looked like a bovine social hour.

"I miss the farm itself, even though I can go there any time I want since Jess still lives there. But I don't miss how hard the work was or how endless the days were. I know when I close the tearoom, I have to open it up again the next morning and that I'm probably going to be baking both after hours and before opening time. But I also know if I'm sick or something happens, I can put up the Closed sign and call the pastry customers and it won't be that big of a deal."

It was a big deal to her, although she didn't want to admit that—not even to Tucker. When she failed, and it seemed to her she failed often, the depression hovered ever closer. In her mind, she knew being ill two days a year or even four or five wasn't a failure. She was the first one to tell Neely to stay home and get some rest when she needed to, because the other woman's fibromyalgia was no joke. However, she found her own weaknesses nearly unforgivable.

"You're right," he said. "It's not a big deal, but I think you're faking it when you say it's not. Go on with what you were saying." He waved an impatient hand without taking his eyes from the road.

She scowled at him, hoping he sensed it even if he wasn't looking at her. "Milking cows, on the other hand, is a show that absolutely must go on. When my mother and father died, those cows had to be milked no matter whose world had come to an end. You remember." Her throat closed up, and she had to struggle to find her voice. "Dad was milking when Mom died, and he finished before he came to the house. Two years later, the cows were in the milking parlor before the sheriff and the ambulance even got there the morning I found Dad." The memories were crushing, taking her breath with their painful intensity. "But you were there before any of them—you knew I was alone." He'd come tearing up the driveway of the farm as if the devil were chasing him. She'd been standing at the door of the barn, rigid, as if the reality of that awful morning would reverse itself if she just didn't move.

She'd folded when Tucker ran toward her, and he'd caught her before she went down. He'd been catching her ever since.

He nodded, reaching over to squeeze her

fingers. "I remember the day the trucks took the cows away when you bought Seven Pillars."

She did, too. It might have been the last time she'd cried, because as much as she'd hated milking them, she'd still loved the huge, gentle-eyed girls. Jesse had put his arm around her and said, "If you've changed your mind, we can stop this right now, give the money back and go on the way we've been."

It was the first time in either of their lives they'd ever known absolute freedom. Libby was shocked by how much the autonomy hurt.

"That was a hard one." She took a deep breath, then another, staring out the passenger window at the fallow fields, just starting to green up with spring's early hope.

She didn't think the word *hope* went well with spring. As far as she was concerned, T. S. Eliot had it right when he proclaimed April the cruelest month.

And it was only a little over a month away.

GAVIN AND MARI ran to the car to greet them when they pulled into the driveway. "Wait till you see the new baby," said Mari, hugging them indiscriminately. "His name is Carson. He poops all the time and doesn't have any hair. Daddy says he'll lose all his, too, if I don't quit talking so much. I think that's goofy, don't you?"

"I don't know, kiddo. I had hair to my shoulders when we started the drive up here and Libby talked all the way. Now look at me." Tucker pointed at his recently cut hair and caught Gavin in a headlock, scrubbing his knuckles over the boy's scalp. "Can you carry the pizza?"

Alice and Dan were in the kitchen. Alice, looking tired but radiant, sat at the table holding a gorgeously bald baby. Dan, his still-thick hair pulled back into a ponytail, was staring at a jug of milk in consternation. His expression lightened when he shook hands with Tucker and hugged Libby. "Do you know what that is?" He pointed at the glass container.

Tucker smiled at the baby in Alice's arms and stroked a finger down his tiny cheek. "You are a good-looking kid. I may have to borrow you." Then he looked back at the gallon-size Mason jar. "I've been wrong before, but I'd almost swear it was milk. It doesn't look very good," he added.

"Making butter?" Libby got plates from the cupboard, handing them to Gavin to set on the table.

"Yes." Dan got out the silverware. "We'd been sharing Joanna's milk with the community food co-op, but Alice had too much downtime these past few days, what with only having a baby and getting an article written for a magazine. She found a butter churn in the attic and decided we should take further steps toward living off the land."

Libby folded the flatware into cloth napkins, showing Mari the way to do it. "How old is the milk?"

She looked so natural in this homey, sort-of-messy kitchen, interacting with an eager little girl but not missing a thing that went on around her. This was the kind of place she belonged, not chasing adventures with a buddy—even a best buddy. Tucker knew that as well as he knew himself, but he also knew too much of her life had been outside the lines of what she could control—he wasn't going to try choosing directions for her.

"Two days. I researched." Alice grinned at her. "I may be a pioneer, but I'm not doing it without the internet."

"Good. Got buttermilk?"

"We do. And cheesecloth. And some really good herbs from our own greenhouse to add to a batch."

Tucker raised his eyebrows at Dan. "Does this mean the next time we come, you'll be wearing suspenders and the kids will be calling you 'Pa' and doing their chores without being told?"

"I actually have the suspenders. I don't remember where they came from, but I have some." Dan took the snoozing baby from his wife, laid him in the Moses basket on the counter and withdrew a bottle from the wine rack. "Rhubarb? If you have even an iota of wine snobbery in your soul, you'll hate it, but it's Alice's favorite. Not that she's drinking any right now."

They demolished the pizza, wine and cupcakes, then Gavin and Mari went off to watch television while the adults stayed at the table.

"You are really living the pioneer lifestyle, aren't you," said Tucker, looking across the table at Alice. "We know that Dan was a bank vice president who wore suits in a former life, and your byline is well-known. How do you go from that to a farm an hour away from anything?"

Dan laughed, exchanging glances with his wife. "I came home from work one day to find Alice extremely upset—"

"With good reason," she interrupted, accepting the coffee he handed her.

He ignored her and went on. "—because she'd driven all the way across Fort Wayne to buy Gavin pants for school. Everyone in our neighborhood, it seems, was buying this particular brand of jeans for their third graders, so obviously we needed to, as well. She was sitting in traffic on Coldwater Road with Mari crying in her car seat when she had an epiphany."

"It wasn't an epiphany." Alice and Libby got up in unison to clear the table, and Tucker wondered if it was a woman thing that they all moved at the same time. "It was a meltdown. I decided life was too short for my kids to wear hundred-dollar jeans and for me to sit in traffic when it was ninety degrees outside. We'd bought the farm as an investment when Dan's cousin retired to Arizona, plus we had a ton of money saved because Dan's salary was…pleasant, to say the least. He'd spent some of the happiest times in his life here, and I wanted a simpler life. It seemed like the perfect solution."

"She's right about the happy times—I loved it here. When it comes to the salary, I wanted to keep on making it, as a matter of fact. But I didn't much like being a weekend dad. The commute was doable, but sixty hours a week at the bank didn't allow family time, so I resigned." He grinned. "Now the kids are homeschooled in jeans that cost a lot less, I teach at a university fairly nearby and Alice still writes articles. She also makes butter. Or is about to."

From his basket on the counter, the baby made his presence known. Libby picked him up and exchanged a few nuzzles and cross-eyed grins with him before handing him off to Alice. "You feed. I'll churn."

"Life on the farm will be the perfect adventure if we don't kill each other first." Alice arranged blanket and baby with a sigh of relief. "Or die of being tired."

"Nah, you won't." Libby's gaze met Tucker's, their laughter silent yet heard by both of them. He wished they were touching but realized they didn't have to be to make their connection as tight as the proverbial tick. "Tired is good medicine."

Tucker snorted. "Libby's brother, her friends and I all threatened to kill her before she got the tearoom up and running, she worked us so hard. If tiredness is good medicine, we were cured of many ills." He gave in to the need and stroked a hand over her silky brown hair. It felt as if it held the warmth of midday sun in it, and the sensation rippled through his fingers.

What was he thinking? This was Libby. He pulled away so suddenly she gave him a startled look that asked, *What's wrong?*

He nodded toward the glass butter churn, the movement jerky. "That's sounding pretty thumpy. Is it butter?"

She lifted the churn to look at the contents. "I think it is. Everybody ready to try it? Do you have homemade bread, Alice, since you haven't been doing anything this week?"

"Fresh from the co-op. And cinnamon bread, too."

It was a great dessert, fresh butter spread on warmed homemade bread with blackberry and strawberry jams on the side. The coffee was hot and rich. After the kids had eaten their fill and gone off to bed, Dan brought out a couple of board games. The four of them played games and talked until nearly midnight.

Marriage and family were on the short list of things he wanted from life, but Tucker tended to daydream more around the *Leave It to Beaver* option than a modern-day *The Waltons*. Dan and Alice's chief support system seemed to come from the food co-op they participated in and—more importantly—from themselves. Unlike the Amish who lived near Lake Miniagua, the Parsons' chosen way of life was vastly different from the one they'd grown up in or expected to maintain. That it wasn't always easy was obvious in the watching, but the often noisy and seemingly dissonant unit that was their family seemed to work.

Something else that was obvious was that throughout the disarray of the house-in-progress and the disorder wrought by a family of five ran a deep and enduring love. As different as the families were, it reminded him of Jack and Arlie and the family they were building. Love was the ballast in both situations.

That was what Tucker wanted—ballast.

It wasn't very exciting, he guessed, walking to the car with Libby's hand in his. But as far as adventures went, tonight had been a success.

CHAPTER SEVEN

THE PLAY WAS FUNNY. Tucker laughed most of the way through it and tried not to care that Meredith wasn't paying attention to the comedy on the stage or him. At intermission, he stood in line for drinks while she went to the restroom. He waited in the lobby for her, sipping his beer and feeling uncomfortable.

He wished he knew where to go in this relationship that seemed to be stalled at an emotional crossroads that had hills on every single side of a four-way stop. No matter how much he liked her—and he did; she was smart and funny and the chemistry between them was very real—he couldn't see over the next hill from their present position.

"Would you like to go?" he asked when she rejoined him. "If you don't like the play, we can have a late supper somewhere or go hear some live music and dance."

She looked surprised by the question but

sipped from her drink before answering. "I like the play." She looked around at the opulent interior of the old theater. "For that matter, I like being back in Indy, where everything is so available. You don't have to drive eighty-seven miles for a professional-quality performance or access to every kind of cuisine or shopping you want. I didn't think I'd miss it as much as I do."

He nodded. "The amenities at the lake are a little lacking," he admitted.

Her eyebrows rose. "A little? I have to drive twenty miles to take Shelby to dance class. Sawyer has one supermarket. *One.* The only grocery at the lake is the bulk foods store. If there's a fire at the lake, it better burn slow, because chances are the volunteer firemen will be in the fields when the alarm sounds. I've yet to figure out what I'll do if we have an actual emergency at the same time as a basketball game, because all the first responders will be in the gym at the high school yelling, 'Go, Lakers.'"

He thought of a freezing Sunday evening last December, when Llewellyn's Lures could easily have burned to the ground but didn't because of the volunteers who'd fought a fire for hours in an ice storm. He opened his mouth to defend...what? They didn't need defending. And Meredith wasn't listening anyway. Her attention was focused somewhere across the room. He wondered fleetingly if she saw someone she knew. Or wished she knew. And then he realized he didn't really care.

She shrugged. "I know it's a nice community with nice people, and I'm everlastingly grateful to Arlie for the job at a time when I didn't know what I was going to do, but I'll never feel at home there. Finding culture at the library, the local theater and bingo at the lake clubhouse just doesn't work for me. I don't mind ordering clothes and makeup online, but I don't want to *have* to."

They went back inside then, and it wasn't until he was driving home later that Tucker thought about what she'd said. He liked cities, too. He loved the convenience of living in them. But Miniagua was home. He could live with driving two hours to a Colts game or to the airport easier than he could handle being that far away from Jack and Charlie.

Or Libby.

That addendum to his thoughts startled him. What was going on here?

"YOUR CHOICE. The White Sox, the Cubs, the Indians or the Reds. They're all having pre-season night games, and we can make it to any of them." Tucker poured coffee from the pot Libby had made when he stopped by after church.

Libby had to give it some thought. The only baseball that really interested her was played at the local sports park and the high school campus. It came with buttery popcorn and fountain soda that sold for a dollar. She knew almost everyone there, both on the field and off, and had sponsored a softball team called Libby's Longarms ever since Seven Pillars opened.

"Where would you rather go?" she asked, stalling for time. She knew he didn't care, or he wouldn't have offered such a wide range of choices. She wished a little resentfully that he'd offer to take her to a play. She loved anything that took place on a stage, probably because her greatest dramatic talent had to do with selling tickets at the door.

But the theater and concerts—those were places he took dates. Places he dressed up for, even occasionally stopping by Libby's to ask which tie he should wear with which shirt.

He shrugged. "I'm not big on baseball unless I'm playing it or I'm watching Charlie. I just thought it might be something different for you." He handed her a cup and sat at the table, waiting for her to join him.

She did, sipping her coffee and fighting back the ill temper that was pushing to make itself known. "I'm not crazy about it, either." There was a play at a local theater in the county seat, less than twenty miles away. If she suggested that, would he think she was asking him on a date?

"Want to go to Peru?" he asked. "I think Ole Olsen Theater's having a matinee, although I don't know if there are any tickets left."

Oh, thank goodness, he'd saved her from herself. "I'd like that. Why don't you check for tickets while I make you a sandwich?"

The theater building was Peru's old depot, a former station of the C&O Railroad. It had fewer than a hundred seats and lots of restored paneling. Libby was charmed by both the venue and the production. She and Tucker leaned into each other and laughed at the comedy onstage, and when they moved back to their original positions, he laid his arm across the back of her chair, his hand occasionally stroking the soft knit of the cotton sweater she wore. He left his arm where it was until the end of the show, when they rose to their feet with everyone else in a standing ovation.

After shaking hands with the cast, they stepped out into the chilly afternoon. "Let's walk awhile." He gestured toward the paved path beyond the gazebo by the depot. "You're not wearing heels, are you?"

"No." And if she had been, she'd have gone anyway. It was disconcerting, she had to admit, this sudden, deeper enjoyment of Tucker's company. Actually, *enjoyment* wasn't a strong enough word. If she were being completely honest with herself, it probably wasn't sudden, either.

She thought maybe it had started with that unexpected kiss on their birthdays, the one that had landed on her mouth and lasted a little longer than usual. That had certainly given her a new awareness of him as more than her best friend.

After that, he'd held her hand more often than not when they went walking. Their goodbyes, which had always included cheek kisses and brief hugs, had become a little self-conscious. Mari Parsons had referred to her as Tucker's sister once, and Libby had blushed and Tucker had looked away, turning studious attention to Gavin's calf.

Then had come that little niggle of relief Libby felt when none of the introductions on his hunt for a wife had worked out. There hadn't been the chemistry he'd mentioned at least once in every conversation until she'd threatened him. At least until Meredith, when he didn't *have* to mention it because it came off them in waves every time they were together. He saw her nearly every day and was uncharacteristically quiet about her, although he talked about the kids.

Meredith was perfect for him. Libby knew that. The nurse-midwife was bright and beautiful, with a certain aura of sophistication Libby couldn't match, even if she was trying to. Which she wasn't.

They walked the nearly mile-long path, stopping to sit in a swing that hung from a crossbar just because it was there. At an enclosed playground farther down the path, they stood for a minute and watched the children playing. They climbed, swung and slid, shouting and running the whole time. The late-afternoon sun shone golden in its descent.

The beauty of it all was enough to make Libby's heart ache.

She looked at Tucker. He was watching the kids, his mouth lifted in a crooked smile. When a timid little girl made her reluctant way to the top of a slide and slid down into her mother's waiting arms, he raised his hand in a thumbs-up, and the little girl clapped her hands in response.

This was what he wanted and needed. Kids and playgrounds and a wife who felt the same way about such things. This was Tucker's chemistry.

They walked on. He pointed at a building near the end of the path. "It used to be a bowling alley."

She squinted at the sign. "Tuck, that's a mortuary."

He nodded. "And an event center."

"So if you die at the event, they just haul you into the next room?"

"I don't think that's quite the way it works."

She laughed. "It's a small town. It might. Remember after the accident? The fire department took Arlie and Holly's dad's casket to the cemetery on the back of the fire engine after his funeral. He'd been a volunteer firefighter for years, and they were happy and honored to do it, but the truth was, every hearse in the county was already in use."

Of course Tucker remembered. His father had been both the cause of and one of the fatalities in the accident. One of the county hearses had carried his body to the cemetery in Kokomo. "Oh, Tuck." She stopped, horrified at what she'd said. "I'm sorry."

"It's okay." He pulled her to him, holding her and watching the sun sink below the building that housed the funeral home and event center. "Jack and I have talked about it, and as awful as it all was, it would have been even worse if our father had survived. If he'd still been walking around in an alcoholic stupor, responsible for Dave's and Linda's deaths and everyone else's injuries, I don't know how anyone could have stood it."

Libby didn't, either. She leaned into him without meaning to, and his arms tightened. "You need to forgive him," she said quietly. "Jack has, since he and Arlie got back together. You need to, too."

He shook his head, his chin rubbing the

top of her head. "Like you've forgiven your dad, Lib?"

She stiffened, and his arms tightened even more. "He chose to leave us, and he knew I'd be the one to find him." Her voice sounded brittle. She *felt* brittle.

She also felt the familiar hopelessness stirring inside, feeling cold and crawly under her skin. It was usually easy to push back when she was with Tucker, to keep depression's insidious presence the secret she needed it to be, but sometimes it was hard even then.

"I know." He turned her so that her cheek rested against his shoulder, and stroked her hair back from her face, leaving warmth on her skin where he touched it. It would have been a romantic moment with anyone else, but this was Tucker. It couldn't be romantic. It couldn't.

"I can't take that away." He chuckled, though the sound was more harsh than humorous. "I guess I haven't forgiven him, either. Maybe we should make a new pact. We'll be thirty-five on our next birthdays— by then we will have found a way to forgive our fathers. What do you think?"

I think I'll never forgive Dad. For what he

did to Jesse. What he did to me. But Tucker would be disappointed if she didn't agree. She didn't think he understood how much harder it was sometimes to forgive someone you loved than someone you didn't.

"Okay," she said. "Let's do that." It wouldn't be the first pact either of them had ever broken. He'd sworn not to tell the story of the bats in her attic, but one night at the Grill after three mugs of hot chocolate, he'd told everyone there. It had been the day the Indianapolis Colts had played in the Super Bowl, so the bar had been full and everyone there had heard it.

So she owed him one.

They stepped apart and continued their walk, looping back to the car, singing "Sundown" and at one point playing a rousing game of hopscotch on a grid someone had chalked onto the path.

"Did you know that song was about the writer's girlfriend at the time?" Tucker looked ridiculous hopping on the grid, which completely charmed the little girls who'd come over to play with them.

"I did. We learned that when we sang it in high school choir." Libby took her turn, knowing she looked just as silly jumping with the skirt of her dress flipping around above her knees as he did in his jeans and sweater.

"It's about fidelity."

She knew that, too.

They waved goodbye to the little girls and their waiting mothers and walked on, reaching the car a few minutes later. "I'm looking for that." He opened the passenger door for her and walked around to get in the other side. "I don't mean the whole sexual faithfulness thing—although I want that, too—but I'm talking about mental and emotional loyalty. Like what we have." He started the car and buckled his seat belt, then put a finger under her chin to turn her face toward his. "Means you can't renege on that pact, Miss Libby. If I'm going to forgive to make myself a more whole person, so are you. I'm not playing that particular gig alone."

She sighed, then did it again more heavily to ensure he knew what a pain he was being. "Fine. I can't believe what I have to go through just to make you a better husband for someone else."

They both laughed. Then he told her he was thinking about buying a boat in addition to the pontoon he shared with his brother, and they spent the ride home discussing which of them was the better water skier. She was, but he certainly wasn't going to admit that. He was still getting over the shame of having fallen—several times—while roller-skating.

CHAPTER EIGHT

"Isn't it hard for you sometimes, coming in here?" The barn at the family farm had fresh red paint on its exterior, with big white letters above the original front entry that said Worth Farm, 1915. Inside, however, it was unrecognizable. Jesse's veterinary practice took up most of the ground floor. Downstairs, where the stables and milking parlor had been, were boarding kennels. The loft held an exercise room and Jesse's art studio.

"Not anymore, and it's different for me. I didn't see what you did." Jesse talked Pretty Boy into standing almost still on the scale. "Ah, good. He's gaining some weight. No table food, right?"

"Not much. He has an affinity for chicken salad. Since I do, too, we share it sometimes."

Libby's older brother scowled at her. She beamed back, not holding the expression long because her chin would tremble if she did.

"How's Elijah?" He gave the dog a rub and a treat, then led the way out of the clinic.

They walked across the parking lot to the redbrick house. "He's fine. He's decided Pretty Boy can stay." She stopped at her car. "I'm going home."

She'd been here for forty-five minutes. They'd shared coffee and Jesse had given the dog a cursory once-over. She knew her brother would be impatient to be by himself again.

He looked at her, surprised. "You sure? I have broccoli soup in the Crock-Pot. I don't mind sharing, especially since you made it in the first place." His somber gaze captured hers, and she couldn't look away. "Come on, Lib." His voice was as quiet as always, his face as unsmiling. Almost. There was a barely imperceptible lift at the corner of his mouth and just the slightest twinkle in his eyes. "I'll even let you load the dishwasher."

Other than a few distant cousins who lived in other states, Jesse was her only relative. She wished they saw each other more, but it was Jesse's choice to hold himself apart. Yet he was inviting her to supper. She had cinnamon rolls to bake, but it wouldn't be the first time she'd gotten up at three to do it.

"All right." She went inside with him, grateful as always that, like the barn, the house looked almost nothing like it had when they grew up in it. The kitchen had been expanded into the old dining room, with custom-built cabinets and granite countertops added. The walls were painted red, the windows replaced with bigger, mullioned ones and left uncovered. Sycamore Hill's orchard and grape arbors were visible through the one over the big sink.

Dad would have hated seeing them. He'd fought the sale of so much as a square inch of land until the day he died, even knowing selling the winery acreage to the Grangers would save the rest of the farm.

He'd been so wrong.

"Mom would have loved this." Libby said it every time she visited. She never added the other part: that their father would have hated it. Change, in his eyes, had never been good.

Jesse stirred the soup. "She would. You want to make us some sandwiches? A client brought me part of a ham today."

Libby nodded, smiling approval at the

sourdough bread she found in the drawer. "Homemade?"

"Holly brought it by. She got it at the new Amish bakery at the lake. It's good."

"Holly, huh?" It wasn't the first time they'd been together, although Holly was as quiet about Jesse as he was about her. "Anything you'd like to confide there, big brother?"

He gave her a look that should have singed her eyelashes off, and she opened the loaf. She had tried the pastries from the bakery. They were at least as good as hers. Their coconut cream pie was better. She frowned, spreading mayonnaise on the dense bread. "I wonder."

Jesse set bowls of soup across from each other on the breakfast bar. "Wonder what? What do you want to drink?"

"Water's good. I wonder if I could afford to give up baking for the Grill and the Silver Moon." She cut the sandwiches in neat triangles and put them on plates—her mother's beloved supermarket-premium china—and carried them to the counter. "I love what I do. I love the tearoom. But I'm tired, too."

Jesse glanced at her, and his gaze sharpened. She wondered what he was seeing. "I can help you. At least give you a loan on your half of the farm income if you won't take money straight out."

She shook her head. "Thank you, but I don't need help. However, I don't want to work myself to death, either. We saw Dad do that. I mean, he obviously chose to die when he did, but he never saw anything in life beyond work. That was why Mom didn't have a nice kitchen and her dishes came from the grocery store. She couldn't buy dishes at the department store or have a new faucet because Dad wanted to buy 'just one more cow.'"

"I think not working yourself to death would be a good idea." It was there again, that hint of a twinkle in his eye. "What are you thinking of doing instead?"

"We're putting the party space in the carriage house, but the truth is that's Neely's baby. I don't want to give it the time or interest it requires." She took a taste of her soup. It was really good; maybe she should give everything up and make soup for a living. But, no, she loved the tearoom. She just wanted more. Or different. Something.

"I don't know." She set down her spoon. "I

. don't have an 'instead' lined up." Jesse had one—he was an accomplished artist. Nearly everyone she knew had a talent or skill with which they either made their living or enhanced their lives. Arlie made beautiful quilts. Holly wrote romance novels. Jack did woodworking.

Libby made good soup. She didn't think that qualified.

"How are the adventures coming?" Jesse refilled his bowl. "Tucker was talking about it when we played poker."

"Fine. They're fun." Although she wondered if they were the root reason for her discontent. If they were the fuel feeding the depression viper. She'd had to go into the restroom at work and take deep breaths just the day before when a customer was rude. If the tearoom hadn't been full, she would have screamed, too.

Well, no, she wouldn't have—Libby wasn't a screamer. But she might have taken an extra dose of the anti-anxiety medication hiding behind the pain relievers in her medicine cabinet.

"I think Tuck's liking them, too. He said you were more fun than we were. We all took exception to that, but Jack and Sam both admitted he was probably right."

Libby grinned at him. "You don't think Holly's more fun than playing cards and drinking beer?"

He gave her the look again, the eyelash-singeing one. "Since we've evidently delved into the dark underworld of minding each other's business, little sister, how's your love life?"

She was startled that he'd asked and thought about making something up, but he'd probably have figured it out, or gleaned enough from conversation with Tucker to know the truth. "Nonexistent."

Sympathy flickered in Jesse's dark eyes but went unspoken. "Do you want some pie?"

"From the Amish bakery?"

"Yes. Coconut cream."

"Then I'd like a great big piece. As big as the one you're eating." She got up to make the coffee.

Jesse walked her to her car when she left, telling Pretty Boy to stay away from too much chicken salad. He patted her shoulder, the gesture awkward—they hardly ever touched each other. "Whatever you decide you want to do, I'll help you however I can."

Driving home through the early spring coolness, she thought having supper with her big brother was probably good for her soul as well as her heart. Not to mention, coconut cream pie was an excellent adventure in and of itself.

"I KNOW YOU want more grandkids, Mum, but Charlie makes up for a whole flock of them, you know."

Tucker's mother's laugh, crisp and British even across the ocean that separated them, made him yearn to see her. Ellen Curtis had moved back to her native England when Tucker had graduated from college, although she made annual trips back to Lake Miniagua to spend time with her son and stepson. Tucker thought he might take a long weekend and go to England—it had been a year since his grandmother died, when Ellen had made the long flight to attend her funeral.

"Charlie's a delight," said his mother, "and so is Arlie, but I'd like to see *both* my boys settled down before I'm completely in my dotage."

Tucker rolled his eyes at his brother. "She's talking about her dotage again."

Jack laughed. "Remind her Charlie's spending a week with her during our honeymoon. There'll be no time for dotage then."

"I heard that." She was laughing, too. "You two just take care of each other and I'll see you at the wedding. All right?"

"All right. We both love you, Mum." Tucker pushed the button on his phone that broke the connection and dropped it into one of the pockets on his cargo pants. "There. I'm sure we've scared all the fish away by now. What do you say we take a ride around the lake?"

His brother shook his head at him. "We're testing lures. You know that. It's one of the charms of our company that no product ever hits the catalog unless everyone on staff who knows how to cast a line into the water has tried it out."

Tucker leaned back in his chair on the deck of the company's fishing boat. "So, here we are, like the Manning brothers—only we're fishermen instead of quarterbacks. I guess that's cool."

"Unfortunately—" Jack detached a very small bluegill from his hook and tossed it back into the water "—we're no better at fishing than we would be at quarterbacking. It's the thought that counts."

"Have I mentioned that it's barely March and I'm freezing?"

"Only four or five times."

These are the best days. The thought lodged in Tucker's mind when he was filling their cups from the thermos that sat between their chairs. The long years after the accident, when his relationship with Jack had been nominal at best and too often contentious, seemed far away now, but he never took their closeness for granted.

They'd been extraordinarily close before the wreck, born only ten months apart to different mothers. In sober moments, their father had referred to them as his Irish twins. When Jack's mentally ill mother died—by suicide, which gave him and Libby an unhappy connection—Ellen reared both boys in the little yellow house on the lake she'd once shared with their father until the Llewellyn money and their grandmother's indomitable will intervened and they went to live at the Albatross. The boys had been each other's lifelines.

Now they were very close again, and Tucker loved it. They shared the CEO position at the company and drove each other crazy and he loved that, too.

"How did you get over worrying about being a good dad?" he asked, setting his fishing rod into the pole rest and giving his coffee the attention it deserved.

Jack snorted. "Who gets over it? But Arlie's influence and Charlie himself convinced me I did more harm trying to stay on the child-support-paying periphery of his life than I'd do if I waded in, mistakes and all." He caught Tucker's gaze, holding it. "What's on your mind, little brother? You and Meredith?"

"No." Tucker was surprised at how quickly the answer came. "When I was traveling all the time, I didn't miss having a family like I do now. If I had an itch, you loaned me Charlie until I got over it. But you guys, and Sam and Penny, and Dan and Alice Parsons—you all make me want what I don't have. That's why Libby's doing the thing introducing me to her friends. And Arlie's friends."

Jack stared out across the lake, his expression thoughtful. He sipped his coffee. "What about Libby?"

Tucker frowned and straightened in his chair. "What do you mean, what about Libby? She's okay, isn't she? Do you know something I don't know? I just saw her the other day." Panic surged, making his heart thump fast and hard against his ribs.

"She's okay as far as I know. What I meant was, what about you and Libby, as in...you and Libby?"

"You mean, like a couple?" Tucker reached to pull his brother's cap down over his face. "In the first place, she barely knows I'm a guy. In the second place, I want a family and she doesn't—I thought she was going to have to go to counseling before she got a dog. In the third place, there's not an iota of chemistry between us." Well, there probably was, but not any he was admitting to. "In the fourth, I've known her since we were born—the idea of there being anything boy-girl between us is just creepy. In the fifth—"

"Whoa!" Jack pushed his cap back into place and raised his hands in supplication. "Enough already. It was just a thought. We all love Libby. She already feels like family. I just thought—"

"Stop thinking. Just shut up." Tucker

pointed. "You have a bite. Reel in your fish and leave me alone. And shut up," he added, in case Jack hadn't heard it the first time.

"THERE ARE TIMES I feel as if I'm the only one who doesn't have any issues." Arlie spoke breezily, turning in a circle in the tearoom, her eyes wide and sparkling with delight. "If I'd known a bridal shower would be so much fun, I'd have gotten married years ago."

"Not only that, you get presents." Holly stopped her midtwirl and pushed her away from the table where the gifts from people unable to attend had been arranged. "However, if you say one more time that you don't have any issues, Libby and I will be happy to start reminding you of what they are."

"Yes, we will." Libby set a tray of sandwiches on the buffet and covered it with a plastic dome. "We might even make some stuff up." She accepted a glass of wine from Holly, clinking gently against the one her friend still held. "To friends with issues." She sipped, then set her glass down to go for another tray.

She pushed back through the door a minute later. "Speaking of issues, my brother is being even more secretive and silent than usual concerning his social life." She covered a cracker with Gianna's spinach dip and took a bite, then spoke into Holly's silence, spraying a few crumbs. "That dip is so good, I think I'll take it back into the kitchen and eat it later all by myself. Out of a cereal bowl. With a really big spoon." She beamed at Holly. "I'll tell your mom Arlie took it. She's getting away with murder these days."

Holly rolled her eyes. "Isn't that the truth? She's going to be the favorite daughter now, at least until I find a boyfriend. Which I haven't. Exactly." She took the bowl from Libby's predatory hands. "But she wouldn't believe Arlie took it, because she doesn't even like it. And, no, I have no idea why Jesse's being more taciturn than usual."

"Hmm. Only a romance author would use the word *taciturn* instead of just saying he's grumpy," said Libby. She chewed thoughtfully, trying to figure out the extra ingredient in the dip.

"He's not grumpy—he's private." Holly spoke instantly, sharply, then went to survey the items on the gift table, her cheeks a bright and becoming pink.

Arlie's friends from the lake, all the women who worked at A Woman's Place and mothers whose babies she had delivered had been invited to the shower. They all either attended or had dropped off gifts earlier. During the shower, nearly all the food was eaten and the punch bowls were emptied. By the time the last guest left, the tearoom had been booked for two more showers, a birthday party and a tea for the women of Miniagua High School's class of 1967. It was good for the business. It made Libby tired.

When she locked the door, Arlie and Holly went into the kitchen to help with cleanup. Neely took the vacuum cleaner into the two rooms where the party had been held.

"You don't have to do this." Libby stood at the sink, filling it with hot water to wash the glassware.

Arlie bumped her to one side. "Sure we do."

Libby scowled at her. "You do remember that Holly paid for this shower, right? Cleanup is part of what she paid for."

Holly snorted, carrying napkins and tablecloths into the laundry room. "Holly didn't pay a whole lot. Besides, Mama would ground us if we didn't help. Even her precious little angel Arlie. Do you wash these all together?"

"The white ones go in by themselves. The others can be together. But you don't have to do it. Let's just sit and drink coffee and talk about what great gifts li'l Arliss got."

"I'm telling Mama that you two are being mean to me," Arlie threatened with no heat whatsoever. "You know I'm only her favorite right now because when I marry Jack, we get Charlie."

"A good thing, too," said Holly, "because we certainly weren't taking Jack into the family without him."

They laughed together, and Libby leaned into the sound. Holly's laugh was musical, evocative of the silver bells in Christmas songs. Arlie's throat had been hurt in the accident so that even now her voice was husky, her laughter throaty.

Spring was upon them. It was when Libby could never outrun her emotional nemesis. It was when her mother had died and two years later, her father. April of the year between their deaths was when the accident had happened that had ended three lives and forever changed so many others.

She had to force herself to breathe normally, to laugh at the right times, to pay attention to these women who'd been sisters of her heart for most of their lives.

They drank coffee even knowing it might keep them awake, looking at the gifts again, oohing and aahing over everything from the Anything Goes gift card to the dish towels with crocheted trim. They looked doubtfully at a set of eggplant-colored towels.

"When those fade," Holly predicted, "they're going to look exactly like beets do when you pull them out of the ground."

Arlie nodded agreement, then brightened. "Yeah, but if I put them in Charlie's bathroom, everything's going to end up the color of mud anyway—his mother warned me about that in the card with the gray towels she sent. They'll fit right in."

Holly looked up from the list she was making for thank-you notes. "It's great how you and she are becoming friends."

Arlie shrugged, looking at the set of fuzzy socks for every day of the week that had accompanied the sheets from Libby. "It's what's best for Charlie. And besides, I like her."

"Are you scared?" Libby helped pack the

gifts into the totes Arlie had brought. "Of sharing your life with someone, I mean."

"A little," Arlie admitted. "Getting married in your thirties means getting over being set in your ways in some aspects. It's hard to leave my house. Plus we have a long, long history and we have to figure out which parts of that history to embrace and which parts to let go. Tracy and I are becoming friends, but the truth is that Jack and I had to learn to be friends, too. It's not enough to be in love— we had to fall in like. And in trust—that was harder than anything."

Arlie and Holly left a little after that. Libby took Pretty Boy out, walking down to the edge of the lake and looking out over its dark surface. She was happy for Arlie and Jack, and the look in Holly's eyes when she'd defended Jesse's disposition had given Libby an internal charge of sisterly joy.

Tucker was still seeing Meredith. He didn't seem the kind of blissful his brother was, but he did seem satisfied. That was what he'd wanted. He was sure love would come in its own time. Libby *wasn't* sure of that, which gave her pause—she wanted only the best of everything for her best friend—but he wasn't a boy; he was a man who knew what he wanted.

Libby listened to the lake lapping against the shore and whistled softly to keep Pretty Boy from going too far. She wished she knew for sure what she wanted. Although she was single and perfectly all right with staying that way, she was glad she had friends who were constant presences in her life. It was nice, having a business where she'd lived all her life. The lake with all its beauty was a constant source of comfort.

Except for sometimes late at night, when it was dark and lonely and silent. And she was afraid the depression and hopelessness were going to surround her before she could get away.

CHAPTER NINE

THEY WALKED ACROSS the bridge at the end of Miniagua's business district with Pretty Boy prancing happily on his leash in front of them. "I want you to come to England with me," said Tucker. "Just for a few days—not long enough to consider it a real adventure. Mum would love to see you, and it will give you a chance to use your passport."

Libby shook her head, moving quickly. She'd lived at Lake Miniagua her whole life and had never gotten over being scared of this bridge. It had been the subject of way too many "it was a dark and stormy night" stories told at slumber parties and by her brother's ornery friends. "I can't afford to go to England. I'm not letting you pay for me to go. And Neely might be getting tired of covering for me at the tearoom. There have been weeks since the first of the year that she's worked more hours than I have. That's not fair to her."

"She loves it."

Libby knew he was right about that, but she wasn't all that eager to use the passport. She'd gotten it several years before to go on a cruise with the library's book club and had come down with a raging case of intestinal flu instead. She'd spent the week of the cruise in bed at home. That lovely memory, combined with just how bad her passport photo was, made her reluctant to travel outside the country. She was afraid her sense of adventure was purely domestic.

"What if I get sick while I'm there?" Not that she got sick often, but once had been enough.

"I think they have doctors there. As a matter of fact, Mum's married to one."

Libby knew that, although she'd never met Grant Monahan, Ellen's husband. "Does he ever come to the States with her?"

"He has a few times, but Grant hates to fly, so he gets out of it any time he can. He'll come for Jack and Arlie's wedding, though."

They reached the other side of the bridge, and Libby breathed easily again. They could go back the long way. It took an extra half hour, but she was good with that. Maybe

Pretty Boy would be tired enough he wouldn't feel compelled to wake her at three o'clock in the morning for a walk.

"I'd like your company."

"Why don't you take Meredith? It would give you a chance to get to know each other better and your mother would be so happy to meet her." Libby smiled at him, wanting him to cheer up.

He hesitated. "Actually, I need a little time to think about that." He looked around and came to a stop. "Are we going the long way around?"

Her cheeks warmed. "I don't like the bridge."

He sighed. "I know. Arlie doesn't, either. I don't know how she walked across it in that ice storm when Charlie ran away in December."

"She had to, so she did. She was brave. I have no idea why I walked across it with you today, because I'm not the least bit brave."

Tuck gave her a disbelieving look. "You pulled a calf."

"That's not brave. It's messy."

"I'm not carrying Pretty Boy the last ten minutes if he gets tired."

"We can stop at the Hall and you can drive us the rest of the way home if you and he are that tired."

That got him. He recognized a challenge when he heard it. "He and I will be fine. Now, about that trip…"

"How long are you talking about?"

"Five days in all, and two of them will be mostly in the air. We'll fly into Birmingham. From there we'll rent a car and drive on the wrong side of the road to Hylton's Notch, the village where Mum and Grant live. It's beautiful there. She walks to the market every day and buys what she's going to cook."

"It sounds perfect."

"It pretty much is. There's a nice pub and a little place that serves a 'lovely tea,' to quote Mum. You'd like it there."

"I would," Libby admitted, thinking how natural his assumed British accent sounded. Whenever he visited his mother, he came back with a lilt that stayed in his voice for weeks. "But, honestly, do you really think Meredith would go along with that? I know you and I are just friends, but we're close ones—if I were her, I wouldn't want the guy I was seeing taking off with some other woman on a jaunt halfway around the world."

The look he gave her bordered on insulting, and Libby glowered at him. "Yes, Tucker, I am a girl. I know that's a little beyond your comprehension, but if you think about it, you'll catch on."

"Meredith knows we're friends. She hasn't had any problem with anywhere we've gone so far."

"Really? Have you asked her? Maybe she's not taking her relationship with you seriously because she thinks there's more between us than friendship." Even though there wasn't. There couldn't be.

"We've talked about having really close friends. I don't know that we ever assigned genders in the conversation." He raised an eyebrow. "Are you telling me if you hook up with some guy, you're going to give him a vote in choosing your friends?"

"Well, no, not a vote, exactly, but I probably won't go jetting off to Europe with you if I have a significant other, either."

"If I tell Meredith you're going and she doesn't have a problem with it, do you want to go?"

Libby didn't answer right away. She walked on and gave a startled yelp when Pretty Boy nearly jerked her off her feet. She was thirty-four years old and had been in only five of the fifty states. Going to England was so near the end of her bucket list she couldn't even imagine it. Admittedly, she wanted adventure—she'd gone far too long without it, but…England?

Not only England, but England with her best friend, the person who knew her—other than her secret—better than anyone else. "I can't afford the ticket," she said again, shaking her head. "Or I probably could, but everything extra is earmarked for the carriage house right now. And if I spend that money anywhere else, something in the tearoom is going to break down." Because it always did. That was something the rich kid next to her didn't always understand.

"I know. I don't want you to buy your ticket."

They sat on a bench that overlooked the lake's public beach, looking out over the choppy waves being blown about by the wind. "I'm not playing the poor card," she said patiently, "but single people who aren't inde-

pendently wealthy do need to watch what
they're doing with their money, Tuck. You
know enough of us to be aware of that. You
paid my way to Tennessee and you gave me
money to gamble with, which was wonderful
of you, but you being my financial godfather
wasn't part of the adventure agreement."

He frowned at her, then out at the lake, then
down at the dog, who was slobbering joyfully
on the knee of his jeans. "How many cups of
coffee do I drink at your place that you don't
charge me for?"

She snorted. "Not enough to pay for a plane
ticket."

"Hey, I'm serious. I probably average at
least one cup a day, taking into account the
days I miss and the days I come in and drink
a whole pot. You've been open close to ten
years. If you charged just two bucks a cup,
which is pretty cheap by today's standards, I'd
owe you about…what…seven or eight thousand dollars?"

He was being ridiculous. They both knew
he was.

England.

Fine. Just this once.

"Okay, if Neely agrees and it doesn't put

her out and if she'll take care of Elijah and Pretty Boy and if I don't have to buy any new clothes, I'll go."

His eyebrow rose again. She wished she could do that. "Are you sure there aren't any more conditions?"

"No laughing at me when I get airsick."

He grinned at her. "Now, there's a deal breaker."

Pretty Boy had lain quietly between their feet after soaking a large spot on Tucker's jeans. He'd even snored when their conversation must have gotten boring. However, when a pair of squirrels appeared to be playing hide-and-seek around the trunk of a nearby cottonwood tree, he wanted to play, too. "Whoa." Tucker tightened his hold on the leash, but the overeager puppy still pulled him off the bench, barking all the way.

Tucker sprawled in the new spring grass, the leash still wrapped around his hand with Pretty Boy tugging at him as he tried to chase the squirrels up the tree.

Libby called to the dog, but she was laughing too hard to be very effective. When she went to help, Pretty Boy ran around the tree in search of his prey, wrapping the leash around the backs of Libby's knees so that she fell, landing on Tucker.

She'd never been close to him in quite this way. While she'd always known he was an attractive man—she'd even told him she named Pretty Boy after him—she'd never been physically close to him. When they hugged, it was quick. If they held each other for comfort, that was as far as the embrace went. Even the kisses they'd exchanged that had made her heartbeat erratic and warmed her from the inside out hadn't been like this. They just… hadn't.

"Oh." She pushed away from him, or tried. The leash had her lashed against him. "I'm sorry. I…"

"Hang on." He shifted to his side, moving her with him so that they were face-to-face. His eyes, the blue of the wildflowers starting to bloom on the roadsides, were thickly lashed and surely sexier than any one man was entitled to. He held her gaze, smiling lazily. "Now, as my grandfather used to say when he was trying to keep Jack and me out of trouble, isn't this a fine how-do-you-do?"

She wanted to look away from him but couldn't. "Tuck, we need to get up."

He nodded. "We probably should. You want to tell your dog? He's not listening to me."

"Pretty Boy." She raised her voice and tried again. "Sit, Pretty Boy."

He did, right beside their heads, having evidently decided the squirrels didn't want to play. He looked down at them, then licked each of them lavishly while they tried to turn their faces away from his eager tongue.

Tucker pushed him away, laughing, then looked back at her. "Ah, Lib."

That was all he said, and then he was kissing her. His heart beat hard and fast against hers, and she knew even as she kissed him back that they shouldn't be doing this. Not now. Not ever.

"No," she said, drawing away at the same time as he did.

"No," he agreed, but he took just a moment to shape her cheek with the palm of his hand and smile into her eyes. "But sometimes I wish…"

Wish what? But she was glad she hadn't said the words aloud. Glad he hadn't finished the sentence. Glad this had happened here and now, before she went however many thousands of miles it was to England with him.

Pretty Boy snorted impatiently and they unwrapped themselves, Tucker helping Libby to her feet but keeping her hand in his. "Okay."

She brushed dirt off her clothes. "Okay?"

"Okay, I won't laugh at you when you get airsick."

"SERIOUSLY? YOU'RE ASKING me to tell you about all my first dates that didn't result in second dates?" Libby took off the sleep mask Neely had given her that was driving her crazy anyway and moved the back of her seat forward. "It's not enough I have to introduce you to women—now you want to live vicariously through my dating mistakes?"

Tucker considered that, finishing the last of the corn chips she'd meant to eat later. "Yeah. Pretty much—don't forget we've got something like eight hours on this plane. You can skip high school, though. I was there for that."

She snorted. "You were one of them." But she backtracked immediately. "Not fair. We've had more than one real date, and they were always fun. We just didn't have any—" She stopped.

"Chemistry. Yeah, I know." He smiled at her, there in the dim light on the plane somewhere over the Atlantic. The expression faded, though. "Only that's not exactly true anymore, is it?"

"We're going to make it true." She held his gaze. "You're my best friend. I'm not giving that up for a fling we both know would never work out."

He sighed. "Me, neither. Besides, you're an older woman—that would make you a cougar. We can't have that."

She hid her face against the shoulder of his sweater to stifle laughter. Everyone around them was asleep except the baby and her parents two rows forward. Libby and Tucker spoke in stage whispers, not wanting to disturb anyone's rest.

"I still can't believe Meredith didn't object to this. She even called me and told me to make sure you took me to Stonehenge." Libby leaned back to scowl at him. "You've gone and blown it, haven't you?"

"I haven't blown anything yet." He frowned back at her. "Did she mention that she's always hated to travel? Evidently the ex does a lot of it with his job, which wasn't good for the relationship. So she hates it double."

Meredith had mentioned that when she called. She'd also seemed completely unconcerned about Libby and Tucker traveling together.

"Okay. Now let's get down to business. We'll take turns. Your first date was—who, Sam Phillipy?"

"I never went out with Sam."

"Sure you did. A whole bunch of us went sledding and he paid for your hot chocolate at that old-time sundry shop that used to be where Arlie's clinic is now."

"Tucker, we were *nine*."

"So?"

"So, does it count as a date that you walked Marie Williams—well, she was Marie Sargent then—home from Arlie's birthday party when we were ten?"

"I did not."

"Did, too."

"She lived just down the street from the Hall. I *had* to walk home with her because we all left at the same time."

"Jack didn't. He walked down the lake side."

"Right, and if I'd crossed the street, I'd have had to walk with Jack. He'd probably have pushed me into the lake. You know what it's like with older brothers."

Yes, she did. Most of their childhood, except for a few times when he'd had to defend her pigtailed honor, Jesse had pretended she didn't exist.

"Did you kiss her?"

Tuck's expression went from smug to horrified. "No! I didn't even know how at that age. I didn't learn until—" He stopped, giving Libby a speculative look. "I don't know. How do I do now?"

She felt the heat climbing her cheeks and cursed her complexion. You'd have thought freckles would have been enough, but no, she had to blush every time she was the least bit…no, she wasn't at all embarrassed. He was just flirting and being cute. That was all. And there was no way she was going to tell him he was probably the best kisser she'd ever known.

But she still blushed.

"You do okay for a beginner," she said.

"A beginner, huh? I'm hurt by that."

She pushed his arm, creating a little needed

space between them. "Sure, you are. Now, moving on. Who'd you date in college?"

"I met a girl named Sabrina my first day at Vanderbilt. She was from Idaho. Neither of us knew anybody, and we dated the whole first semester. When we went home for the holidays, she remembered she had a boyfriend, and I asked out a girl who'd come to the lake to spend Christmas with her grandparents. When we got back to school in January, Sabrina and I never went out again." He grinned. "We are friends on Facebook, though. She married the boyfriend."

"The girl from the lake was related to Cass, wasn't she?"

"I think so."

Libby thought for a moment of Cass Gentry, the survivor of the wreck who left the lake the summer after it happened and never came back. No one had ever located her.

"I wonder what happened to her," Libby murmured, not for the first time. "Do you remember the girl's name?"

"Susan? Sharon? Something with an S."

"Last name? It wasn't the same as Cass's, was it?"

"No. They were steprelatives or something.

They knew each other, but it wasn't a close relationship."

"So you probably don't remember enough to find Cass."

He just looked at her, and she nodded. "Yeah, right," she said. "That really didn't deserve an answer. We've all looked off and on ever since she left."

"If she wanted to be found, she would have been. Isn't that basically what her aunt said when we called out at the orchard the family owned? Now, who was your worst date?"

"A summer guy from the condos over on the east side. He thought I was twenty and I thought he was twenty-two. I was eighteen and he was twenty-eight. You remember that one. You came and got me at a bar in Sawyer."

"Oh, yeah." Tuck closed his eyes, snickering. "They threw us both out."

She pushed his arm. "Your turn."

By the time they were two hours into the eight-hour flight, they had rehashed their entire dating history, embellishing here and there just to keep it interesting. Then Tucker fell asleep and she watched a movie, wide-eyed and queasy. The Dramamine she'd taken in Chicago helped, though, and she kept down the three cups of tea the flight attendant gave her. Past the six-hour point in the flight, Tucker woke up and they made desultory conversation until they landed.

When she realized Tucker was going to drive a car in a foreign country on the wrong side of the road, she wished she'd slept on the plane—she wasn't all that sure she'd ever feel safe enough to sleep again.

CHAPTER TEN

"Darling!"

No one in Lake Miniagua called anyone "darling," but it sounded perfect when Tucker's mother said it in her pleasant Yorkshire accent. "I've missed you so much," she said, hugging him before he'd even gotten the door to the rental car closed behind him.

"I missed you, too." It was true. Ellen was the only parent he and Jack had, and they both loved her. She'd had a rough time when they were little—their father and grandmother had seen to that—but her life was better now, and she was happy. He hoped. "All good, Mum?"

"All good. You?" She held his gaze, making sure he told her the truth. "And Jack. He's as over the moon as he sounds on the telephone?"

"He is. More so. And Charlie can't wait to come and get even more spoiled than he is by Gianna."

His mother beamed. "I can't wait to do the spoiling, too."

Tucker's stepfather came from behind his wife, giving Tucker's arm a squeeze as he passed and approached Libby. "We're so glad you've come. Do call me Grant. I'm so sorry not to have met you before when Ellen came to the Colonies to see the boys, but I'm the original cowardly flyer."

"I'm happy to meet you." Libby offered her hand. "Colonies? Really?"

"Grant's just trying to get you going." Tucker moved back so his mother could hug Libby. "Any minute now, he'll refer to George Washington as an upstart and the entire central United States as an uncharted wilderness."

"And don't even get him started on politics," begged Ellen. "Come in, darlings. Tea's just ready, Libby, and then you can have a little lie-down if you like while Grant and Tucker go off and check the quality of the Guinness at the pub."

The house Grant and Ellen lived in belonged in a movie, with its thatched roof, wavy mullioned windows and thick white-washed walls. "We'll have to have the thatchers this summer," Grant grieved, pushing open the heavy dark green front door. "Good thing I'm not in any hurry to retire—keeping this house up is more than a pension could bear."

By the time they'd had their tea from Ellen's beloved bone-china cups she'd taken to the United States as a young woman and then packed up and brought back to England with her after Tucker graduated from college, Libby was barely holding her eyes open.

"I think Libby had better go to bed, Mum. She got a grand total of twenty minutes' sleep on the plane."

Libby pulled herself up straight at the sound of Tucker's voice. "I'm so sorry. What a terrible guest I am. The tea was wonderful, and I love the cookies…biscuits, I mean. We have them at Seven Pillars, but they're not the same."

Ellen laughed. "Go ahead and take her up, love. We'll have a late supper when you and Grant come back. Or, better yet, Libby and I will walk down and join you."

"Come on, Lib." Tucker picked up her purple suitcase, and walked up the stairs with her, ducking his head. "You get the married-people guest room. It has a comfortable bed. My room is the 'boys' room,' complete with twin beds. I imagine she'll put Jack and me in it forever, with a trundle or something for Charlie." He gestured toward the end of the hall. "There's the loo, and here you go." He opened a door and gave her a little push inside the bedroom. "Take a nap."

"Oh, it's so pretty." She looked around the room with its low, slanted ceilings. "I hate to waste time sleeping. Maybe I could go down and visit with Ellen after I brush my teeth and change."

He shook his head at her. "Sleep. I'll see you later at the pub." By the time he'd closed the door, he thought she was already lying down.

It was the only eight-hour flight he'd ever enjoyed, he reflected, although the one when he'd watched two Harry Potter movies with Charlie hadn't been bad.

When he got downstairs, the room his mother called the front room was empty. Laughter floated from the kitchen, and he followed the sound. His parents were washing up the dishes from tea, and he leaned against the thick door frame and watched them. Grant was probably ten years older than Ellen, although it didn't show in either his looks or his demeanor. He adored his wife, and that was all Tucker and Jack had ever cared about.

She adored him, too, but Tucker didn't think she always had. He thought she'd married him for companionship and because she was tired of being on her own.

He could understand that, but he wondered almost every time he saw Meredith if that was her reason for being with him. Was he just a good-enough alternative to changing her own tires, someone who would play catch with Zack and teach Shelby to fish?

Of course, questioning her motivation gave him an uncomfortable opportunity to look at his own. He'd been nearly as surprised as Libby when Meredith hadn't objected to the England trip. He had thought, after the fact, that he should have invited Meredith to go first, but he'd known right away he wasn't ready for that. He wasn't ready for his mother to meet her.

He and Grant walked to the pub, discussing the economy, politics, Jack's wedding and how much a thatcher charged.

"Was it hard when you married Mum?"

Tucker asked abruptly, following his stepfather into the Blue Rooster, the establishment where he'd learned to appreciate shepherd's pie and love Guinness.

"Was what hard?" Grant's eyebrows, a bushy mixture of blond and silver, rose over the small lenses of his glasses. "Everything about marriage is hard, lad, except for making the vows in the first place. That's easy, when you're head over heels for someone. It's the day-to-day part that separates the doers from the talkers." He raised two fingers to the landlord behind the bar. "Guinness, Will, for my American boy and me."

"Mum was the walking wounded when you and she got together. My dad had made her life miserable the whole time, and when she finally came back to England, it was with no job, no money and no family left here."

"But she got a job. She was the best nurse I ever had working for me, and you know your mum—she made family of everyone in Hylton's Notch. She doesn't hold grudges against your dad, either. She has you and Jack and Charlie, and she has lifelong friends from the States—do you know she and Arlie's mother do that Skype business on the computer for at least an hour every Sunday? They have the wedding planned right down to the last flower in the aisle of the church."

Tucker laughed. "That's probably a good thing, since Jack and Arlie aren't all that interested in the wedding."

Grant laughed, too. He nodded his thanks when the pints of Guinness were set before them, then led the way to a booth against the wall. "This'll be a good seat when the ladies join us for supper."

"That's if Libby wakes up before morning. She was pretty zonked."

"She seems to be a lovely young lady. Your mother was thrilled she was coming with you." Grant sipped from his glass, wiping the froth from his mustache with a paper napkin. "Is she the reason you're asking about marriage?"

"No." Although the denial didn't come as quickly as it should have. "I've just been thinking about it. I'd like to be married, to have a family, but falling in love doesn't seem to be something that happens on demand. I don't think—" He hesitated, embarrassed and worried he would offend this man who'd been nothing but kind to him in all the time he'd known him. "I don't think you and Mum were in love when you got together, but you certainly are now, so I'm kind of hoping it happens that way for me." He shrugged. "I'm blaming Jack. Being married and a father never got important to me until lately."

"I see." Grant hesitated. "I was a goner by the second time she came into the office to work. It took her longer, and she told me straight off that she had no interest in falling in love with anyone, especially a persnickety old doctor who loses his glasses and is set in his ways. She insisted on keeping her own last name." His voice thickened a bit, and he took off the glasses to wipe them carefully on his handkerchief before meeting Tucker's gaze again with a smile. "But it has worked out rather famously, hasn't it?"

"It has," Tucker agreed, raising his glass to clink against the other man's. "To you both."

He thought about Meredith, as they talked about football and cricket and how things were going with Llewellyn's Lures and Grant's practice. She wouldn't like this little backwater village, with its narrow streets and cramped little houses. He remembered asking, on his first trip here after Ellen and

Grant had married, what there was to do at night. His stepfather had looked surprised, then said, "You just do more of what you do in the daytime, and sometimes you do it at the Blue Rooster."

He was getting ready to remind Grant of that conversation when the door opened and his mother came in with Libby. She didn't see him—she was too busy looking around the room. She left Ellen's side and stood at the bar to watch the landlord build a Guinness. "My goodness," Tucker heard her say, "I think I've brewed pots of tea that didn't take that long."

The man behind the bar chuckled, handing the glass to his customer. "The tea probably didn't do quite as much to warm your insides then, either, did it?"

She laughed, the sound ringing out so that other patrons turned to see where the sound had come from. "Probably not."

The landlord looked as captivated as Tucker felt. "Would you like a pint, miss, to be sitting down with?"

"I would. Thank you so much."

While she waited, she spoke to the barmaid and to the farmer nursing his ale at the bar beside where she stood. She asked a question about the glasses and listened eagerly to the patient answer. Then she asked if many Americans visited Hylton's Notch and was rewarded by a mutter of, "Too many by a far piece," from a man at the end of the bar.

She smiled at him anyway, and he looked a little as if he didn't know what had hit him.

Tucker, getting up to let her slide into the booth beside him when she had her drink, knew exactly how he felt.

THE BED UPSTAIRS in the cottage was comfortable. Libby had rested well during her earlier siesta. But when she slipped between the sheets after their return from the Blue Rooster, sleep eluded her.

Being exhausted made depression worse— the doctor and her therapist had both told her that—so she tried to avoid it as much as someone who owned a business could. She didn't usually take naps, but she did allow downtime while she worked. She never baked immediately after closing the tearoom. She usually slept enough at night, especially at this time of year when the enemy seemed able to take two steps to her every one in its pursuit of her.

But other than the twenty minutes or so, she hadn't rested on the plane. She hadn't slept much the night before the flight, either, when she vacillated about whether it really was okay to take such a major trip with Tucker. She wasn't worried about her reputation—she was an adult, after all—but she worried about Meredith's reaction regardless of the other woman's phone call. And then she worried because Tucker didn't seem at all concerned.

She'd taken her medication, but maybe it had been too little, too late. The anxiety dragged at her, scraping her skin and making her itch. She finally got up and went to the bathroom at the end of the hall. She drank some water and swallowed another pill. Maybe. Later, after sleeping fitfully for a while, she wasn't positive it had gone down. It was tempting to take another just in case, but she knew better than that, so she hunkered down between sheets gone wrinkled and damp with her distress, and tried to sleep again.

It was a dream. She knew that even while it was happening, but she still couldn't wake from it. No amount of urging Crystal to eat could stop her mother from dying. Trying to shout, "Dave, watch out! Watch out!" from a throat closed by horror couldn't undo the collision on Country Club Road that had cost three lives. She couldn't stop herself from walking into the barn and finding her father. In the dream, the events didn't happen over a period of a few years; instead, she walked through doors that led from one tragedy to the next.

Again. And again. And yet again.

"Lib?" She didn't know where the voice came from or even whose it was, but it was as calming as her mother's had been. "Wake up, honey."

She woke, but she didn't want to open her eyes. "Sometimes when I dream," she whispered, searching for memories that would make being awake bearable, "she's still alive, singing 'Coat of Many Colors' while she cooks. And Dad's going out to milk, calling all the cows by name. 'So, Cherry,' he'll say. 'So, Billie Jo and Arletta.' They all come so he can scratch their necks while he fastens the stanchions."

"Libby?" She felt herself being lifted into a sitting position, and the mattress sank as someone sat beside her on the bed, pulling her close with a bare, muscled arm. A bristly chin brushed her temple lightly, and she knew whose it was. She knew and trusted Tucker's scent and touch more than anyone's in the world.

But she still didn't want to open her eyes. "Sometimes I can warn Dave before the wreck happens, too, you know? I yell, 'Watch out! Watch out!' and I'm fast enough that he can swerve to the side even on that skinny, curvy road."

Beside her, holding her, Tucker drew a deep breath. And then a couple more. "We all do it," he said quietly, his mouth near her cheek so that the words were like a caress. "Jack dreams that he and Dad didn't fight before the prom so the old man didn't get drunk and cause the accident. Holly dreams she still has both her feet. Arlie can still sing. Sam has both eyes. I can hear out of my left ear. Nate's not held together with thumbtacks and cotter pins, so he's on the pro golf tour. Gianna and Dave got to grow old together. Linda's folks probably dream she didn't go to the prom at all, that she'd been able to grow up and have a family of her own. Somewhere, Cass probably hides from it in her own way, too—I imagine that's why we've never been able to find her."

So Libby wasn't alone. She wasn't the only one who still mourned. "Gianna says we have to let go," she murmured, then repeated the words when he ducked his head closer, not able to hear her.

"I know, and she's right, but she knows we all still have bad times. She has them, too." He nuzzled Libby's already-messy hair. "Hey, Mum swears by hot milk. You want some with chocolate and maybe a little of Mollie's additive in it?"

"That would be good. No additive, though." She couldn't mix alcohol with the pills she took. "Can we get it without disturbing your folks?"

"Probably, although they keep wonky hours—they may already be up." He got off the bed, leaving her somehow bereft, and reached for her hand. "Come on."

She tugged a robe on over her nightshirt and left the room with him. He held her hand as they went down the narrow staircase, and she had to stifle a laugh when they were half-way down.

"What's funny?" he whispered when they got to the kitchen.

"It just struck me what you said about Nate being held together with thumbtacks and cotter pins."

"Oh." Tucker laughed, too, although he was searching her face with unsmiling eyes. "That's what he always says."

Grant and Ellen, dressed in bathrobes and yawning, joined them before the milk was hot. They all sat together in the warm kitchen and watched the sun come up.

Libby was exhausted by the travel of the long day before and by the dreams in the night that had just passed. She couldn't tell if she'd taken more anxiety medicine than she should have. But for now, in this place and with these people—especially the best friend whose arm lay across the back of her chair—she was in a safe place. A good place.

She took in the cozy kitchen with its appliances that looked somehow different from her own and the ferns that hung in front of the east windows. It was, she thought, a virtual Venus. A safe place.

"I'm so glad you came with Tucker," said

Ellen at one point, covering Libby's hand with her own. "It's such a pleasure seeing you."

"I'm glad I came, too." She smiled first at Ellen and Grant, then at Tucker. "It's the grandest adventure yet."

CHAPTER ELEVEN

MEREDITH TEXTED TUCKER at work his first day back from England. How about dinner? I'm cooking.

He sat for a moment, thinking. He was tired from both the trip home and the long day in the office. He'd started before daylight with a breakfast meeting with the managers, and the sun had been doing its daily tumble into the western horizon when his phone pinged.

Jack had offered to work late today to take the video meeting Tucker had scheduled, but Charlie had a practice baseball game that night. As Tucker was mulling over how to respond to Meredith's text, Jack poked his head in his office and asked if it was still okay to leave.

"You go watch that kid, and remember if he does good it's because I helped him."

Jack snorted. "Yeah, right." A little pride

gleamed in his eyes, though. "Actually, I think he's going to be better than either of us."

"I wouldn't be surprised, and I'm glad for him, too. He has so much fun." Tucker grinned, thinking of his nephew. "Tell him I'll make the next one."

"Will do." Jack sketched a wave. "See you tomorrow."

When his brother had gone, Tucker tapped into his phone, Sure, but I'll be late. Eight or so if that's okay. What can I bring?

Just yourself was the response, and he frowned at the screen. What might have been flirtatious just…wasn't. He wondered what was on Meredith's mind.

She'd been so willing for him to spend the long weekend in England, as well as completely unconcerned that Libby had traveled with him. He didn't know what any of it meant, and he wasn't sure why he wasn't more concerned.

Whatever it was didn't become obvious right away when he got to her place. Zack and Shelby, who'd already eaten, commandeered him into playing fifteen minutes of video games while Meredith finished dinner preparations.

"Bed!" She came into the living room and clapped her hands. "Ten minutes to read, five to drink and pee, then lights out. Got it?" She hugged and kissed them both, Tucker gave high fives, and they went upstairs.

Tucker moved to kiss Meredith, and she turned her head so that his lips touched her cheek. She hugged him, holding on for an extra moment, and he drew back to look at her. She was as beautiful as always, but there was excitement in her eyes he'd never seen before. He'd felt it when she'd been in his arms. But it was different. "I do believe," he said, "that this is a farewell dinner. Am I right?"

She hesitated. "How would you feel about it if that's the case?"

Oh, come on. I'm not the one breaking up here. He had to push back the irritation her question caused. "Why don't you tell me what's going on?" he suggested. "Then I'll know how I feel about it."

"Let's sit down."

He thought with a touch of dark humor that his heart wasn't broken, because he was still hungry and the pork chops she'd put on his plate looked excellent.

She took a bite of salad, then put down her fork. "I took the kids to their dad's this weekend while you were in England, then I went to my folks' house rather than come back here."

There was nothing new in that—she did it more often than not.

He'd been right. The pork chops were wonderful. He wondered if she'd ordered them from Anything Goes Grill. Meredith wasn't long on cooking, which he fully understood. He didn't know how anyone could handle everything that went with working full-time in addition to being a full-time mom.

"So, was it a good weekend?" She didn't ask about his, he noticed. The thought made him remember his mother and Grant, sitting across from each other with a cozied teapot and a plate of sandwiches between them while they asked about each other's day.

The string beans were good, too. Tender and crisp the way the chef at the Grill did them so well.

"Their dad took them to the zoo on Saturday and Shelby got sick. They went to the urgent care clinic and I met them there." Excitement made Meredith's voice higher.

"She's okay, right? Why did she get sick?"

Meredith waved a hand, the dismissal that of a mother who'd treated many children's illnesses. "It was the zoo. He let her eat everything she wanted. It made her sick."

Tucker frowned. "So then what?"

"I went back to the house with him and the kids to put Shelby to bed. Zack went to spend the night with a friend down the street. Brad and I got into a huge argument."

She sounded happy about that "huge argument," and she'd called her ex-husband by his first name. As long as he'd known her, she'd only ever referred to him as "my ex" or as "the kids' dad." Tucker shook his head, confused.

Or maybe not.

"So," he said, "did the huge argument result in a huge making up?"

"Not exactly." The sadness was there in her eyes again, although not with the magnitude it had been before. "But it did end up with us talking instead of yelling. We made apologies instead of casting blame." She leaned toward Tucker, her elbows on the table. "I don't know if we can make it work or not. There was a lot of hurt on both sides. But I do know we don't have a chance if I'm seeing a really nice guy who the kids think hung the moon."

You knew this all along. Tucker was surprised at the surge of anger that was his immediate, but thankfully silent, response. He didn't know whom he was angry *at*.

While it was true she'd "led him on," in the vernacular of his high school years, acting eager for every forward step their relationship had taken, she'd never spoken of love or even affection. She'd never mentioned sharing a future. Nor, he had to admit, had he.

She hadn't minded him spending a weekend in a foreign country with another woman. She'd even called Libby to make it crystal clear she didn't mind.

He'd known that even with the attraction they shared and the parts of their budding relationship that had meshed in a way that had him thinking about looking at rings and land for houses, something was lacking. He hadn't mentioned love, affection or the future, either.

Sometimes he'd been more entertained by her kids than by her. He'd thought that was a good thing, considering that Arlie's unabashed adoration of Charlie had little or nothing to do with how she felt about Jack. She loved his son for himself.

But Arlie wasn't marrying Jack because she loved Charlie. If he and Meredith had married, it would have been because he wanted a family, not because he wanted to spend the rest of his life with her.

The certainty of that brought him up short, and he knew with sudden clarity exactly with whom his anger rested. It was himself.

He smiled across the table. "I hope you're happy. All of you."

Back to square one.

"WE NEED TO give the whole thing a rest for a while." Libby peered into the eyepiece of her telescope, releasing a sigh of satisfaction when she zeroed in on the light show that was her quarry. "I need to think about work and how I'm going to pay for remodeling the carriage house. You need to meet someone naturally, without me saying, 'I know just the girl for you.' Don't you think?"

"Maybe." Tuck bumped her aside with his hip so he could look. "You don't own the sky, you know."

"No, but I should have been an astronomer. And don't forget Venus is my guardian planet. See the cloud bands on Jupiter. Aren't they spectacular?"

He met her enthusiasm with silence. "I'm sure they are, if I knew what I was looking at. I'm here strictly for all the pretty lights." He moved away, reaching for the beer he'd set on the table between the chairs in Libby's backyard.

She looked back at the stars.

"You probably would have been a good astronomer, though. Are you sorry you're not?"

"I guess not. I'm sorry I didn't go to college, though. Jesse offered to help me go after Dad died. He was actually pretty insistent about it, thinking it would be good to get away from the farm. But someone had to be there, and he couldn't stay because he was in the navy."

"You could always go now."

She thought about that for a minute, studying the brightness in the sky. "It's hard to realize that what we're seeing isn't really what's there now because it takes the light so long to cross those billions of light-years." She could feel him looking at her, so she stepped away from the eyepiece. "What?"

"I think I know you so well," he said, "and then your mind goes off somewhere like that. Who *are* you?"

She shrugged. "I'm who you think I am, and you must admit that the real Libby Worth is pretty boring. Do you know I've stopped wearing brown because I'm afraid I'll stand up against a tree trunk and disappear because that's how monochromatic I am? Do you know what people say when they look at our high school yearbook? They say, 'Who's the girl standing between Tucker and Arlie? She looks familiar but I can't place her.'"

She stopped, uncertain why she'd gone off on that tangent. She wanted to cry, she who never wept no matter how insistent the depression monster got, but she wouldn't. Not now. Not over this. "You're right. I could go back to school now, but it wouldn't be the same, and I don't have the money or the time to give it. Plus, what was there then isn't there now, just like what we see through the telescope. It's not that I'm unhappy. I'm not. I'm just... I don't know... I think I'm just tired."

Her voice trailed away. She wasn't sure where her whole poor-me soliloquy had come from, but she wished she could take it back.

She stood stiffly, keeping herself apart from him. He'd come to talk about Meredith and their breakup, and Libby had turned things around until it was all about her. What kind of friend was good old Lib now?

"We still have over three months on our agreement." He didn't address what she'd said, but he put an arm over her shoulders and stood there with her until her heartbeat settled down and she was sure her embarrassed blush had faded back into her freckles. "See?" He pointed. "The Big Dipper. You didn't even have to tell me where it is. Everyone gets lucky sometimes."

And she couldn't help it. She elbowed him, then burst into laughter that had her leaning forward holding on to her knees. He laughed with her, and if he heard her sob a few times, he didn't say so. He just kept his arm tight around her and she tried hard to pretend his embrace didn't feel different than it used to.

They took the telescope inside and went for a walk, Pretty Boy heeling nicely on his lead.

"I'll miss her kids the most. I guess that should be a clue it wasn't right in the first place, shouldn't it?" Tucker stopped, spinning a couple of flat stones over the calm surface of the lake.

"I don't think so. You were attracted to the whole package, not just Meredith. You're a kid person. It makes sense you'd miss them a lot."

Libby thought of Kendall Williams, the girl whose ordinariness so disappointed her feuding parents that neither of them wanted primary custody of her.

"I'm going to fat camp for six weeks after school's out while Mom and Dad work," Kendall had confided to Libby that morning in the tearoom while Marie was having a meeting in the side parlor. "I told them I didn't need to—I'm already fat—but they didn't laugh. And when the camp's over, I have to spend the rest of summer with my grandparents. Do you know how *old* they are?"

Libby had chuckled and hugged her. "You'll have fun. Want to ask your folks if you can help in the tearoom sometimes after you come back?"

"Can I really?"

"You bet, but it will involve washing glasses—they don't go in the dishwashers—and dusting the shelves. Not fun work at all."

"I don't care. I love it here."

Libby had regretted the offer several times since she made it—she and Neely had a pretty seamless routine—but now, hearing the sadness in Tucker's voice when he spoke of Zack and Shelby, she was glad she had. There were a lot worse things than doing something good for a child. Especially a child she sensed might have a viper chasing her.

"I was just thinking," said Libby. "Have you ever gone out with Mollie?"

CHAPTER TWELVE

ON THE SECOND Sunday in April, when people were still finding Easter eggs hidden the week before, Arlie swore a moratorium on anything to do with her wedding.

The ever-changing circle of friends who met many Sunday afternoons in the sewing room over her garage sat back as a unit and gestured for her to hold forth. Holly offered her a ladle to use as a microphone.

Arlie ignored her sister and lifted her chin. "I've had it with wedding stuff. With satin and tulle and underwear that costs more than I spent on my wardrobe my entire last year of college. With wondering what I'm going to do if my biological mother shows up. With worrying about the weather. I mean, seriously, are we going to be any less married if it rains on May 26?"

Holly leaned forward, looking concerned, although her dark eyes danced. "Actually, I think what you should be worrying about is whether your maid of honor is going to out-shine you in that gorgeous dress she's wear-ing."

"That's right," said Libby quickly, "or one of the bridesmaids could show you up, for that matter. Who knew I was going to look that good in yellow?"

"Actually, Tucker did. He picked it out, re-member?" Arlie's expression was thoughtful when her gaze rested on Libby, which was better than how frantic it had been a few min-utes before. "So how is it he knew better than anyone else what would look good on you?"

"He's *known* me longer than anyone else has—even Jesse didn't come on the scene for a few days after I was born, and I'm pretty sure he wanted to send me back. Plus, Tucker's spent half our lives bemoaning the fact that I care nothing about clothes even though, in his charming words, it's obvi-ous to almost everyone that I'm a girl. We were leaving for dinner once and he said he wouldn't go if I didn't change my shoes."

Holly's eyes widened. "Did you do it? Change them, I mean."

Libby grinned. "Sure I did. I had on one black one and one brown one."

"You could worry about Charlie losing the ring, too," suggested Gianna. "If he gets to clowning around with the groomsmen back there in Father Doherty's office, he could drop it and it could roll under the desk and never be seen again."

"And what if I walk out with Jess instead of Sam?" said Penny Phillipy. "Sam will get mad and stomp off to his hardware store. Jess and I won't match because I'm wearing mint green and his tie is the same blue as Mollie's dress, so it'll be an aesthetic nightmare."

Libby raised her eyebrows. "Since when did we start using words like *aesthetic*? Except for Holly, I mean, who tries to sound like a writer just because she is one."

Penny laughed. "Since I just read that word somewhere...probably in Holly's latest book."

"Oh, and did I tell you the photographer I recommended intends to take all the wedding pictures with his phone?" Mollie added.

Arlie looked from one to the other of them. "You are a bunch of—"

"Ah, ah. Don't say it." Gianna shook her head and a warning finger at her. "I can still put you in time-out. Believe me, my girl, I can."

"I had no doubt." Arlie sat down. She didn't look either frantic or thoughtful now, just a little pensive. "It's not about the wedding, is it, Mama? It's about the marriage. And Charlie."

"That's it, honey." Gianna, who'd loved and been happily married twice, and was in love again a third time with Max Harrison, leaned toward her. "The best part of your dad's and my wedding was laughing at you girls because Holly was picking up flower petals as fast as you could drop them."

"My favorite part was my dress and the fact that you let me wear cowboy boots to the wedding before they were in style." Arlie's smile was a little watery.

Libby, Holly and Penny exchanged a look of alarm, although Mollie appeared pleased—she was fonder of boots than heels. "She's going to make us wear them this time, too, isn't she?" Penny sounded resigned—painfully so.

Arlie laughed. "Nah. Jack's too conservative. And he's got this thing about stilettos."

In the end, they made popcorn and went

down to Arlie's living room and watched *My Best Friend's Wedding.*

"Are we still going to have our sister Sundays after you get married?" asked Penny, standing at the back door when they were leaving. "You won't be living in this house anymore."

"We'll still have them. Tuck will probably be here, and he won't mind us coming over," Arlie assured them, hugging everyone as they left.

Libby and Holly walked together, sharing melancholy feelings as they sauntered through a light drizzle to Seven Pillars, where Holly had left her car.

"I never like change," Holly admitted, "and Arlie being married is a biggie."

Libby nodded. "It is. We've all been so close for so long, I'm afraid it will be different."

Holly laughed. "We were saying the same thing when we went away to college. It didn't change then." She stopped. "Oh, Lib, I'm sorry—that was thoughtless. I know you wanted to go and couldn't."

"I went vicariously, though. You and Arlie either came home or I went down to Ball

State more weekends than not, any time I could get someone to do the milking." Libby bumped shoulders gently with her. "And I'm okay with the way things turned out. Really, I am." She laughed, the sound catching in her throat with the memory. "Though just the other night I was telling Tuck about how I should have been an astronomer."

"We all have deferred dreams, don't we? Like in that poem by Langston Hughes." Holly smiled, her dark eyes so bright Libby thought she saw the stars reflected in them. "I was going to open a dancing school, then got sidetracked by writing books. Arlie wanted to sing. Jesse wanted to study art in Europe, then live in New York. Jack—"

"Wait a minute." Libby interrupted her, standing stock-still. "Jesse wanted what?"

"You knew that, didn't you? Not that he probably ever talked about it."

"No, I didn't." She should have. She and her brother had had each other's backs from the day of their mother's diagnosis when Libby was in eighth grade. But they hadn't talked about dreams; they'd talked about survival. About who'd milked which cows and who'd fed calves the night before. About who was going to ask Dad for lunch money.

But still. "I can't believe I didn't know."

Holly tucked Libby's arm through her own and walked on. "I wouldn't have if I hadn't gone into his studio in the barn one day when he didn't know I was there. Which was a big mistake, by the way, even though I only went in because I was looking for him. He was so mad at me he wouldn't even talk to me for a few days."

"What was in there? I haven't been in it since he built the new studio."

Holly hesitated, and Libby held up a hand to stop her. "No, don't tell me." She smiled, but it felt wobbly. "But I'm glad you know. I think he's safe with you, isn't he?"

Holly nodded, moisture brightening her eyes even more. "He is. I promise."

"You can't be her. We were just talking about you two weeks ago." Tucker stared at the blonde woman who'd just approached him at the bar in Anything Goes. "I mean, I know it's you, but...how long has it been, anyway?"

The woman laughed, showing astonishingly white teeth. "It's been fifteen years. I think you were in kindergarten and I was in nursery school at the time."

"Obviously." He gestured at the stool next to his. "Won't you sit down?"

"Thank you." Susan…Sharon…whatever her name was—she hadn't said it yet—sat down. "It's spring break where I teach in Wisconsin. I know it's not beach weather in Indiana yet, but I thought it would be fun to take a nostalgic trip back to the lake anyway. I haven't been here since that summer when we went out. I couldn't believe it when I walked in and saw you. You're about the only person I remember from spending that Christmas with my grandparents."

"Are they still here at the lake?"

"No, they've both passed away, and my parents sold the lake house. It never occurred to me to come back until I went to a conference in Michigan and saw the Llewellyn's Lures plant there. It brought back some sweet memories." She smiled when the bartender set a glass of wine in front of her on the shining mahogany bar. "Thank you."

Mollie nodded. "You're welcome. It's nice to have you back, Sandy. I hope you have a good time while you're here."

Sandy—that was it! Tucker felt like leaping across the bar to hug Mollie. He hated to forget names, even ones he hadn't thought of for fifteen years.

"How about dinner?" he asked.

She smiled. "I was going to get some carry-out, but I'd rather share a meal and old times with someone. Thank you."

"Go ahead and get a booth on the lake-view wall before it fills up," Mollie suggested. "I'll bring your drinks over."

Tucker nodded his thanks and escorted Sandy to the table. "You live in Wisconsin? Is that where you're from? I really don't remember."

"Yes, I teach first grade in the town where I grew up."

"Married?" Might as well get it out of the way. "Kids?"

"Divorced and yes, twenty-one of them." She grinned. "I'd like to have kids, really, but sometimes I think there's not enough of me to go around. I love teaching with every fiber of my being, but it absolutely *takes* every fiber to do it well." She leaned her elbows on the table. "What about you? Did you go back to the girl at Vanderbilt?"

"No. She had an old boyfriend."

"Married?"

"Never. Close a few times, but no cigar."

It was an enjoyable evening. Conversation never flagged. He began to think he'd be able to let Libby off the hook, because he'd done just fine at meeting a woman all on his own. They even had sugar cream pie after dinner. "I'm on vacation," Sandy said. "You *bet* I'm having dessert."

It was then that he noticed Libby standing at the bar, her silky hair in its usual loose braid. She was wearing a short black skirt and a sleeveless teal sweater that showed off her freckled and toned arms. And a pair of those skinny heels that made her legs look a mile long even though they weren't.

He wondered what she was doing at the Grill so late and if she had a ride home. Unless he was mistaken, she had a wineglass in front of her. She usually walked home if she was going to drink, but she sure wasn't going to do any walking on those strappy black stilts.

She wasn't alone. Jim Wilson, the high school football coach, was standing beside her. Really close. They were both looking up at the TV behind the bar and laughing. Libby never watched television—why was she suddenly completely entertained by it? Or maybe it wasn't the TV but Jim. Who was a nice guy but wrong for Libby. Completely wrong.

Sandy's voice reclaimed Tucker's attention. "That's Libby Worth, isn't it? Standing at the bar, I mean. I remember her. Is that her husband?"

"That's Libby. She's not married."

"That's too bad. She was always so nice to everyone. Sometimes that's the way it goes."

He frowned, not getting her point, and pushed his empty dessert plate aside. There were many reasons sugar cream was Indiana's state pie, and he'd just enjoyed every one of them. "The way what goes?"

"The nice girls who aren't very pretty or thin enough too often don't get the guy or the two-point-however-many kids. They end up being the bridesmaids, the babysitters, the stereotypical spinster librarians. Average seems to be the new word for socially unacceptable."

What she said was far too often true. Tucker knew that. His father had even laughed at him once for dating a girl who wore thick-lensed glasses.

Are you trying to prove some kind of point, son? Don't you know it's just as easy to like a pretty girl as one who's not?

"Lib's single by choice," Tucker said mildly. He shrugged, trying to shake off the annoyance Sandy's words had caused. "She thinks running her own business is enough trouble without adding a husband to the mix."

"Oh, well." Sandy blinked. "I'm sorry if I said the wrong thing. I don't like being single and tend to take it for granted other women don't like it, either. It's not that I can't take care of myself—of course I can—but I liked being married. I like always having a date to the dance."

He didn't know why he was so irritated. She felt exactly like he did. Or thought he did. He wanted to be married, too. He wanted the date for the dance.

"Hey." He got out his wallet, paying their tab and leaving a hefty tip for the server who'd brought their meals. "I came over here on the pontoon boat. It's a nice night. Do you want to go for a ride?"

She smiled. "I'd like that. You can drop

me off at the condos if you would—I walked over."

They stopped on the way out to speak to Libby and Jim. Tucker almost asked if they wanted to join them for the moonlight ride, but held back. Libby didn't need him playing big brother if she was interested in the coach.

And he didn't even want to consider why that thought bothered him so much.

The night was perfect for a boat ride, but it was a little cool. Tucker got jackets out of a storage box and offered Sandy one. When he held it for her to slip her arms into, she leaned back against him so slightly he might have imagined it.

She smelled good, like something floral he couldn't identify. Her clothes were expensive, her purse a brand that Libby once said she'd like to carry but would have to sell the tearoom to finance. He only remembered because he'd said at the time that he thought it sounded more like a name that belonged on a gym bag.

"What do you do when you aren't teaching?" he asked, moving slowly away from the Grill's dock and waving at the pilot of the boat waiting to take his place.

Sandy laughed. "Lesson plans."

"Public or private school?"

"Oh, private." She shuddered, so slightly that once again he might have imagined it. "I love to teach and I love my students, but I don't think public school is within the scope of my abilities. Don't you remember the difference between public and private school when you were a kid?"

He didn't remember because he hadn't gone to private school. It was one battle his mother had won. His father and grandparents had wanted him and Jack both to go to the same boarding school all the other Llewellyn males had attended, but Ellen had held her ground.

"I have to admit," Sandy continued when he didn't answer, "Cass Gentry loved going to the public high school here, and she got into a better college than I did—even though she ended up not going. You remember her, don't you?"

CHAPTER THIRTEEN

"SHE'S REALLY PRETTY. As pretty as Meredith." Libby hilled fertile soil around the spindly new tomato plants in Gianna's garden. "I think he likes her." She squinted at the sky. "I also think we're going to get another frost and all this effort will be wasted."

"I couldn't tell how he felt about her." Arlie spoke from where she was planting green beans a few rows over. "He's not secretive, but Jack is, and all he said was that she was a teacher and Tucker said you'd like her purse." She straightened, groaning. "Mama, when are you going to shrink this garden to a manageable size?"

"When you girls start refusing to help with it." Gianna frowned at the package in her hand. "Although I must admit, I think peas are more trouble than they're worth."

"Oh, absolutely." Arlie and Holly spoke in unison, and their mother burst into laughter.

"All right. Just one row. That way there will only be enough for a couple of messes—no one will have to help freeze them."

"Good thinking." Arlie nodded encouragingly. "And you can take them off the list for next year."

"Well, no." Libby shook her head. "I serve pea salad in the tearoom for as long as they last, and it's really popular. Maybe two rows, Gi."

Holly pointed an accusing finger in Libby's direction. "Then you're picking and shelling them."

"She does anyway." Gianna dropped the wrinkly seed peas tidily into the row. "You and Arlie disappear when it comes to pea-picking time every year."

"Which explains why I'm her favorite," said Libby airily.

"Only because you're dating Jim. Mama likes it when we have boyfriends." Holly grinned at Libby and ducked the handful of dirt her mother tossed in her direction.

"We went out twice. That's not actually dating." She liked the football coach but had no illusions about having a relationship with him.

"Did Tucker mention what Sandy said about Cass?" asked Arlie, rescuing Libby from a subject she wasn't ready to discuss, even with the Sunday sisters.

"Not much, I guess. She doesn't know where she lives, although it's out west somewhere. Sandy's uncle used to be married to Cass's cousin, or something like that. It wasn't a close relationship, and it ended when that marriage did."

"At least it's a clue," Holly said. "I'll bet Sandy's uncle could find out, anyway."

"But if she doesn't want to be found," said Arlie thoughtfully, "should we even be looking?"

They carried their tools to Gianna's garden shed, then sat on the deck to drink iced tea and look out over the lake's shining surface, pretending the April sun was warmer than it actually was. "I don't know," said Libby. "It's been so long and so many things have happened to all of us. Maybe it's better to just let it go."

But she knew they wouldn't. The wreck had made them members of a club none of them could ever really leave. Most of them had remained friends, but even when they weren't, they kept track of one another. They did things for each other that were never acknowledged. Several of them had been angry with Jack for years because he'd left town without a word after the prom accident, unable to face what his dad had done. But they'd stood solidly behind him when his grandmother died and he'd made a reluctant return to Miniagua.

"I can't help worrying about her." Gianna went into the house and came back out with a platter of sandwiches. "I remember how troubled she looked. When you girls were in two different hospitals, she'd sometimes sit with one of you while I sat with the other."

"Jesse said she sat with me, too." Libby had been in a coma for days. She'd missed the funerals. By the time she woke, the worst of everyone's physical trauma had been over and their surgeries and reconstruction had begun. In a strange and dreadful way, she'd felt as if they'd gone on without her and that her grief was always going to be ten days behind theirs. Sometimes it still seemed that way.

They were still healing from the mental and emotional wounds, but the others in the club remembered some rawness that she didn't.

"She did sit with you, too—I remember. I think she felt some of the same guilt Jack did, because she was hardly hurt." Gianna looked haunted. "When I asked the cemetery sexton who took care of Dave's grave before I ever got to it, all he knew was that it was a young girl. It had to have been Cass—none of you were well enough."

"By that time, she'd left, hadn't she?" asked Holly.

Gianna nodded. "Yes, and that's why I've always worried about her. She did her best to look after everyone after the accident, just as Jack did, but who looked after her?"

"LET'S GO." TUCKER had come straight from the office. He was wearing a suit and white shirt, and his necktie was hanging out of his side pocket. It must have been a meeting day.

Libby shook her head, lifting chairs onto tables. There was occasionally a night when she didn't have to mop the tearoom's hardwood floors—this wasn't one of those. "Can't do it. Tomorrow's a workday, and I have to bake for Silver Moon before I open. Or at 3:00 a.m. if I happen to wake up then."

"This won't take that long and we don't

have far to go. Lock up and let's go. I'll help you clean when we're done." He looked at his watch. "Come on, Lib. We're burning daylight."

She rolled her eyes at him, recognizing the line from an old John Wayne movie. "Do I need to change before we start herdin' those cattle?"

"Nope."

He was right—they didn't go very far. Except for during the fair, the county fairgrounds were usually deserted in the late afternoon, but today there was activity on the infield of the racetrack. Tucker parked close to a van, and Libby leaned forward in her seat, peering through the Camaro's narrow windshield. She gulped.

"Oh, no."

"Oh, yes."

"You can't make me."

"Wanna try me on that? I'm bigger than you, and I could probably be mean."

She almost laughed at that one. He didn't have so much as a mean pinkie finger in his whole body. "Okay, you *won't* make me. I know you."

"Well." He shrugged and reached for the keys. "If you're scared—"

"I most definitely am that."

"—and if you're going to cry—"

"I never cry, Tucker Darby Llewellyn. You know I never cry."

"I do know that, but when I tell this story, I'm telling it my way." He started the car.

She reached over and turned the key to the off position. "I hate you for this."

"I know."

Thirty minutes later, she clutched his arm inside the basket of the hot air balloon. "Oh, Tuck, it's wonderful." She leaned in to kiss his cheek. "I love you."

If she could have taken back the words in that instant, she would have, because they didn't mean the same thing they had all the times she'd said them before. When it had been purely friendship, before hormones and her heart had made themselves known.

He laughed, tucking his arm around her. "I know."

She relaxed in the casual embrace. Of course he knew, just as she knew he loved her. The deep affection had been there between them all their lives and she hoped it would be there forever. Soon, she would convince herself it was enough. Soon.

But not yet.

"I've never heard this kind of silence." She held on to the side of the wicker basket with her free hand and leaned over its edge, no longer the least bit afraid. "Oh, look at the fields. There's the back of the farm down by the creek, my favorite place ever. And there's Sycamore Hill. Have you ever seen anything more beautiful than a whole field full of grape arbors? Dad would hate that part of the farm became a winery, but Mom would love it—you can see it right through the kitchen window at the house." She beamed at the pilot. "Thank you for bringing me up here." She pointed. "There's Miniagua. You can see the whole lake from here. How big is it?"

"Six hundred acres."

"Oh. I knew that." Everyone did. It was in all the tourism pamphlets free for the taking in every business in town, including her own. *With businesses named after songwriter Cole Porter, who grew up in nearby Peru, Lake Miniagua's six hundred acres is a utopian oasis here in central Indiana.*

The silence was like a magnet, and she settled into it. *Is this what death is like? Beautiful and silent and fearless.*

It was the closest she'd felt to her mother since the day she died. *You're okay, aren't you?* The peace of knowing the answer to that made Libby smile and close her eyes and rest her head against Tucker's shoulder, feeling the crisp cloth of his suit jacket against her cheek. *What about me, Mom? Do you think I'll be okay?*

There was no answer forthcoming, and she didn't expect one. Even when she talked to Venus, she didn't get any answers. It was enough, right then, to feel close to Crystal in the soaring musical silence of the sky and to lean into the warmth and affection that was Tucker Llewellyn. It was a grand adventure.

All too soon, the balloon wafted its way toward the ground, chased by the van from the fairgrounds.

The sun was setting over the lake when they drove back to Seven Pillars. The radio played quietly, and Tucker sang along. Libby watched the red ball sink through the streaky sky into the lake.

"I think that's the most awesome thing I've

ever seen," she said when he pulled into an angled parking place in front of the tearoom.

"The sunset? It was a beauty."

"No." She touched his arm, feeling its strength. "I'm talking about the ride. Seeing the sky on an adventure with my best friend." She leaned over, brushing his lips lightly with hers.

He turned his head before she could draw away, capturing her mouth with his and keeping it, teasing and whispering wordlessly, coaxing the kiss to a deeper, warmer place. His breath was a mixture of mint and coffee, and his arms slipped around her. This wasn't a best-friends hug or a comfort hug or a hold-each-other-up-when-they-were-laughing hug—no, it was a man holding a woman, and there weren't any words there in that cramped Camaro to describe just how good it felt.

Libby had no idea how long the kiss lasted. She only knew that when it ended she wanted more, and she leaned in so that their lips met and clung again. Her heartbeat thumped hard, keeping time with his. "Tuck."

She drew away, but she didn't want to. Oh, dear God, she didn't want to. But they couldn't do this. *She* couldn't do this. Tucker wanted to be a husband and a dad. He wanted to have a wife who would be there with and for him forever and ever.

There would be no forever and ever for Libby Worth. She knew that as surely as that glorious red sun had set over the lake. Because as splendid as tonight's adventure had been and as much joy as she'd felt in having her mother close in her heart, the viper was still nipping at her heels. It was coming closer and closer, and rather than give in to it and suffer depression's tenacious grip, she would find the peace of that silence in the sky.

"We can't." She made her voice firm.

"I know." He let her go, but his hand slipped through her hair, catching on the band that held her braid. "Sometime, though, we need to think about how strange the reason is that we can't."

"What do you mean?" She frowned and tried not to think about kissing him again.

"We can't because neither of us wants anything more in the world than for the other one to be happy." He pushed her hair back, his thumb catching in her hoop earring. "We both know we'd make each other miserable.

If we were in our twenties, maybe we could make it work, but we don't have all that much time at this point to make our dreams work together. The thing with kids is just too big, and it's not something that calls for compromise. You can't have half a kid."

She nodded agreement. As reasons went, that was at the top of the list. At least the heart she was trying to convince to stick to friendship understood that particular issue. But it still ached.

He stopped at the Hall to change into a T-shirt, shorts and flip-flops before he took her home, picking up pizza and bread sticks on the way.

"You don't have to help clean," she insisted as they stepped inside the tearoom.

"Sure I do." He set the pizza box on the table under the front window and went to get plates, forks and napkins from the buffet near the kitchen door. "You can bake while I mop floors." He grinned at her, accepting the beer and glass she handed him. "It will keep us from getting too used to high adventure."

She sat across from him. "So how's it going with Sandy?" The idea of him with a woman other than herself created a sinking sensation inside, but that wasn't something she was prepared to think about. The kisses in his car had been...well, pretty wonderful. But they'd also been a mistake, one they shouldn't make again.

"It's not."

She'd lost track of the conversation. What was he talking about?

"She'll go back to Wisconsin at the end of the week, and I doubt we'll keep in touch."

Oh. Sandy. Libby didn't like herself for the nudge of pleasure his words gave her, but she still felt it.

He took a bite of pizza, gazing moodily at the cold fireplace. "I don't know why I'm sizing up every woman I meet as a potential wife. It's not that I hate being single. I don't. Maybe I should just let it go at that. I could even adopt kids as a single dad. Jack has been a good one—he could give me lessons."

She watched him, wondering at the melancholy in his expression. He wasn't usually sad. "You'd be a great dad."

He smiled at her, holding her gaze. "You're biased, I think."

"Maybe a little."

He finished his beer. "You'd be a great mom, too, you know."

She thought fleetingly of Kendall Williams. "Actually, I'd be a better aunt, so go ahead and adopt those kids you were talking about. Speaking of which, what do you think's going on with Holly and my brother? They're both super touchy, and Jess is even more clammed up than usual."

Tuck looked around the deserted room as if to make sure no one could hear him. "All I know is that Jack mentioned Holly's name on poker night and Jess jumped right down his throat, so I just looked innocent and won seven bucks from your brother on the next hand. That tells me something was definitely on his mind, because I *never* win when Jesse plays."

"Sounds interesting. I'll have to talk to Arlie when Holly's not around." She finished her second piece of pizza and looked regretfully at a third one that was calling her name. Maybe after she got the rolls in the oven…

"I tried doing that with Jack on the way home from playing cards. He told me to butt out."

"Arlie probably will, too, but since Jess is

my brother, she'll probably say it in sweeter words." She got up to head for the kitchen. "If you don't want to help me, it's okay. I can mop while the dough rises."

He pushed back from the table. "Or you can mix up the second batch."

It was peaceful, being in Seven Pillars alone with Tucker. They were in separate rooms, but they could both hear the music playing softly over the sound system. When they knew the words, they sang along; when they didn't, they faked it and sang along anyway, their laughter at each other's attempts at lyrics floating between the rooms.

The rolls were in the oven when the floors were done. Libby went into the dining room to help set the chairs back on the hardwood. "Thank you for doing this." She smiled, turning to him. "Thanks for every…" Her voice faded away, because he wasn't standing near the door with his keys in his hand. He was standing right there, so close she could feel the heat of him.

"Maybe," he said, "it's time we went on another real date. What do you think?"

What she thought was that if she went on

even one "real date" with Tucker Llewellyn, she was asking to have her heart broken.

And even worse was the chance that she might break his.

CHAPTER FOURTEEN

"So, LLEWELLYN, THIS is your idea of a real date? It's no wonder I can't find you a wife. I'm surprised I even found anyone who'd go out with you twice." Libby hefted a case of canned goods into the back of a pickup and hoisted herself onto the tailgate behind it. A tearing sound reminded her of the fact that she'd worn her very newest dress pants, the ones she'd never worn in the tearoom. She hadn't thought, when she got dressed, that she'd be spending the day riding around in the back of a truck while gale-force winds did their level best to blow central Indiana off the map.

"The spring food drive has been on the third Saturday in April for as long as there's been a lake association. The post office has theirs in May. You're as guilty of forgetting it as I am." Tucker stacked a milk crate full of boxes of cereal on top of her canned goods.

and sat beside her, thumping the truck bed with his knuckles to let his brother know he could take off again. When Jack pulled away with a jerk, Tucker clamped his arm around Libby to keep her from sliding off the end of the tailgate. "Can we get arrested for riding back here?"

"Probably, if the wind doesn't blow us into the lake first. Is jail the next stop on our date?" She smiled sweetly at him. "I know you like to go all out."

"Might be. You never can tell."

At the next stop, they picked up two rusted cans of Vienna sausages and a box of cereal that had already been opened. They rolled their eyes at each other and poured the cereal out on the roadside, inviting the birds to dine. The rusty cans went into a trash bag. The next house, belonging to an elderly couple known to be generous during trick-or-treating, netted twelve packages of multicolor marshmallow treats, a case of tomato juice and two bottles of Sycamore Hill wine with a note stipulating it was for "you sweet young people who volunteer."

"Maybe this isn't so bad as dates go." Libby

reached for one of the packages of marshmallows and got her hand slapped for the effort.

By the time the annual food drive was done and the local food pantries had been filled, they were both dirty and exhausted. At the clubhouse at the lake, they ordered in pizza and ate dinner, complete with wine, with the rest of the volunteers. After that, they dropped the borrowed pickup off at the dealership in Sawyer.

"We can make the late movie," said Tucker, "and it's one we'd both like. Want to go?"

Was he out of his mind? Libby was filthy, her pants were torn and she'd dribbled pizza sauce down the front of her sweater. Her hair, which had looked pretty good when he picked her up, had been riding in the back of a pickup all day and looked like it. Her makeup was just gone.

There could be no doubt about it. He'd completely lost it.

"I'll buy, and you can have popcorn and as big a drink as you want." He grinned at her. "It'll be almost as much fun as going off the road in the snow or pulling a calf."

"Have I told you recently that you're out of your mind?"

"On a daily basis, I think."

"Okay."

When they got to the theater, they were blessedly late, which meant they'd miss the blaring previews of coming attractions. No one would see them skulk into the theater except the cashiers.

When Tucker handed over his debit card, the machine wouldn't take it. It didn't like it the second or third times around, either. Libby thought if the machine could have rolled its eyes and called him a loser, it would have. Gleefully, she told him so.

He ignored her and scrounged through his wallet in search of cash or a credit card. He found three dollars and a rewards card from the gas station at the lake.

"Man," said the kid behind the counter, whose mother worked at the plant, "I am so sorry, Mr. Llewellyn. The machine has been weird all night, but your card is the first one it completely refused to take. I know you're good for it, though."

Libby dug her wallet from the very bottom of her too-large purse, smiling conspiratorially at the teenager. "I've been out with this guy before—I'm not sure you should count on him being good for it." She handed over cash that had been earmarked for the collection plate at church—she hoped they could find an ATM that was working. Once they had their tickets, she picked up their popcorn and he grabbed their drinks. "At least this time you didn't try to convince the kid you're too young to attend an R-rated movie."

"I didn't tell him you were old enough for the senior discount, either. You should thank me." Tuck bumped her shoulder gently with his. "That twenty-seven minutes counts, you know."

"You really *are* a loser, aren't you?"

"You bet."

"I've always liked that about you."

"Thought so."

The movie was probably good. Libby couldn't have said, because as soon as the popcorn was eaten and the soda cup empty, she fell asleep, with the sweet warm feel of Tucker's sweater against her cheek. She woke when the lights came on, the top of her head coming in sharp contact with his chin as she straightened.

"Libby?" he murmured drowsily, putting

his hand on her arm when she was halfway up so that she fell back into her seat.

She pushed him away. "What?" She didn't care at all that she sounded grumpy. She *was* grumpy. And sleepy. And probably a few more of the Seven Dwarfs while she was at it.

As if on cue, she sneezed. One more dwarf added to the count.

He handed her an unused napkin. "This means we've slept together. We either have to get married or I'll need to kill Jess before he kills me."

She scowled at him. "Neither of those works for me. Let's go before they call the police on us for loitering. We were only one step ahead of them this afternoon when we were riding around in the back of that truck, remember?"

The wind nearly blew them off their feet when they stepped out the doors of the theater. Libby, searching in her bag for the house keys she knew were buried down there with her wallet, lost her balance and stumbled against the side of the building.

"Whoa!" Tucker grabbed her hand and pulled her toward the car. "Are there any storm warnings tonight? This wind is fierce."

"We've been together all day," she reminded him. "I haven't heard anything you haven't."

They drove around the lake going home, talking about everything and nothing. They discussed stopping at the Grill but went back to Libby's instead to sit on the porch off her living room with cups of hot chocolate and watch the clouds make fierce paths through the sky. Pretty Boy lay at their feet and Elijah curled up in Tucker's lap, his nose tucked into his tail.

"You're feeling restless, aren't you?" Libby searched out his gaze and held it. "Are you tired of being in one place?"

"No." The answer came without hesitation, but he didn't look surprised by her question. "I know this won't come as a surprise to you, but I'm sort of a spoiled guy. I haven't had to wait very often for things that I wanted, although trying to rebuild a relationship with my brother required patience I didn't know I had. When I decided I wanted the whole marriage, house and family thing, I thought it would be easy."

She'd thought it would be, too. He was a kind and handsome man, generous to a fault, who'd never had trouble attracting women. While he'd never been particularly good at long romantic relationships—Libby could count them on less than one hand even if she started the count in the seventh grade—the women he'd loved were still his friends. She'd thought when he decided on permanency, someone wonderful would appear like a genie from a bottle.

He smiled, hooking little fingers with her. "Especially with the person who knows me better than anyone helping in the search. But I think maybe I underestimated my own dream. I've been looking at Jack and Arlie together. I watch this great new thing going on between Holly and Jesse. And Nate—have you ever seen him so pumped in all the years we've known him?"

"Never." She smiled back at him, but sadness settled like a weight on her chest. "It'll happen, Tuck."

When it did, where would Libby be? Would she be his kids' favorite aunt, the one who bought the best presents and knew the most about the stars even if she was afraid of bats? What if his wife was resentful that Tucker's buddy was a woman and wanted to push the friendship far back into the couple's locker, only to be brought out for occasions like baby showers and parties where Libby brought her own date.

It would be all right—of course it would. She had plenty of friends, and she was closer in many ways to Arlie and Holly than to Tucker. After all, only Arlie knew Libby's secret.

She turned her attention back to the sky. The clouds were frenzied, swirling and dancing on the pressure of the air. She loved the hope and beauty offered by Earth's rebirth in spring, but storms or threats thereof left her unsettled and breathless. Made the weight heavier.

"I think it will happen, too, but I kind of wish I'd started looking when I was a little younger. I'm going to be too old to play catch or crawl around on the floor with my kids at this rate."

"Tucker, you're thirty-four. You've got at least a couple of months before retirement age."

He laughed. "You think?" He leaned back to peer at the sky. "It's spring, I guess. Remember that poem about a young man's fancy?"

"When it turns to love? I remember." She'd liked it when they'd read it in one high school literature class or another. Most of the guys, including Tucker, had snickered at Tennyson's words, but she wondered how many of them still remembered their gist.

"I guess I'm not feeling so young, even if I do have that couple of months."

"We're both young," she said firmly. "I'm not finished with adventures, and your dream will come true. I'm sure of it."

"I hope you're right."

She walked him to the door when he left, stepping out onto the back porch and hugging herself against the chill in the wind. "A strange night," she murmured.

He drew her into the loose circle of his arm. "But a pretty good date, wouldn't you say?"

She laughed, resting her hands lightly on his biceps. "A day in the back of a truck, an evening where I had to pay our way into the movie even though you were the one who did the asking and hot chocolate I made. I may have to think about that."

He bent his head to hers, pulling her in closer so that she could feel his heartbeat, slow and steady. The kiss was long and leisurely and not at all brotherly. Or merely friendly. Or casual in any way.

His heartbeat wasn't slow anymore, either. Or particularly steady.

Neither was hers.

"Yeah," she whispered. "It was a pretty good date."

He kissed her again, then turned her toward the door. "Go inside before you blow away. I'll talk to you tomorrow."

She went in, locking the door behind her. She waited for the faint sound of his car horn before she turned off the porch light and went upstairs with Pretty Boy and Elijah at her heels.

She was glad they were there. The weight on her chest was getting heavier, and it was harder to carry if she was alone.

"ONE OF US needs to go to Vermont for a couple of days. There's nothing wrong, but the fire in December kept us from putting in appearances at our satellite locations. In addition to that, there's a retirement dinner for one of the assemblers tomorrow night. He's been there since before we were born and we owe him the respect of attending. I can go if you don't want to. I need to check on my house and the bike shop anyway." Jack handed a cup of coffee to his brother.

Tucker knew Jack loved Vermont—it had been his home base for years. He still owned a house there, nestled into the shadow of Wish Mountain, though it was rented out.

"You'd miss one of Charlie's practice games, wouldn't you? And Arlie. You'd miss her, too." Tucker sipped from the hot brew, wishing he'd stopped by the tearoom and begged a cup from Libby.

"I would," Jack admitted.

"I'll go then. I wouldn't mind getting some skiing in. The mountain's still open, isn't it?"

"It is. You could always take Libby with you." Jack leaned back in his chair and didn't quite meet Tucker's eyes. "She's never been there, and I don't think she's ever skied, either. It could be two adventures rolled into one."

"Are you and Arlie trying to set us up?"

His brother shrugged. "Maybe. We'd like to see you happy, both of you."

"You've known me my whole life—can you really see me making anyone happy?" Tucker was joking, sort of, but he had a growing sense that he didn't have it in him to actually put someone else's needs before his own on a continuing basis. He and Jack hadn't grown up with good role models, but he was pretty sure that was how a relationship was supposed to work.

Jack looked thoughtful. "I don't think it's about making someone happy. I think it's about sharing happiness with someone."

"That sounds like something Gianna Gallagher would say."

"I think she did. Can you think of anyone whose advice you'd rather follow?"

"Not right offhand," Tucker admitted. "If you'll have the office manager get me a flight, I'll get packed and on the road. Is this the normal evaluation period, or do we have plant closing back on the business plan as a possibility?" They'd talked about it ever since their return to Miniagua a year before. One of the potential buyers of Llewellyn's Lures had made it clear that if they bought the company, the Vermont plant would close and the Michigan one would be reduced to a warehousing facility. The proposition had led to Jack and Tucker not selling after all; however, keeping all the facilities going was a quarter-by-quarter decision.

"I think we go on as we are. It's working."

"Good answer." The differences in their personalities led to differences in administrative styles, too. The Lake Miniagua plant manager, Sam Phillipy's dad, had been known to stride into their offices when they were arguing and tell them to either keep it down or take it outside. For the most part, they'd come to realize that they shared both values and concerns in both their work lives and their personal ones; if they applied those values differently sometimes…well, it kept it interesting.

"Am I mistaken, or are you getting restless?"

"You're mistaken." The two people closest to Tucker had asked the same question in the last three days. Irritation skittered along his nerves, but he wasn't sure whom he was irritated *at*. "Sometimes when you look at other people, it seems as if their lives have just fallen neatly into place, even when they haven't."

Jack nodded. "Yup. I know that one." He finished his coffee and got up. "If you need a week or two away, you can visit the Michigan and Tennessee plants while you're gone, too. Barring unforeseen incidents, that would put us ahead of the game for this year."

"I think I will." Tucker rose, too, and shook hands with his brother, something they did at the end of every business meeting whether they'd reached agreement or not. Sometimes the handshakes were more like arm wrestling than brotherly affection, but it kept them connected. "See you in ten days or so."

He stopped by Seven Pillars on his way out of town. The tearoom was closed, but Libby was baking. He hadn't seen her for a few days, since their date, and she looked terrible.

He filled a to-go cup and told her about his trip, laying it on thick about knowing how much she'd miss him but she'd just have to be strong.

She smiled over her shoulder. "I'll bear up under the strain."

But she didn't really look like she could.

"You're sick." He stopped her from moving around, laying a hand on her forehead and easing it down to rest on her cheek. "What's wrong?"

"Just a headache." She pushed him away and opened the oven door.

He handed her a tray of cinnamon rolls. "Did you take anything?"

"Yes. No." She closed the oven door, set the timer and stopped halfway back to the sink. "I'm not sure. I'll check before I take anything else."

Something was wrong. It was like it had been that day a month or so before, only worse. She'd blown him off then, and he hadn't given it much thought. The next time he'd seen her, it was as if it had never happened. But something…something was off.

"Check how?" he asked. "Do you count your headache pills?"

She hesitated, and the look in her gray eyes was frenzied. He stepped closer. "Lib?"

"No, of course I don't. But they're strong. I have a prescription for them, and I want to be careful." She grinned at him, but it was a splintery expression, nothing at all like her usual cheerfulness. "You know I'm a cheap drunk, Llewellyn."

He did know that. Two mugs of Mollie's

hot chocolate put Libby near the outer edge of sobriety—three had pushed her all the way over at their birthday party. He also knew she had headaches occasionally, so a prescription for pain wasn't out of the ordinary. Or was it? He almost asked but stopped—he'd ask Arlie instead. He used her nursing expertise shamelessly.

"Did you say you're going to Vermont, Michigan and Tennessee?" Libby asked. Her voice was higher than usual. She sounded like she was going to cry, which was crazy. Libby never cried.

"I am. And I'm going to downhill ski in Vermont, cross-country ski in Michigan and go to the Opry in Tennessee. Want to go with me?"

"Not this time. The crew has gotten started on the carriage house. I want to be around to see the transformation and maybe get in the way."

"You're good at that." He gave her a hug. "Call if you need me for anything. I'll only be a flight away."

"I'm good." She kissed his cheek and gave him another push. "Get going. If you're here when the rolls come out of the oven, you'll eat them all. I'll have to bake some more and I don't want to."

"Good point." He stepped outside, hesitating on the back porch because leaving felt like a mistake. Everything felt out of place. He glanced back through the window on the door. She wasn't moving around the kitchen but had taken a seat on a stool at the prep island.

Tucker started to go back in—he even had his hand on the doorknob—but he knew her body language well enough to understand she didn't want him there. Not then. So he wouldn't go. One thing that had made their friendship so strong was their absolute respect for each other's privacy.

But something was definitely wrong.

CHAPTER FIFTEEN

ALTHOUGH IT WAS only April, Libby felt as if it had surely been the longest day of the year. After delivering the rolls, she went for a walk, meeting Arlie at the end of her friend's driveway.

"It's so warm. Doesn't it feel great?" Arlie pushed up the long sleeves of her T-shirt. "How's the remodeling coming on the carriage house?"

"Really well. I'll be glad when I stop having knots in my stomach over the size of the mortgage. It's a good thing they're putting the apartment in upstairs, because I may be living there." Libby knew the loan on the building wasn't what was causing her upset—the payments were manageable even if her business expansion didn't go as planned. But at least it was a reason she could give to how she'd been feeling. She hated *being* clinically depressed, but she hated not understanding its triggers even more.

Of course she had had grief in her life, most of it slammed into a two-year period when she was still in her teens, but hadn't everyone? Why was good old Lib the one who was still curling into the emotional fetal position every time…every time what? She couldn't pin down a time. It was worse in the darkness of winter and in the gloom and angry wind of spring, but she'd been tossed into the viper's grasp on bright sunshiny days, too.

"You're having some trouble, aren't you?" Arlie's voice was quiet and calm.

Libby nodded, a lump working its way into her throat. She cleared it, then cleared it again. "I'm so afraid of taking too many anti-anxiety pills that sometimes I don't take enough. It was almost easy when I just took two pills first thing in the morning—one for depression and one for anxiety—but there's more to it now. We've had to change the combination a few times."

"Do you set them out for the day?"

"I always mean to. I even have one of those little pill cases for three dosages a day, but sometimes I forget to load it. Or I lose track of where I've put it, because I never bring it downstairs with me. One morning I think Elijah and Pretty Boy were playing catch with it. Sometimes I'm convinced I've already taken the dose even when the pill is right there in the case. All ridiculous things." Her heart was fluttering in her chest like a flock of big butterflies.

Was she losing her mind? Was the thing she'd dreaded since the morning she'd found her father in the barn finally happening? He'd been forty-six when he died, her mother only forty-one. None of her grandparents had lived to old age, either; although one had died in an accident and another had been killed in Vietnam, Libby had never expected longevity—it didn't seem to happen much in her lineage. But dying in her midthirties was way too young even if she did follow her father's path into madness. She had far too much to do.

"Tucker left this afternoon. He's going to be gone for ten days or so." She kept her tone casual. No one else needed to know how much she missed him when he was gone. "He'll enjoy it. I think he misses traveling."

"He hired Rent-a-Wife to pack up his things at the Hall while he's gone and put them in storage. The new owners are taking possession." Arlie chuckled, although her eyes still looked wary when they met Libby's. "He'll be living out of a suitcase at Jack's house."

Libby thought of her purple suitcase. Its plastic wheels had gotten some wear on them since her adventures with Tucker. She wondered what the next destination would be.

Or if there would be one. Was it time for them to stop pretending they weren't grown-ups?

A gust of wind made her look up and frown as clouds rolled in. The drop in temperature was immediate. By the time they'd walked past another house, Arlie was pushing her sleeves back down. "This is the weirdest spring. Between what the almanac is predicting and what the people at the old lakers' tables at the Silver Moon and Anything Goes say, I'll be surprised if a storm doesn't blow us right into lower Michigan."

Libby shuddered. "I remember my dad talking about the Palm Sunday tornadoes in northern Indiana. He was from Elkhart, and his family lived in a trailer park that was decimated. No one in his family was badly hurt, but their home was destroyed. He pushed us into the basement every time the wind rose."

"How did you ever get to be a sky watcher?"

"I think that's how. I'm not claustrophobic, but I hated when he closed us in down there, so I started learning about the sky. I studied cloud formations before I ever looked at stars, and I'd say, 'Hey, look, Dad, they're just scud clouds. Nothing's going to happen with them.' After a while, he believed me. I never admitted I was scared anyway—he'd have made us go back downstairs."

Arlie laughed. "Daddy would take Holly and me outside to look at the clouds. Mama would stand at the door saying, 'Dave, I mean it, bring them inside. If you want to blow away, that's up to you, but they're staying here with me.' We'd go in, and whenever it thundered or the wind got loud, Dad would throw himself on the floor, howling that it had hit him."

"I remember!" Dave Gallagher had been a hero to all of his daughters' friends—they'd called him Superdad. Libby mourned him as much as she did her own father.

Libby and Arlie walked all the way around the lake, clinging to each other when they crossed the bridge over the slapping waves below. Libby felt better when they parted in front of Seven Pillars, as if the weight on her chest had been lightened by being shared.

When it was fully dark, she took the telescope out and looked at the stars. She wished on Venus, the plea whispered into the silence of the night, and tried to feel her mother's presence as she had on the balloon ride.

It was late when she went to bed. She could barely keep her eyes open, but she was afraid to sleep. Afraid of the dreams she sensed were coming, pushed into her subconscious by the monster she couldn't control.

Elijah curled into his usual space at her back. Pretty Boy left his rug across the room and leaped agilely onto the bed, settling himself at her feet. Almost asleep, she rested her fingers in the dog's fur and took comfort in not being alone.

TUCKER SKIED EARLY and not well, giving up midmorning and going back to the inn for a late breakfast. He went to the plant that occupied an old brick building in downtown Fionnegan, Vermont, and spent the rest of the day talking to employees and seeing if he could still do the jobs he'd had during summers while he was in college. He found he could do them, but he was in no way good at them.

"I wouldn't hire me," he admitted, laughing.

"You know we have good people, and the business is important to the town," the plant manager assured him at the retirement dinner at McGuffey's Tavern, "but if we don't change equipment soon, we're not going to be able to produce enough to stay sustainable."

Tucker was glad he and Jack had argued and come to a decision on this already. "We have room here for another production line without crowding the building, too, don't we?"

"Sure."

"Do you think if we were able to make that kind of investment—including new equipment for the products you're already making—we could get any tax breaks until we recoup the costs?" It was a game he hated playing, and his brother did, too, but if Llewellyn's Lures was to stay profitable, it was a necessary one.

"It's something we've never asked for, but

we're a valuable and philanthropic part of the community. I don't see it being a problem."

"Do you want us to handle it at corporate or do you want to take care of it here? If you'd rather gather information and present it yourselves, we'll offer any kind of support you ask."

"The city council will probably want one of you to be there, although I don't know why it would matter. They know Jack owns property here. You not only make money here, but you spend it, as well."

After dinner, Tucker walked back to the bed-and-breakfast. He'd missed a call from Libby last night, but when he'd called back this morning, she hadn't answered. He'd left a voice mail, but all he'd heard from her since was a one-word text that said, BUSY! He knew she was—Hershberger Construction was working on the carriage house—but it seemed odd not to have talked to her since he'd left for the airport the day before.

He'd never lost the sense that something was not right in her world, but he also hadn't been able to pinpoint the source of his unease.

When Jack called, Tucker filled him in on the events of the day, then said, "I'm headed to Michigan tomorrow. I was going to drive over, but I think I'll fly instead. I don't feel much like being away right now."

"Whatever you want to do." Jack sounded surprised, but not unhappy. "It grows on you, doesn't it, being settled into one spot?"

"It does." More and more, Tucker realized Miniagua was his spot. Sometimes he wished he'd never left, but then he wouldn't have known. He wouldn't have understood how much of a laker he truly was, and how much the little community and all its idiosyncrasies meant to him. He wouldn't have understood the axiom "no friends like old friends" if he'd never parted from the old ones.

That made him think about the Parsonses. They weren't old friends at all, but it seemed as if they were. Gavin texted him and Libby every time Liberty the calf made a forward stride in the bovine scheme of things. Mari sent crayon drawings through the mail that decorated their refrigerators. Alice and Dan were coming to Miniagua for dinner and a boat ride the first week of May.

There was, Tucker was starting to realize, a common denominator in the long problem that was his life.

It was late and she'd probably be asleep, but that was too bad. She should have called him back today. He reached for his phone and tapped the place on the screen that would connect him to Libby.

THEY SAT ON the bleachers at Charlie's baseball game on Tucker's first night back in town after a week away. Jack and Tucker were side by side between Arlie and Libby. Holly and Jesse sat on the next row down. Gianna and Max were working in the concession stand. Kendall, who had come into the tearoom after school to help in the kitchen, sat beside Libby.

"Don't embarrass him." Arlie scowled at Jack and Tucker.

The two men exchanged a look of such outrage that Libby had to bury her face against Tucker's sleeve to hide her laughter.

"I am not the one who tried to climb the backstop when Charlie slid into home at the last game," Jack said mildly, "nor am I the one who texted his mother with a high-five emoji and a link to Queen singing 'We Are the Champions.' I also didn't cave and buy him the new bat he just *had* to have."

"We bartered for the bat."

"Him admitting to the entire eighth grade that you helped Tucker, me *and* him with algebra is not barter." Jack grinned at her. "Neither is the fact that he let you kiss him when you dropped him off at school."

Arlie sniffed. "Sure it is."

"If you feel like arguing, ask Libby what skinny-dipping is first," Tucker advised his brother. "You won't win either argument. They learned their thinking from a much higher power than we did."

"That's right." Libby beamed. "Gianna taught us all. Too bad you guys weren't listening. But we won't talk about the skinny-dipping question, will we, Llewellyn? I may have been a little wasted at the time of the original discussion. Besides—" she covered Kendall's ears "—I am nothing if not a good influence."

"That's what I've always said about you, too," Holly volunteered. "Jesse seems to think otherwise."

"Older brothers are seldom either truthful or appreciative," said Tucker righteously, "which explains why Libby and I are the way we are." He hesitated. "I guess you could take that however you wanted to, couldn't you?"

"Yes, they could, so let's just leave it at that." Libby joined in the laughter.

After the ball game, during which Charlie and his new bat proved themselves in a base hit and a double, they went to Anything Goes, sitting in the dining room instead of the bar because Charlie, Kendall and the Phillipy children were all part of the group.

When Libby and Tucker walked Kendall home, the house was dark.

Kendall reached under a rock, coming up with a key in a plastic sandwich bag. "When Mom left this morning, she said she might not be back tonight. It's okay." She met Libby's eyes. "Really, it is. I've stayed by myself before."

Libby understood that sometimes children had to take care of themselves. She had friends who left their adolescent kids alone or in charge of younger siblings while they worked the overnight shift at hospitals or factories because they couldn't afford child care. She was on the emergency call list for a few of them. Those children were left with cell phones, and a deputy's patrol car made extra trips past their houses. Their parents were home by the time their teeth were brushed in the morning.

She knew very well that even in Miniagua not everyone had a safety net, but most people kept watchful eyes on others' children. Not everyone even had a home, but there were vacant buildings with unlocked doors and blankets and pillows inside so that no one ever had to sleep under the proverbial bridge.

No matter how utopian its residents considered the little community to be, occasionally someone slipped through the cracks of its boardwalks. A child was abused, a spouse battered, a homeless person found half-starved.

"I'll text your mom," said Libby, taking her phone out of her pocket. "You can run in and get some pajamas, then you're coming home with me. I have a guest room that never gets used."

Tucker checked the house quickly before allowing Kendall to go inside to collect her belongings. He pulled Libby in close, kissing the top of her head.

"No, ma'am," he said. "Absolutely not."

She looked up. "No, what?"

"No, you wouldn't be the kind of mother

Marie Williams is. You'd be more like Crystal Worth or Ellen Curtis or Gianna Gallagher."

Libby hadn't been wondering that. Unlike Arlie, who'd wanted children and worried that she'd never have any, or Holly, who intended to have at least four, Libby hadn't even wanted them. They didn't fit in particularly well with adventures. At least, not the kind of adventures she hoped to have.

However, she had to admit she liked that Tucker thought she'd be a good mother.

The guest room in the apartment was small but cozy, and Kendall was charmed by the window seat that matched the one in Libby's room. Elijah and Pretty Boy, being polite hosts, joined Kendall when she went to bed, and they were all asleep within minutes.

"How's the carriage house coming?" Tucker asked when Libby rejoined him in the kitchen.

"Come on out and see it. Neely's so excited. We already have at least ten events scheduled for the summer, and we've barely advertised."

They toured the building that sat at the lake end of Seven Pillars's driveway. "Look at this," she said when they'd climbed the stairs at the end of the large room. "Isn't it a neat apartment? I can't decide whether to rent it for someone to live in or as a vacation condo, since the lake is right out the back door." Her voice echoed in the empty space.

Tucker asked questions and she answered them. He promised Llewellyn's Lures would bring business to the Seven Pillars Event Center. She thanked him. They stopped on their way back to the house to listen to the sounds of the lake, and Tucker's arm came around her shoulders, scooping her into him.

"Now that we've been so extraordinarily polite and correct with each other ever since I got home, when are you going to talk about what's wrong?"

CHAPTER SIXTEEN

"SHE'S MAD AT ME," Tucker said flatly.

"I know." Jesse gave him a sidewise glance from where he sat beside him at the Thursday night poker game. "I asked her if she wanted me to beat you up, and now she's mad at me, too. What did you do, anyway?"

"I asked her what was wrong. I said we'd been too good friends for too many years for her to be shutting me out the way she is. She said she wasn't. It became a battle of 'am not' and 'are, too,' and I appear to have lost. She hasn't spoken to me in two days. She even let me pay for my coffee at the tearoom." That had been the biggest shock of all. "I have absolutely no objection to paying for my coffee, but in the ten years she's been in business, she's refused to take a dime. Suddenly, because I showed what I considered to be natural concern for her well-being, I'm paying full price." He glowered at the cards in his hand—the game wasn't going so great for him, either. "If I wasn't mad right back at her, and if my feelings weren't hurt, I'd think it was funny."

"I've been married a long time," said Sam, laying down cards and holding up two fingers. "I've learned to just say I'm sorry and that I didn't mean it." He flinched at the cards Jack handed him—Sam didn't have much of a poker face. "For what it's worth, that's exactly the same story Penny tells about me."

Tucker frowned. "Is that supposed to be helpful in some way?"

"Probably not, but if you were married to Libby, you would just expect these things and not be talking about them on poker night when we should be talking about NASCAR and football and beer."

"Libby's dating the football coach at the high school. I don't think marrying me is on her list of adventures." Saying that stung some. Tucker thought he knew why it did, but he didn't want to go there in his mind, at least not while she was mad at him over nothing and definitely not while sitting at a table with a bunch of guys who knew them both way too well.

"See, he got football into the conversation, Sam, so we're good to go. Besides, that's my little sister you're talking about. Her marrying Tucker isn't gonna happen." Jesse's voice was even. His gaze went from his cards to Tucker in another sidewise glance.

Tucker looked hard to see if there was a smile in his eyes and didn't see one.

"Lib could do worse than my little brother," said Jack. "I'm not quite sure how, but she could."

Sam snorted. "Seems we said the same about Arlie not too long back."

"You know what?" Tucker tossed down his cards. "It's not funny. I'm sorry I started the conversation and that I kept it going, but we're not talking about Libby anymore. I won't marry her because she's too smart to have me, so no worries, Jess. And there's never been any question in the world that as far as husband material goes, I'm the scrapings from the bottom of the barrel." He got up, pushing his chair under the game table in the Dower House's den. "I'm going for a walk. See you guys later."

He might have let the door slam on his way out.

Wind gusts were whipping the lake into frilly whitecaps again. Clouds scudded across the sky, their edges lit by the moon. This was the stormiest spring Tucker could remember. He walked into the breeze, his eyes drying and his face beginning to burn. His hair peeled back from his face.

Another storm was coming. He could smell it on the wind. Hard, driving rain that kept the farmers out of the fields. Wind damage. Power outages. Warnings on television. "Seek a place of shelter" had been said so often this year that people had stopped paying attention.

Turbulence. Not just in the weather, but in everything. Nothing felt right. "Count your blessings," his mother always urged him, and he did. He had an embarrassment of them to count and he knew it, but still...

Turbulent was how he felt, and he couldn't seem to shake it. He was not a profound individual. The reason he'd decided on pursuing marriage and family without necessarily falling in love was that he didn't think falling in love was in his DNA. No, that was wrong— he fell in love just fine; it was the staying that escaped him.

Sam and Penny had met the first day of

their second year of college and never looked back. Jack and Arlie had loved each other since they were in high school. They denied it, insisting they'd fallen in love again when Jack moved back to the lake after sixteen years, but Tucker didn't think so. He thought their love for each other had kept a firm hold on both their hearts.

Other than his mother, Jack and Charlie, Tucker didn't think he'd ever loved anyone for very long.

Except for Libby.

"I DON'T WANT to talk about it." Libby served quiche, salad and coffee to her brother and glared at him all in one smooth motion. If she could have figured out a way to kick him at the same time, she would have. "You never eat lunch here and now suddenly you are?"

"I was hungry." Jesse hesitated, then grasped her hand and pulled her into the chair beside his. "Last night, Tucker walked out on the poker game. You've been mad at me all week. I admit to not being the sharpest knife in the drawer when it comes to anything requiring emotion—Holly has told me that more than once—but even I know something's going on. Can I help?"

Libby would have been fine if it hadn't been for that last question. But she couldn't let go. What if the viper broke free and unleashed the pain and anger that were consuming her? What came out would hurt. She would not only reveal her secret, she'd use words she couldn't unsay.

"You know, it's a little late for the devoted-brother act, Jess."

Oh, no, where had that come from after her stern admonishment to herself? Of all the people in the world, her brother was the last one she'd ever want to hurt. He'd had her back nearly as long as Tucker had. He was the only person she absolutely knew loved her. Maybe he just did it because he had to, but he loved her nevertheless.

"I'm sorry," she said immediately. "I didn't mean that. You're a very good brother."

"No, I'm not. I'm an emotional vacuum. I know that." He turned his cup around and around on the saucer. Then he stopped and turned it back the other way. "I wasn't there for the awful things. I was in the barn when Mom died. I was stationed in San Diego when you found Dad. Even after the accident when you were in a coma, I wasn't there. I was milking cows and planting corn and swearing into the navy."

"You were supportive every way you could be." He had been. She hadn't always given him credit for it, but he'd done all he could. If it hadn't been for his support of her dreams, Seven Pillars would still be a series of sketches and notes on lined yellow paper.

She had wanted more from him. She still did. She wanted affection. She wanted to believe that if he knew her secret, he wouldn't judge her for it. She wanted conversation more often than the couple of times a year he took care of her animals.

She wanted to know he'd miss her if she was gone. God help her, she wanted to know if *anyone* would.

Dismayed that she had hurt Jesse and frightened by the panic that was rising in her throat, she moved to get up. The lunch rush was over, but a private party was still taking place in the side parlor. She had to see if they needed anything. If she could just get out of the room long enough to catch her breath and force back the scream that was choking her, she'd be all right for a little while longer.

But he stopped her. His hand grasped hers again and his eyes held hers. "Libby, let me help."

For just an instant, she hesitated. Maybe she should tell him. It would take away part of the load. Sharing it with Arlie made it bearable most of the time; maybe it would be even better if her brother knew. She didn't want to drag him down the viper's path with her, but he had emotional strength that she obviously didn't. Surely he did.

But then she remembered how he'd described himself. *An emotional vacuum.* He had baggage of his own to carry—she couldn't add to it.

Someone came into the room, and she pulled her hand away. She couldn't do this now. Maybe not ever.

"Hi!" Holly approached the table, limping slightly. She wore ragged sweatpants and a faded Ball State University sweatshirt. If she'd combed her shiny dark hair lately, it wasn't noticeable. Instead of contacts, she wore horn-rimmed glasses that sat crookedly on her face and no makeup. She had a zit square in the middle of her chin. "It's going to rain again—my leg is telling me so. I realize I look like hammered poop, and I just can't make myself care." She approached them, hugging Libby when she got up from the table.

Libby hugged her back, holding on a second too long and too tightly. Holly drew back and looked hard at her. "I'm sorry. You're having a private conversation, aren't you?" She clasped Libby's hands, holding her gaze. "I'll see you both later."

"You will not. Sit down here. You're just in time to stop me from embarrassing myself and Jess from swearing he'll never come in here again. Want some lunch?"

"I'd love some. I swear I haven't eaten since January. But why don't you let me get it? You two go ahead and—"

"No, ma'am." Libby gave her hands a squeeze. "Sit. Do you want the special?"

"Yes, and if you have an extra-large serving or a piece that fell out on the table, I'll take that." Holly took the chair Libby had been sitting in and turned her thousand-watt smile on Jesse. "Good afternoon, Dr. Jesse. How are you?"

He frowned at her. "I thought you couldn't go anywhere today."

"I couldn't." Holly's beaming grin might have dimmed a little, but not very much. Libby envied her that—a scowl from Jesse could make his sister whimper like a puppy.

"So how do you happen to be here?" he asked, nodding when Libby held the coffee carafe up in question.

"Well, about twenty minutes ago, I typed 'The End' and have given myself a break before I go back to the beginning and decide which half of what I wrote is trash. You want to be a reader for me, Lib?"

"Sure do." Libby could use a dose of the happily-ever-after Holly's books always promised. Plus the vicarious trips to Regency-period England were worthy of being compared to an adventure with Tucker. "I'll get your food. Is there enough cream and sugar on the table?"

She needed to walk away, because thinking of Tucker hurt. As she filled a plate, adding an extra half slice of quiche, regret lodged under her breastbone much as the panic had only a few minutes ago. She laughed out loud, surprising herself. For someone who was healthy as a horse, swallowing was becoming a real issue.

She owed Jesse an apology, but she didn't know how to apologize without explaining why she'd gotten angry. And she didn't think she could. How could she explain her condition to someone else when she couldn't make sense of it to herself?

When she carried Holly's meal back into the dining room, her brother and her friend were holding hands, their dark heads together. Libby stopped in the archway, delight pushing through the panic, anger and regret that had defined the days since she'd stopped speaking to Tucker. As she hesitated, Holly threw back her messy dark head as her laughter rang silvery and loud into the quiet space. For just a second, Jesse looked shocked, and then his laughter joined hers, mingling and lifting until the joy filled the room.

Libby had to set down the tray of food. She couldn't remember the last time she'd heard Jesse laugh aloud. If she hadn't walked in at that moment and seen it, she wasn't sure she'd have recognized the sound.

It was enough to get her through the day.

"I'M TAKING CHARLIE to South Bend this morning to spend the weekend with his grandparents. He doesn't want to go because he's afraid he'll miss something, but he has to. How do you feel about spending an hour and a half in a car with a grumpy twelve-year-old? After we drop him off, we could catch the train and ride into Chicago for the day." Tucker took a deep breath. "If you're still mad at me, you don't have to talk to me."

She stood silently, blocking his way into her apartment. Her eyes were large and shadowed in the dim light of the hallway. He'd hesitated before letting himself in downstairs even though he'd texted her first to let her know he was coming up. When he'd tapped on the apartment door, she'd opened it immediately. But she hadn't let him in. He could see why through the crack in the door—she was wearing a tank top and pajama pants and all the hair on the right side of her head was standing straight up.

No wonder she hadn't answered his text—she'd been in bed. He wasn't going to examine too closely at how that made him feel, but she looked cute with her hair pushed all out of shape like that.

She pushed the door open all the way, stepping back to let him in. When she spoke, it was in a rush, the words tumbling over each other. Her hands were in front of her, palms up. "I'm so sorry. I don't know how… I don't know… I'm just so sorry."

"You don't ever have to be sorry for anything with me." She knew that. Of course she did. They'd been insulting and forgiving each other their entire lives, all without apology. He knew, without either of them saying it, that this time was different, but he couldn't begin to define how. All he was sure of was that her pain was so intense he could feel it with every beat of his heart.

Her arms came around his neck, and she held on. He drew her into him, saying nothing, absorbing the tremble of her body. Feeling each breath she took, the rise and fall of her chest slowing as he held her. *It will be all right now. Everything will be all right now.* He didn't say the words but hoped she understood them anyway. Things were changing between them, and it seemed as if they were changing too fast.

"We need to talk," he said.

"I know."

"You want to go to Chicago?"

"Do I get coffee and breakfast on the way?"

"Yes."

"Sure." She pulled away, and he let her go, feeling bereft.

He knew, with that sudden emptiness, exactly how to fill the void he'd been denying was there. He understood exactly why he'd been unable to commit to any previous relationship. He got what Meredith had meant when she said *just one* when he'd asked her if she had "friends like that."

Because there was just one for him, too.

How had he gone thirty-four years without knowing who it was?

"Will you take Pretty Boy out while I get dressed?"

"I will." He took the leash from its hook inside the entry closet door, and the dog immediately began a dance around his feet. "Arlie said she'd come and take him out tonight and in the morning if we spend the night somewhere."

"Oh, good." Libby looked relieved. "Do you need to go get Charlie or is he in the car?"

"He's in the car, hopefully asleep. We're

driving Jack's SUV, so it will be a comfortable trip for him."

By the time Tucker and the dog came back upstairs, Libby was dressed and her hair braided. She had on makeup and was in the kitchen, stuffing pastries into a zippered plastic bag. "He'll need these for between breakfast with us and lunch at his grandparents'. Kendall told me boys can only go something like twelve minutes between meals."

"Kendall's right. Put an extra one in there for me."

He watched Libby move around the apartment and was amazed he hadn't done it before. How could he have known someone his whole life without really seeing her, memorizing how she moved, how she felt, the scent that was hers alone? If anyone had asked him what she looked like, he'd have shrugged and said something like *She has brown hair and gray eyes and freckles on her nose. And she's short. A little heavy. She smells like soap.*

He wouldn't have mentioned the silkiness of her hair—it was so smooth it slipped right out of her braid if she didn't spray it with stuff. He wouldn't have told anyone else about the blue sparkles in her eyes that she insisted weren't really there. She was five foot five—short only because he was over six feet. She wasn't heavy, either, just shaped so that her hips had more curve to them than she liked.

She was the one, as she said herself, whose name people forgot when they looked at pictures from days past. She was the survivor of the prom night accident who bore the fewest scars, either physical or otherwise. She'd been good old Lib all their lives before and had wakened from the coma as good old Lib again. By her own definition, she was neither beautiful nor talented.

How could he not have seen the beauty and the heart and the generous spirit that was the real Libby Worth? She'd been his best friend since the minute of his birth, they'd loved each other that long, and he'd never once seen the person she truly was.

And why had he been so blithely sure she didn't have any scars?

Anger toward himself wasn't something Tucker indulged in very often. He did his best to be a problem solver instead of a problem causer and never failed to take credit for his own transgressions, but he also forgave himself for them.

He wasn't sure how soon he'd be able to do that this time—if ever.

"You look great," he said.

She gave Elijah a farewell pat and shot Tucker a narrow look. "You don't have to be *that* nice to me, Llewellyn. I may have thrown a tantrum of sorts, but I'm not a delicate flower."

He grabbed her purple overnighter and went down the stairs ahead of her, thinking that even if she wasn't a delicate flower, it wouldn't hurt to treat her like one once in a while.

In the car, she tossed the pastries back to Charlie, who'd wakened when the door opened.

"You'll have to share with your uncle," she warned.

"We're going to Chicago while you're at your grandparents'," said Tucker, backing into the street. "I'll pick you up tomorrow night, so your period of torture will be short."

"I'd rather go with you. Libby likes having me around, don't you, Libby?" Charlie's smile, laden with braces though it was, was as charming as his uncle's.

"I do," she agreed, "but putting myself

in your grandmother's shoes, I'd want you to hang around, too. Because she was one of the people you scared to death by running off in December, and you need to be a really good grandson to make up for it. You should probably even offer to wash her car today or do something equally helpful. When she pinches your cheeks, you shouldn't complain, and when she calls you Chugga-chugga-Charlie, you should just smile and pray you outgrow it or she does."

Tucker choked on laughter. "I'd forgotten all about Chugga-chugga-Charlie. Thanks for the reminder."

"Yeah, Lib, thanks a lot." But Charlie was laughing, too.

Tucker felt the tension leave him as they drove. They ate breakfast at a truck stop, with Charlie finishing off his uncle's pancakes and stealing bacon from Libby's plate. *This is what it would be like with a family.*

Back in the car, he looked over at Libby, trying to gauge her mood, but she was playing Name that Tune with Charlie. She was laughing, and had been all morning, but was it forced? Was she trying too hard to convince both him and herself that all was well between them?

"You can't possibly use any songs that have come out in the last five years," she said when she lost a round. "They don't even *have* tunes!"

"You're dating yourself," Tucker warned, "but you can get him next time. Remember when Gianna beat all of us by naming 'A Hard Day's Night' on one note after we laughed at her for not knowing our stuff?"

They left Charlie at his grandparents' house with warnings to behave. The boy hugged Libby, and the look in her eyes made Tucker's heart ache.

He'd always believed her when she insisted she didn't want kids. He'd understood when she said she was single because she'd never found anyone worth giving up her independence for—he felt the same way, after all. Or he had until recently.

They didn't lie to each other. That was one of the unspoken, unbroken rules of friendship. It went along with keeping secrets if they had any and having each other's backs no matter what. Their pacts were different—

they broke them way too easily to take them very seriously. Not so the rules of friendship.

But had she broken that rule? Had she been less than honest when they talked about kids and families? Did she have a lot more baggage left over from the accident than she admitted to?

And finally, there was the question that had been eating at him ever since the other night: Why had she gotten so angry?

"I DON'T THINK I've ever been to Chicago when I wasn't either on a field trip with chaperones or being a chaperone on someone else's trip. Are we going to the museums?" Chicago had great museums, but Libby didn't want to go to them.

"Not unless you want to. I only have one place in mind. After that, the rest of the day is up to you. Remember we can't stay in Chicago, though—we left our bags in the car back at the train station in South Bend." He grinned at her, but the expression in his eyes told her something was still off between them. Her apology hadn't smoothed the rough edges her unreasoning anger had placed on their friendship.

She had to be more careful. She'd been controlling the depression for half her life—she couldn't let it control her now.

She also didn't have any idea how to spend the day. She didn't know how to be a tourist without a premade schedule.

She was surprised when they got off the train at the Museum Campus station. "I thought we weren't going to the museums."

"We're not going to the ones we've been to before." He pointed ahead in the direction they were walking. "We're going to that one."

"Oh." She stopped midstride, her hands clasped in front of her as she stared up at the dome of Adler Planetarium. "I've never been to a planetarium before. Tuck, did you know that?"

"I did know that, and I feel like a real idiot because I never thought of it before."

"Do you know what they're like? All I've done is read about them."

"I've been to Dyer Observatory at Vanderbilt. It's pretty cool." He caught her hand and pulled her forward. "Come on. It's farther away than it looks."

"Did you like it?"

"I did." He hesitated. "Although other than

looking through the telescope with you telling me what I'm looking at, I'm not much of a sky person."

She'd known that, of course. "Why don't we go somewhere that you'll enjoy, too?" she asked. "Adventures don't always have to be all about me."

He laughed. "We've been to a Louisville Bats baseball practice, a Pacers basketball game and a Colts football game. I don't think any of those were about you, do you?" He tugged at her braid.

She was so enthralled with all the exhibits the planetarium had to offer that she lost track of him for fifteen-minute periods, only to turn and find him standing at the back of a group watching her or sitting at a table in the café with a man with a walker, sharing coffee and laughing out loud.

When it was time to go into the auditorium for the *Skywatch Live* program, Tucker appeared at her side. "Dan said he fell asleep when he brought Alice and the kids here, but they loved it," he warned. "You already know so much about the sky I don't know if you'll like it or not, but I'm going for the nap."

They made themselves comfortable in the

reclining chairs inside the auditorium and went on a guided tour through the sky. She loved it, and so did he. It was the last exhibit they visited, and they talked about it all the way to the taxi line, on the ride to Navy Pier and while they waited for pizza in the first restaurant they found.

"So, as adventures go, this was a good one?" he asked.

"It's been perfect. I can't thank you enough." She smiled at him, feeling more like herself than she had in days. She didn't even have to force the expression or fold one of her hands into a fist to keep herself from trembling. "Now, if we can just find you a gi—"

"We're not looking anymore," he interrupted. His voice was abrupt, but not angry or cold. Just…firm.

"We're not?" She wasn't about to examine the leap her heart took with his statement. "I know we haven't been as successful as we'd hoped, but don't give up." She reached to push his hair out of his eyes—it grew so fast that it needed cutting every few weeks. "You're cute, Llewellyn, and you're one of the good guys. It will work out."

"Actually, we have been successful." He

caught her hand before she could pull it away. "Meredith was perfect. Cindy was fun. Risa was better at algebra than Arlie and good at volleyball—she was great. Allison's a terrific girl. Even Sandy…well, no, that wouldn't have worked. But there was nothing wrong with any of them, and there's nothing wrong with me, either. What's wrong is trying to do the equivalent of shopping for a wife at the supermarket."

"We weren't doing that."

"Yes, we were." He nodded as if to make his point. "Do you remember what Gianna said after the accident? No, of course you don't—it was while you were still in the coma. We met in the hallway outside Arlie's room one night and Gianna said, 'I keep going into rooms and they're empty because he's not there.' I want to love someone that much. I want someone to love *me* that much."

Libby met his eyes across the table. They were summer-sky blue, the lashes so impossibly long that she'd begrudged him having them all their lives. She used to tell him if he'd put on mascara, he'd look like he had an alpaca's lashes. Those eyes were always bright, always laughing.

Except now. Now they were dark and serious.

"I want that for you, too." And she did—it wasn't even hard to say the words. The next ones didn't come so easily. "I wish I could have helped you find it."

"Who knows?" He rubbed his thumb over her fingernails. "Maybe you have."

CHAPTER SEVENTEEN

"How do you think it's going?" Libby stood with her hands on her hips and looked around the ground floor of the carriage house. "Is it what you had in mind?"

"I think it's perfect." Neely Warren beamed. "I never thought I'd be happy again when I got divorced after all those years, but I have to say, Libby, this makes me happy. It'll be great for the lake, great for us. There's no downside."

The mortgage payment made Libby think there *was* a downside to her business expansion, but that had been her choice. Besides, the revenue Nate's golfing associates had just brought in during the soft-opening week had taken a great deal of the pain out of that particular bottom line.

"What's up next?" She went to the calendar at the reception desk near the French doors that provided entry into the facility.

"The class of '87 is Saturday night."

"Servers and menu all set? Who's catering?" That had been the topic of a big discussion when they'd talked about opening the event center. Neely had wanted Seven Pillars to do all the catering, especially since there was a good kitchen in the venue and another in the upstairs apartment, but Libby hadn't agreed. One of the things that made businesses in Miniagua successful was that they supported each other.

"Anything Goes, with the Amish bakery doing desserts." Neely didn't sniff, but Libby thought she wanted to.

She grinned at the other woman. "We need a name for the center, a Cole Porter title— I'm still in trouble with the chamber of commerce because Seven Pillars is a place on the Mississinewa River instead of the name of a song. Got any new ideas?" She'd pitched calling it the Beguine after the song "Begin the Beguine," but a visit to the dictionary had taught her the beguine was a dance, not the delightful respite of the mind she'd always assumed it to be.

"I like Come On In, but the hardware store already used it. Let's give it some time and not name it until the perfect title presents it-self."

"I think you're right." Libby looked at her watch. "I also think it's midnight, the place is clean as a whistle and it's time to call it a day. I'll see you in church."

"You will if I get out of bed in time." Neely stretched and groaned. "My mind is still twenty-two, but the body gave that age up forty years ago."

The omnipresent wind was whipping as they walked across the newly paved parking lot to the house. Neely waved and got into her car. Libby went up to her apartment. She took a shower, made sure the animals were all right and fell into bed. It had been a very long day.

At two thirty, she sat up in bed. She had no idea how she *knew* it was two thirty, be-cause there was no power. The darkness in her room was absolute. Beside her, Elijah me-owed plaintively. That was alarming in itself, because he'd been silent ever since Jesse had brought him to her as a starved and abused kitten. Even when he purred, she could only tell if she was holding him.

"What's wrong, kitty?" she murmured,

shoving her hair out of her eyes. "Can't read the clock?"

Across the room, Pretty Boy woofed.

Libby turned on the flashlight she kept in the nightstand and got out of bed. She went to the bathroom, came back and petted the disturbed animals, and started to crawl back into bed.

She'd just gotten the pillow into the right position under her head when she realized what had awakened her in the first place. When she'd come into the house, she'd left the money bag lying on the reception desk in the carriage house. She thought she'd locked the door and set the alarm, but had she? She'd been talking to Neely as they left the building, and no one had ever accused her of being a multitasker even on her best day.

While Nate had paid for the use of the facility with his credit card, most of the other expenses had been paid in cash. In addition to that, she kept a bank of small bills for people who needed change. There was a lot of money in that bag, and that was important when it came to her new mortgage payment.

She couldn't go back to sleep. The lights didn't come back on, and she was wide-awake. Elijah meowed again. Pretty Boy leaped onto the foot of the bed and lay there in silent wakefulness, much like Libby's own.

"Okay." She got up again, tossing a robe on over her tank top and pajama shorts and pushing her feet into flip-flops. "I can't sleep until I get that money into the house, and obviously you guys can't, either. You coming with me?" She grabbed the flashlight and shone it on her watch again.

Two forty-five.

It was eerily quiet when she stepped outside with the animals beside her. No birdsong, no wind, no rustle of leaves. No cars drove past on the gravelly street. She didn't even hear the muted slapping of the water, the "laker's lullaby."

Into the soundlessness came the strident wail of a siren. Not the usual whoops or blats of fire trucks or ambulances or police cars, but an insistent one that hurt her ears as it bounced off the water. It was the kind of noise Tucker heard even if his good ear was covered. She recognized the tornado siren—they checked it at noon on the first Monday of every month, driving everyone crazy for three minutes.

This wasn't noon. Or Monday.

She'd always heard that fear caused a metallic sensation in one's mouth, although she'd never noticed it. Until now. She stood still on the paved drive between Seven Pillars and the carriage house, listening. Waiting for the sound to stop.

When it did, she relaxed. It was just a warning, that was all, to make people aware and watchful. Not everyone woke on their own at two thirty. But when the siren stopped, the silence was back. Heavy and unnerving. Elijah, held firmly in her arms, meowed again. Pretty Boy leaned against her legs.

And then it wasn't silent at all. It was like the stories she'd read about the long-ago Palm Sunday tornadoes in the issues of the *Elkhart Truth* and the *South Bend Tribune* her father had kept from 1965. It was as if she were standing on the tracks with a freight train bearing down at full throttle. The air was oppressive, and stinger-like twigs and gravel blew against her bare legs.

She looked wildly between the house and the carriage house. The house had a basement, but the carriage house was closer and two of its restrooms were in the center of the building, built where the tack room used to be. No windows, just vents that went…where did they go? It seemed important to know, but she didn't.

The sky was unnervingly black, but when relief from the gloom came, it was worse. She could see the rotating funnel as it roared across the lake. It was coming straight toward her, and she wondered with no small amount of terror how it could see her in the darkness. She shouted at Pretty Boy to "Come on!" but didn't wait to see if he followed as she dashed toward the French doors of the carriage house.

They were locked. Oh, dear God, they were locked! And what was the combination? She knew it as well as she knew her own…that was it! She punched in the scrambled digits of her Social Security number with a trembling finger, vowing if she lived through this night she'd change the combination to something shorter. Two digits, a two and a seven. That way, Tucker would remember it even if she didn't, because that's how much older than him she was.

Oh, Tucker. The roar was surrounding her, pushing her and the animals inside the building and taking her breath away with its suffocating force. "Come on," she said again, gasping, holding Elijah so close he struggled against her. *Oh, Tuck, I wish I'd told you—*

IT WAS AN unusual Saturday night. Restless and empty. There was almost always something going on at the lake during spring and summer, but this week was different. Even the Saturday night acoustic jam session at the clubhouse, which he hardly ever attended, had been canceled this week.

Tucker hadn't realized how much time he'd spent with Libby on their adventures until he asked her to go on one and she told him she couldn't because it was the first week of business for the event center. His first thought—thankfully one he didn't voice—was that she should have gotten more people to help, because it was going to be too much work for her and Neely. But then she told him about the two women she'd hired from Rent-a-Wife.

Tucker was much more business minded than his brother. When they decided to share the CEO position at Llewellyn's Lures, one of the reasons was that their skill sets differed so much that each of them brought something of value to the table. Jack was hands-on and practical, keeping operations going and growing; Tucker was the idea guy who got bored as soon as things were up and running.

He wouldn't have wanted to run a business without his brother, much less stick around long enough to help make it grow. He admired that Libby, with her high school education and handwritten business plan, was so successful.

He wished she was happy, because he knew as surely as the sun had risen and set today that she wasn't. Not really. Most of the time she put up a good pretense, but the mask was growing thin.

He walked to Anything Goes early in the evening, finding Jesse at the bar. They ate dinner together then played darts, nursing draft beer and watching the water react to the wind lashing at its surface. "Tornado watch," Mollie called from behind the bar, watching the television closest to her, "till four in the morning."

"Nighttime ones are the worst." The observation came from one of the men in the dominoes corner. He sounded morose. "Recall that'n that went through Evansville in aught-five? Twenty-some people killed just like that. My missus can't fall asleep if there's watches or warnings going on."

"Sounds like Dad," Jesse murmured. He tipped his mug to drain the last of his beer. "Some of us just order another beer and pretend not to worry."

The door to the grill swung open, and Holly came in. She waved at everyone, but her eyes were solely on Jesse. Tucker had to bite back a wash of envy.

Someone who looked at him like that. Yeah, that's what he wanted. Someone with dark gray eyes and a short nose and a smile that lit up his soul.

He put money on the bar and stepped away, handing Holly his darts. "I think I'll head for home. Dr. Jesse here probably needs a driver—or will when he finishes that one. You going to stay around?"

She smiled at him. "I thought I would. Are these darts lucky?"

"Not so far." He gave her shoulders a squeeze and waved at Mollie.

The parking lot between Seven Pillars and the carriage house was emptying as he passed. Golf course builders from all over the country as well as Nate's friends from North Carolina had shown up to play at Feathermoor and discuss design with Nate. The cottages at Hoosier Hills Cabins and Campground on the other side of the lake were full. So were the bed-and-breakfasts that had sprung up in the area over the past few years. The weather had cooperated until now—the weekend had been shorts weather. Tucker and Jack had both taken the pontoon out.

The wind rose and ebbed, and he hoped the impending storms would blow themselves out before doing any damage. The cabins at the resort were particularly vulnerable, but the owner was a lifetime laker; he would never endanger guests. He probably had them in the basement barroom of the building that housed the lobby and camp store, playing pool and poker.

Jack and Charlie were watching a movie when he got to the Dower House. He joined them, ate a piece of frozen pizza he didn't really want and finally went to bed with a book at midnight. The wind was howling when he fell asleep. The last numbers he saw on his clock were one-two-three. He chuckled.

"Tuck! Let's go!"

He came awake immediately at the urgency in Jack's voice, following it into the wide upstairs hallway, because there was no light to lead him there. The full darkness in the house let him know the power was out. His brother and nephew were on the stairs, nearly halfway down from the sound of their footsteps. "Hurry!" Charlie's voice, which had deepened over the past months to the point that Tucker didn't always recognize it on the phone, was childishly high.

It had been years since he'd been in the Dower House's basement. He knew a moment's regret on the stairs that he hadn't taken time to put on shoes. He didn't remember what the floor was like down there.

He was relieved to feel concrete where the stairs stopped. A moment later, a light flickered to life, and then another. He looked from the battery-powered lanterns to his brother's shadowy face. "How did you know they were down here?"

"I don't know," Jack admitted. "Do you have your cell phone?"

"No. I barely have clothes on."

They all barely had clothes on. If fear and worry hadn't entered the basement with them, they'd have laughed at each other. Jack was wearing basketball shorts and a tank top. Charlie had on Star Wars pajama pants and a T-shirt in the only possible color that wouldn't match them. Tucker had on gray sweatpants he might possibly have worn when he went to Vanderbilt.

He watched as his brother hugged Charlie to him and remembered the December ice storm when Charlie had run away from his grandparents' home and Llewellyn's Lures had caught fire. The power had gone out then, too, but he remembered the look on Jack's face when he hadn't known where Charlie was. Later, when Charlie was safe and there'd been time to think about it, he'd wondered what it would be like to risk yourself to such a great degree by loving someone that much.

Standing in the basement of the Dower House, hearing the wind roar overhead, he was pretty sure he already did. He wished he'd told her.

IN THE BASEMENT of Seven Pillars, Libby kept emergency candles, battery-powered lanterns and extra blankets. An extra pantry was full of food, and so was the extra freezer.

Knowing that did her no good whatsoever as she huddled in an eight-by-twelve-foot restroom in the middle of the carriage house. She was glad she'd tucked a rocking chair into the corner of the room beside the cabinet that housed extra toilet paper and paper towels.

"At least," she told the animals, "we'll die in comparative comfort."

She'd always faced life's challenges head-on. She'd done what she had to following her parents' deaths, after the accident. When she'd bought the house that became Seven Pillars and lived for the first few years with the paralyzing fear that she'd made a mistake, she'd dealt with that. When she'd had to acknowledge that her kind of depression wasn't a quick fix, she'd...well, not dealt with it, precisely, but learned to live with it.

It was odd, she thought, sitting there with Elijah in her lap, that although they'd been nearly constant companions lately, panic and anxiety weren't pushing at her mind right now. Her breathing and heartbeat weren't erratic. Not very, anyway.

Because she thought she was going to die and had accepted it. She wouldn't say she'd invited it—she'd taken cover from the storm, for heaven's sake—but she expected it. And was okay with it.

"Living's harder," Gianna had told her one time after a particularly distressing panic attack. "Linda's parents know that. I know that. You know it, too. But it's worthwhile. It's always worthwhile. We have people who depend on us."

But Libby didn't. She had Jesse, but he would be all right without her—Holly would see to that. There was no one in the world Libby would rather trust to love her brother.

"It could end now, in this storm. It could be me who goes instead of someone's mother or father or, even worse, someone's child," she said, her voice a desperate whisper in the dark room. "It's not that I haven't loved people or that they haven't loved me." Her voice caught, and she wondered why she was speaking aloud with no one but two animals to listen, but she went on anyway. "It's just that it's so hard. No one depends on me, not like Gianna meant, and I couldn't help those who did. Not Mom or Dad or even the others in the accident. By the time I woke up, I couldn't help anyone." Her voice cracked. "It would be all right if it ended."

She was wearing her watch, but the flashlight's battery had failed, so she couldn't see it. She didn't know how long they sat there. Even after the roar from outside stopped, leaving the faint sound of sirens in its wake, she was reluctant to leave the dark stillness of the room.

Because maybe it really had ended and this was what it was like.

That was when she heard the voice.

CHAPTER EIGHTEEN

TREE LIMBS AND pieces of roofing were everywhere, so Tucker and Jack didn't bother with a car; they took the golf cart instead. People were already out, some just looking around wearing expressions ranging from avidly curious to horrified. Others were already working in the light afforded by lanterns and flashlights. They stacked branches and twigs into piles at the edge of the road, or worked in yards with neighbors. Chain saws sent up a staccato roar that echoed off the lake.

Arlie's and Jack's texts had crossed each other, so they knew all the Gallaghers were all right. Gianna's house had been slightly damaged and a tree had fallen on Arlie's car, but there were no injuries.

Tucker couldn't reach Libby. He got hold of Jesse, safe at the farm with Holly, and found out he couldn't reach his sister, either. "I'm on my way," said Jesse.

"I'll see you at Seven Pillars."

Jack, driving the golf cart, stopped at the Toe. "You stay with Grandma Gi," he ordered Charlie as Arlie ran out of the house carrying her medical bag. "Don't go anywhere else. Do you hear me?"

Charlie nodded. Arlie nearly knocked him over hugging him, then took his place on the back of the golf cart. "I can't reach her, either." She answered Tucker's unasked question, grasping his arm gently and holding his gaze with steady whiskey-colored eyes. Her throaty voice was soft, steady. "But the tornado evidently went right through Main Street. The sheriff's department already called to tell me there was damage to A Woman's Place. One of the vacant buildings near it was flattened." She bit her lip, as if she might know more, then shook her head and rested it for a minute against Jack's back.

It was surreal. Power was still out, but there was enough emergency lighting to see the damage that had been done. Tucker heard generators start up as they drove toward Main Street. With the sound came more light. More people working.

Lake Road was a mess of tree limbs and

leaves, but no worse than it often was after a spring storm. Main Street, on the other hand, looked like a war zone. The barbershop's roof was gone. The sign that had graced the front of the Come On In hardware store for as long as any of them could remember had been snatched up and lay in pieces on the street. The storage shed behind Rent-a-Wife had been picked up and set neatly in the center of a lot left vacant by the land's new owner.

Jack stopped in the middle of the block when someone called Arlie's name. "Over here," called the unknown voice. "Someone's cut pretty bad."

She jumped off the cart, carrying her bag, and Jack drove on, coasting to a stop at Seven Pillars.

They sat for a fractured moment, staring at what had been Libby's dream. Jack's hand came to rest on Tucker's arm. "She's probably all right. You know Lib. She wouldn't have slept through the storm."

The big Victorian was gone. Its large lot looked as if the swirling razor of wind that had decimated Main Street had taken special aim and exploded the big house. Wreckage covered the front yard. The white fence she'd been so proud of lay splintered beneath the debris. In grim contrast, the gazebo that had sat outside the tearoom's side doors and was used for outside dining in summer was untouched. Even the wrought iron tables and chairs inside it looked ready for occupation, unmoved by the twister that had devastated their surroundings.

Tucker didn't see Libby's car and thought for a wild, hopeful moment that she hadn't been home when the tornado struck. She'd been seeing Jim Wilson—maybe she was with him.

But the hope died when he saw her car lying upside down in the parking lot of the carriage house. He'd gotten out of the golf cart before it stopped moving, but the sight of the car nearly took him to his knees. He went still, and when Jack's arm came around him, he sagged against him for a moment before straightening and beginning to shout.

"Libby!" He didn't care that he sounded desperate and afraid. He *was* desperate and afraid. "Lib!" He moved toward where the house had been, propelled by dread. His brother called, too, but moved in another direction.

They met a few minutes later, their calls unanswered. "Tuck!" Jack stopped him, grasping his arm before he waded into the nightmare that had been Libby's beloved tearoom. "There she is." He pointed in the direction of the carriage house.

Libby was walking across the parking lot, Pretty Boy at her heels and Elijah in her arms. She was moving slowly, her gait wobbly, but she appeared to be all right. She wore short pajamas, a robe and flip-flops. Her hair was tousled, her skin ashen.

As she drew closer, he could see her features, find her eyes. She wasn't all right at all.

He caught her when she fell.

EVER HER BEST FRIEND, Tucker reached her before she could make a complete fool of herself. She hadn't even realized it was him. How had he gotten there so fast? Or maybe it hadn't been that fast—she wasn't sure how long it had been since the storm passed.

She hadn't fainted, although things were swimming around in front of her eyes even after Tucker hauled her up against him. Or maybe she *had* lost consciousness—she wasn't sure. If she had, the episode hadn't lasted long. She could tell from the teeming activity all around that there were people and animals hurt—this was not the time for good old Lib to come out as the wimp she really was.

She couldn't bear to look at Seven Pillars, so she clutched the sleeves of Tucker's windbreaker and buried her face against his shoulder. He held her, not saying anything, but his breathing was as irregular as hers.

"Where...who can we help?" she asked when she could find her voice, drawing back but facing away from what had been her home for the last ten years.

"Gianna just texted." Jack kissed her cheek and kept a hand on his brother's shoulder. "They're going to open the clubhouse for anyone who needs shelter right away. The other side of the lake wasn't hit. We just have to get people over there." He pointed in the direction of St. Paul's Church, across the street and farther away from the lake. People were moving around it, shining bright lights toward its roof. "The church has quite a bit of damage. It's probably not safe."

Libby waved an arm. "The carriage house is right there. It's still unlocked from when I came out. It can be used for whatever's needed."

By the time the sun blazed up over the lake, the community knew there had been no deaths due to the tornado, although one person had suffered a heart attack and Arlie was in the process of delivering a baby in its Amish parents' barn because their house was too heavily damaged to be safe. There were many cuts and bruises, a few broken bones, and some concussions. The damage in the light of day was horrifying, but the lakers were grateful it wasn't worse.

Libby worked alongside everyone else, dressed in clothing borrowed from Arlie. As long as she stayed busy, she would be fine. She avoided looking at Seven Pillars by helping with cleanup at the opposite end of the street and—later in the day—serving food in the carriage house to people who were working or who no longer had operational kitchens.

Insurance company representatives came sometime after lunch. Claims adjusters took pictures and asked questions. Men and women who'd sold policies to lakers put on gloves and helped with cleanup.

Libby answered the adjuster who questioned her as well as she could and promised to do her best to find the additional information that was needed. The bank could provide some of what she needed. Jesse had some of her records, too. It would all work out.

It was the sympathy from all quarters that nearly undid her. Gianna's long, tight hug. Father Doherty's tear-filled eyes and his endless supply of peppermint candy—he gave her a whole handful instead of the two pieces he usually allotted. Kendall came and washed dishes all afternoon and Charlie helped, a process Jack took pictures of for future blackmail purposes. Max Harrison brought loaves of bread to serve with the sliced ham and cookies Jesse's Amish neighbors had donated.

Libby just kept moving. She laughed when people tried to cheer her up to show them it was working, then tried in turn to cheer neighbors whose losses were as great as hers. If there was a rebellious voice in the back of her mind that insisted no one else's losses *were* as great as hers, she kept it silent. Especially since her bathroom was gone—she couldn't get to the prescription bottle that sat behind the pain relievers. She had to remain calm on her own.

No one must know just how certainly she was unraveling. No one.

Even after power was restored in the late morning, the day seemed to go on forever. The streets were cleared of debris. Her car and a few others were hauled away. Repairs that could be made easily and quickly were done. People like Libby, whose homes couldn't be inhabited, would have to wait.

At suppertime, when Tucker said firmly that it was time to stop for the day and eat, she didn't argue. They went to Anything Goes along with Jack, Arlie, Jesse and Holly.

Libby was afraid to talk for fear she would scream instead. Wasn't it enough that she had to survive one more loss without being reminded of all the others? She loved her brother, but when she looked at him today, it was their father she saw. When she'd brushed her teeth with the new brush Arlie had handed her and seen herself in the bathroom mirror, her mother's haunted, pain-filled eyes had looked back at her.

"You'll come out to the farm, right?" Jesse touched her arm from across the table and held her gaze. "I know it's hard for you there, but there's plenty of room and you're always welcome to stay however long you want."

She smiled at him, the emotion that clogged her throat so thick it nearly smothered her, then shook her head. "I'll stay in the carriage house. It will work out." How many times that day had she said that? *It will work out.*

She needed to replace her medication that had been lost in the tornado, but there'd been no opportunity that day to call her doctor or even to ask Arlie for an emergency prescription. She was okay so far, but would she be when she was alone in the empty apartment above the carriage house, when she could look out the windows and see what was left of the life she'd built for herself?

"I don't mean to be the overbearing big brother," said Jesse, "but I really don't like the idea of you being by yourself right now."

Her eyes narrowed. What did he know, or think he knew, about her condition? Had Arlie or Gianna told anyone? She knew before the thought was complete that they had not.

She also knew the time for her secret remaining a secret was winding down. She tried not to panic at the thought of everyone knowing.

Tucker spoke from beside her. "We're having a sleepover. It's the newest adventure."

Libby laughed, although exhaustion made it sound wheezy. "A sleepover? I don't even have any furniture up there, Tuck, much less the flat-screen TV and beer and chips you need to make it through the night."

"Sure you do." He spoke easily. "The new owner of the Albatross offered up any furniture that was needed anywhere and manpower to move it, so you actually have everything up there."

"That's impossible. I was working in there all afternoon, remember?"

"You were working downstairs." Jack was laughing. "They took everything in through the outside entrance. I guarantee, since the furniture was Grandmother's, that you're not going to like it, but it'll work for starters."

"I'm so grateful." Libby knew she didn't have to say anything else. The people at the long table understood—to a certain extent— how she felt now.

Arlie texted her from the other end of the table. Are you all right? Do you need a scrip?

Libby caught her eye and shook her head.

She could do this. She could keep the secret a little longer. She couldn't bear one more thing today.

She and Tucker left the Grill first, stopping by the convenience store near the bridge for snacks, beer and a bottle of wine. A quick run into the Dower House netted clean clothes. Back in the golf cart, she leaned against his shoulder. "I am so tired." It was an effort to get the words out.

"I know." He tucked his arm around her, drawing her closer into himself. "It's been a long, long day."

The apartment was sparsely but adequately furnished. Two bar stools even sat at the counter that divided the small kitchen from the living area.

They took turns showering, then, dressed in sweats, they sat on the floor and leaned back against the front of the couch. "Believe me," he said drily, "it's more comfortable to lean against it than it is to sit on it."

She chuckled, took a sip of wine and hugged her knees, staring sightlessly at the sliding doors at the end of the room. She'd love to do some stargazing to soothe her soul, but her telescope…no, she wasn't going to think about that. Not yet. "If this has been your idea of an adventure," she said lightly, "you need to work on your repertoire, not to mention your delivery."

The look he gave her told her he knew what she was doing. "And here I thought you'd arranged it so I could meet the new EMT from Sawyer. She was pretty cute but looked like she was barely out of high school."

"I know, but you gotta give me credit for trying." It took such effort to talk, even the silly buddy-to-buddy banter that always came so easily.

"Lib?"

Don't ask me. Don't ask me things I don't want to answer. Don't make me tell you things I don't want to tell. But he wouldn't. Surely he wouldn't. He knew she was on her last nerve. "What?" But she didn't look at him. She couldn't.

"What took you so long?"

She frowned. What was he talking about? "Took me so long when?"

"To come outside after the storm. Couldn't you hear us calling?"

He knew.

"I didn't know it was over. There was silence, but I couldn't be sure there wasn't another one coming. Don't tell me you've lived away from tornado territory long enough to forget they sometimes travel in packs." Her laugh was whispery, hurting her throat when she forced it out.

"Not buying it." He was silent for a few beats, as if waiting for her to say something else. When she remained still, he went on. "I'm sure they heard us shouting clear across the lake, but you didn't—or at least you didn't respond. When you finally came out, you didn't even look up. You didn't look anywhere. When I got to you, I'm not sure you knew it was me. It could have all been shock, I guess. I'm no expert. But I just don't think so." He leaned far enough away that he could stroke her hair, still damp from her shower, back from her face.

"The storm's over, Lib." His eyes caught hers and didn't let go. Not under penalty of anything she could think of—not that she had much left to lose—could she have looked away. His hands were so warm, she didn't want to move away from his touch, either. "It's time to talk."

CHAPTER NINETEEN

"I'M REALLY TIRED," Libby said again. "Can't we do this tomorrow?"

Tucker hesitated, still holding her gaze, still stroking the hair that felt like warm silk between his fingers. "I don't think so. We were going to do it after you got mad at me last week, too, but we never got to it." He moved his hand from her hair to her face, shaping her cheek. Her skin was even softer than her hair. "You're the most important person in my life, Lib. Our friendship is the only relationship I've ever had that has never broken down, no matter how much we've both abused it from time to time. But I can feel you slipping away. Not for the first time, but I always waited before. I tried to give you time to come back when you were ready. I'm not doing that now."

She tried to turn her head, but he wouldn't let her, placing his free hand on her other cheek. "I'm not letting you go," he said, "but I don't know what's going on. I don't know how to help."

"I don't need help. I just need us to go on being friends like we've always been."

He shook his head, thinking it might be too late for things to be as they'd always been. Different wasn't always bad, though—it could be downright wonderful. "Still not buying it. My brother distanced himself for years. He hurt Arlie, his son, me and himself most of all. I'm not watching you do the same thing."

"Jack had a huge case of survivor guilt. I don't." She put her hands on his, started to pat them but gripped them instead, her knuckles going white.

He looked at her, seeing the faint white line at her hairline that was her only visible scar from the accident. "Do you still get headaches?"

Her eyes widened for a second. "Oh, you mean from the accident? No. At least, I don't think so. I get…you know…just regular headaches from time to time. Everybody does, don't they?"

Probably, but most people weren't defensive about it.

"Did I ever tell you my mom has anxiety attacks?" he said, keeping his voice conversational. "Scared the snot out of Jack and me the first time it happened. Scared her, too. She thought she was dying, or at least having a humdinger of a heart attack. It was how she met Grant—well, how we all met Grant. It was the year after the accident, and we were at Stonehenge. It was the first time she'd taken us to England, and even though we were all excited, we were suffering aftereffects of the wreck, too. I was ticked off about my hearing. Jack was already buried in guilt and separating himself from everyone as much as he could—I don't remember how we got him to make the trip. Mum seemed fine, at least until she wasn't."

"What happened?"

"She collapsed. Her heart was going a mile a minute, and she couldn't breathe. She was sweating—and this was in England, mind you, and it was drizzling. She shouldn't have been sweating. We yelled for help, and Grant and a few others came charging over. He knew right away what it was, and convinced us all she wasn't going to die right then. By the time he'd talked her—and Jack and me—

off the ledge, he'd also offered her a job in Hylton's Notch. The rest, as they say—"

"—is history." Libby smiled, but the expression was brittle. "What a nice history it is, too. Does she still have the attacks?"

"Not really, because she and Grant both know what to watch for. She insists it's only a 'wee bit' of anxiety, anyway. She calls it a storm in a teacup." He moved, leaning back against the couch again and putting his arm around Libby's shoulders. "So tell me," he said, his cheek against the softness of her hair, "do you have any storms—teacup-size or otherwise—that you'd like to talk about?"

Her inhalation was so deep and long lasting, he found himself breathing with her. "How did you know?" It was that thready voice again, the one that made him feel as if she was slipping away.

It frightened him. "I don't know," he admitted, "but I do know something's wrong." He chuckled, forcing the sound out so she could hear it, since she wasn't looking at him. "And getting wronger, I think, isn't it?"

She nodded. And took another deep breath. And another.

"I have clinical depression and anxiety disorder," she admitted finally. "Neither of them is the teacup variety, I'm afraid. More the why-do-I-have-to-wake-up-tomorrow? type."

"Ah." He nodded, bumping the top of her head. "How long have you had this—these bumps in the road you've chosen to keep to yourself?"

She shrugged. "I'm not sure. It came to light a few months after Dad died. I had a tension headache and, like your mom with the anxiety attack, I thought I was dying. The pain was in my neck, my jaw, all on one side. I called Arlie, who was in nursing school at the time, and she took me to the ER. All the way to Sawyer, I was telling her what to do with everything I left behind, because I didn't have a will." She laughed, although there was nothing funny in what she'd said. "They gave me stuff that helped the headache almost right away, but indicated depression and anxiety were often causes for symptoms like I had. I wasn't surprised—Dad had it my whole life—but I *was* scared. I was afraid I was going to take the same way out of it he did." She shrugged again, just a little lift of her shoulder that Tucker felt against his chest. It broke his heart.

"Then what?"

It was her turn to bump his chin when she lifted her head. "What do you mean?"

"Your dad's been gone seventeen years. What have you done all this time to hide that you have all this going on? And what in God's holy name made you think you needed to hide it from me?"

She moved quickly, getting up and going into the kitchen. "I'm going to get another glass of wine. Do you want a beer?"

"Sure." He didn't, but he thought it would be good to keep his hands busy. He followed her to the kitchen area, taking a seat on one of the bar stools.

He was angry. He was offended. But he had to keep reminding himself this wasn't about him. Whatever anger and hurt he felt could be discussed later, when he could be sure he wouldn't say things that couldn't be unsaid.

"This kitchen really came out nice, didn't it?" she said chattily, setting a bottle and glass in front of him—they'd brought dishes up from downstairs. "I mean, not for more than one or two people, but it's a one-bedroom apartment, for heaven's sake, and thank goodness it's here! Jess and I'd have been at each other's throats within hours if I'd stayed at the farm."

"Lib."

"Do you want something to eat?" She turned her back to open the refrigerator. "I'm sure there's ham here. Maybe some cheese?"

"Libby." He walked around the bar, turning her to face him. The light was brighter in here, coming from a large overhead fixture. She looked even more drawn, her eyes darker, the corners of her mouth tucked in tight. "Just stop. This is me, remember?"

She stiffened. Tucker thought if he'd hugged her then, she'd have broken into pieces in his arms. He reached around her to push the refrigerator door closed, and she flinched away from him, going over to the stainless steel sink. She picked up a sponge and ran water over it, then wiped the sink and the faucet's already spotless surfaces.

"Tell me." He kept his voice low. "You know the rules, even if we never wrote them down. No lies and we don't tell each other's secrets. It's why we're safe with each other. We're *always* safe with each other. Right?"

She stopped moving, then looked down at the sponge in her hands. She wrung it out, twisting so hard the cratered fabric tore between her fingers. "I hide it because I'm broken and I *hate* being broken!" Her voice rose to nearly shrill, then dropped when she went on. "I take medication. Or I usually do. My pills are buried in that mess out there." She swung her arm in the general direction of where Seven Pillars lay in a sharp-edged pile of pieces.

Along with her life. It was in a heap of splintery pieces, too. Tucker understood that. He'd been there the other times she'd survived the wreckage. But she'd been different then. She'd offered more comfort than she accepted. At her parents' viewings, she'd told wonderful stories. At their funerals, she'd offered eulogies to her parents and gratitude to their friends—speaking for both Jesse and herself. She'd been everywhere, like some kind of whirling dervish, helping everyone, working until she was ready to collapse.

Because she probably would have collapsed if she'd stopped. She probably wouldn't have known how to stop crying if she'd ever allowed herself to start. She'd have had the headache she thought was deadly even before she had.

Maybe she hadn't been so different back then after all. He thought of her first comment today. *Who can we help?*

"I'm on the edge a lot." She twisted the sponge the other way. "Sometimes I'll read until daylight, or I'll walk along the lake. I'll call you and then hang up. It's never that you have to come—it's knowing that you would."

"Do you ever slip over the edge?" Jack's mother had done just that. She'd taken enough pills to make sure she'd never wake up, locked herself in the garage and started her car. She'd left her toddler asleep inside the house.

"No." But Libby sounded doubtful. "I've had a few anxiety attacks that were pretty intense, and a lot of the time, I really don't care if I wake up or not. But I never want to do anything to myself."

He didn't believe her—something new in their relationship. "So," he said, "why did you stay in the carriage house after the storm was over?"

She tossed the sponge into the sink—no, *threw* it, so that it bounced off the tall arc of the faucet and landed neatly on the sink's rim as if she'd aimed it there. She stood with her back to him, gripping the edge of the counter.

"It was black dark in there. No windows. I had a flashlight, but the battery only lasted long enough to get us into the room. It was black dark," she repeated, "and silent. I couldn't even hear Elijah and Pretty Boy breathing. And I thought we were dead. I don't... I don't know if it actually *was* silent in there or if that's just what I heard because the pressure was gone. I thought—" She stopped on a gasp.

He stood behind her and pulled her in close, kissing the top of her head. He started to tell her it was all good, that she didn't have to talk about it, but stopped himself; instead, he waited. Until he realized that she was crying. Even though it happened in trembling, noiseless agony, the dam of her grief had finally broken.

She turned, burying her face in his shoulder, and he held her even tighter. If pain hadn't been such loud company in the room, he might have wanted to explore the pleasure he felt with her in his arms, but this wasn't the time for that. He felt his own pain and anger begin to ebb—it wasn't time for them, either. Not now. Maybe it would never be.

They stood unspeaking for a time, during

which Elijah and Pretty Boy came to settle in around their feet. Tucker wasn't that much of an animal person, even if everyone he knew seemed to have pets who loved shedding on him. But he knew the cat and dog sought to comfort the person they loved best.

That was what he wanted to do, too.

He took his handkerchief from his pocket, glad at least a few of his grandmother's admonitions about being a gentleman had stuck with him, and pushed it into Libby's hand.

When she spoke again, her voice was so low he could barely hear it. "I thought my mom would come and find me. I mean, if I truly *was* dead, I knew she would. And then I heard her voice. You remember her voice, Tuck, and how beautiful it was?"

"I remember." His eyes burned and he clamped his teeth down on his lower lip. "What did she say when you heard her voice today?"

"I don't know. I don't even know that I actually heard any words, just her voice, but I remembered her telling me when she was alive that I would never really be alone because she would always be with me." Libby drew back enough to look into Tucker's face. Her eyes were swollen, her face tear streaked.

She was so beautiful.

"But then," she said, resting her palms against his shoulders, "I heard *your* voice. And I knew it wasn't time for me to go."

"I DON'T BELIEVE I've ever had ham and cheese on rye for breakfast." Libby frowned at her plate.

"First time for everything." Tucker set coffee in front of her. "I plan to take credit for fixing your breakfast the day after the tornado and won't let you forget it. Also, take a look at your watch. I know the tearoom doesn't open until eleven, but you've only got a couple of hours, and the kitchen downstairs here isn't nearly as well equipped as the one in the house was."

She set down the sandwich. "Excuse me?"

"The plant's closing today so people can either clean up their own damage or help their neighbors. Jack and Arlie and I will be working right out here, and I wouldn't be surprised if others showed up, too. I think it would be really bad if we didn't have anywhere to go for lunch and coffee when we needed it. Not only that, you have people who eat at Seven Pillars every day—for a while, they're just going to have to make do with the carriage house."

"I wasn't going to open for a while." *If ever. I had my run. Maybe it's time to go another direction.* "We don't even have a name for it yet."

He raised an eyebrow. "You need a name to cook?"

"I don't have anything to cook with," she objected. "Other than the makings for coffee and tea, I don't even have beverages."

"Then you'd better get a move on, hadn't you?"

A few hours later, Gianna had gone to the supermarket and the bulk foods store and returned with enough supplies to keep the tearoom going for a week. Marie Williams had dropped Kendall off to help. Holly was setting tables. Libby and Neely were using both the downstairs and the upstairs kitchens and working nearly as seamlessly together as they had in Seven Pillars.

At eleven o'clock, the first of the customers came in. By eleven thirty, the tables were full. Much of the reason for the full house was probably curiosity, but Libby didn't care. If people hadn't been there before, she wanted to give them reason to come back.

She avoided looking at where the house had been as much as she could, resolutely putting thoughts of her telescope, her mother's Windsor rocking chair and her new commercial stove out of her mind.

At twelve thirty, her doctor came in for lunch. Bryce Kelly peered into her eyes, took her pulse and her blood pressure, and wrote new prescriptions for her medications. Libby asked him if this was a house call and he said no, but he wouldn't turn down an extra-large piece of dessert. He tossed in a lecture about how she should have let Arlie write her an emergency prescription free of charge.

At one o'clock, the door opened and the Parsons family entered. At least, Alice, Mari and the baby came in—Dan and Gavin waved and went right back out. Alice plopped Carson into Libby's arms. "Here. Take a break and give me one at the same time. What can I do to help?"

"You can cut this cake," Holly called from the kitchen. "Libby says I cut crooked, and Neely says the pieces are too big." She came over. "I'll take a break, too, and sit and look at this baby for a few minutes. I just love the bald ones."

"And we were both right, too," Neely interjected, her laughter coming from the other room. "Don't use up that baby before I get out there. I haven't held one in a while."

At the end of the day, Libby put the bank deposit into the money pouch that had started the whole wakefulness episode two nights before and sent it on its way with Neely. The Parsons family hugged Libby and Tucker goodbye and got back into their van. "We're going far enough south that the kids have to wear sunblock, spending three days and heading back," said Alice. "The nice thing about homeschooling is that you don't have to be home to do it."

"Don't tell Charlie that," said Tucker, although his nephew and Gavin had become fast friends while helping with cleanup that afternoon. Charlie was probably already trying to fast talk Jack and Arlie into homeschooling him.

Libby handed the baby over reluctantly. "He could stay here, you know. You'd enjoy your vacation more, and you could stop in on the way back and pick him up."

Alice laughed and hugged her again. "You're not equipped, and he has an unsophisticated palate. Any hint of formula and he screams like he's being poisoned."

"Mom, that is just gross. You have heard of TMI, right?" Gavin rolled his eyes in the way mastered by kids who'd reached middle-school age.

"We'll stop in when we come back through," Dan promised, latching Carson into the car seat. "We're going fishing."

Libby and Tucker waved as the van drove away, then Tucker said, "Are you ready?"

She hoped her eye roll was as good as Gavin's. "I may never be ready for anything again, Llewellyn. What are you talking about?"

"You've avoided looking at Seven Pillars all day—easy enough to do because you were pretty busy. Are you ready to look and make decisions? Your insurance guy said to call whenever you want to talk to him."

She wasn't even close to ready. Ten years of her life and countless tangible memories of the twenty-four years before it had been in that house. But Tucker was there beside her just as he'd been the whole time. If she was going to face it, now was the time.

She'd known there was a large tent over the site. She'd seen the truck bring it and put it up. She *hadn't* expected so much of the wreckage and the resultant rubble to have been removed. The ground she walked on was raked clear. At one side of the house lot, incongruently pristine, stood the white gazebo. Inside its railings, chairs and two round tables were arranged haphazardly, as if the people who'd worked on the property today had taken breaks there.

"Everything that could be saved or restored is in the tent," Tucker warned. "Jess and I made choices on what was repairable and what wasn't. I'm sorry if we were wrong."

"You weren't wrong. I couldn't do it." She stopped outside the entry flap of the tent. "I don't even know if I can do this."

His arm came around her, and she leaned into him, thinking she'd been doing a lot of that lately. Too much, probably, especially since her body tended to sing wherever he touched her.

She straightened. "Let's do it. It can count as an adventure."

It could have been worse, she thought later, getting ready for bed in the apartment over the interim tearoom. Albeit not much. Her new stove had been untouched, protected by the old chimney that had remained standing. A small safe holding important papers and her mother's few pieces of jewelry had done its job. No dishes, tables or chairs from the dining rooms had survived, but the buffet that had sat too close to the kitchen's swinging doors was in good shape, the punch bowls it housed unbroken.

The staircases had both been destroyed, and virtually nothing had been salvaged from upstairs, including anything to wear. Libby, who'd spent her entire adulthood avoiding shopping for clothes, was going to have to make up for it now.

Unbelievably, the stained-glass window on the front stair landing was completely intact. Wherever she lived next, she'd take that window with her.

It was the first time since that morning that she'd considered the possibility that she might not rebuild the tearoom. The knowledge that Neely would buy or lease the remaining building and property in a heartbeat and probably make a greater success of the business than Libby had lingered at the back of her mind all day.

How could it be that she was even thinking of giving up her dream? Was her life like a weird transit of Mercury that happened every ten years or so? At four, she'd wanted to be either a ballet dancer or, when she was with Tucker, a firefighter. At fourteen, she'd longed to be an astronaut. At twenty-four, she'd left the farm and bought Seven Pillars with the conviction that she would stay there forever.

Even then, she hadn't expected her forever to be very long.

She stepped out onto the little balcony outside the bedroom, Elijah winding around her ankles, and looked out at the lake. How peaceful everything looked in the quiet of past midnight.

There she was. There was Venus, lighting Libby's way as she always had. Standing in her temporary home wearing her borrowed clothing, with her hair still damp from being washed with borrowed shampoo, Libby remembered the conversation with Nate about taking ownership of his life. She thought she'd done that, but she hadn't. Not really. She'd only had a long-term lease on that life she'd chosen, and it had just run out.

It was time to start over.

CHAPTER TWENTY

HE HADN'T SEEN it coming. Not in a million years.

"You wouldn't leave the lake." Tucker reached for Libby's hand as they walked the cart paths at Feathermoor. They'd come to play golf, but the course had been so crowded in the late afternoon that they'd walked instead.

It had been a long week since the tornado. He'd spent part of every evening with her, helping with cleanup in the carriage house after long days in the tearoom. With each day, she seemed to slip further and further away no matter how hard he tried to bring her back.

"I might." She looked toward the sun as if inviting its warmth. "I've never lived anywhere but here. Moving away would be an adventure, and you know how I feel about adventures."

"But what would you do? Where would you

go?" He knew he sounded like an overprotective father. Too bad about that. He did feel protective, but he didn't feel at all fatherly.

"I don't know." She faced him, and he saw the emotional damage wrought by the past week. She was pale, the thin skin under her eyes rounded crescents of darkness. Even her hair seemed dull. He wondered if it would feel less silky under his fingers. "I can't face any more loss. The way I see it—at least for right now—if I don't have anything, I can't lose anything."

At the park bench beside the sixth-hole tee box, he sat down, pulling her with him.

"I don't know what to say," he said. Unable to stop himself, he stroked her hair away from her face. It was still soft. "Other than I don't want you to go." *Unless it's with me.* But that wouldn't work. He didn't want to leave the lake. He still wanted the wife, kids and house.

But life had grown more complicated in this season of adventures and stolen kisses under the stars she'd shown him.

"I'm not sure I want to go, either." She pointed. "The trees are so beautiful here. I'm glad the tornado didn't come through Feathermoor."

Their phones made the percolating sounds of incoming texts at the same time. Libby got to hers first. "It's Holly and Jess inviting us to dinner at the farm." She looked at the time. "In a half hour."

He looked at his phone, too. "Right. Since when does Jesse Worth ever invite anyone to his house?"

Libby grinned. "Since Holly Gallagher started running roughshod over him. Isn't it great?"

"Want to walk over? We can sneak right through the vineyard from the seventh hole." It had been a long time since he'd been on the back forty of Worth Farm. Bordered by Cottonwood Creek, which ran through the golf course, the land was one of the prettiest locations in the area.

Boys and girls alike had ridden bicycles as fast as they could on the cow paths that led to the barn. It had been the scene of pickup baseball games, hide-and-seek, class picnics, fishing and swimming parties. Those had ended when Crystal Worth died, but Tucker and Libby had still walked back there to go swimming beneath the little waterfall or walk in the woods. She hesitated, then nodded.

The farm was L-shaped, due to the acreage that Chris Granger had bought for Sycamore Hill Vineyard and Winery. Part of the land was sloped and wooded so that neither the winery nor Jesse's house was visible from the bottom of the L. The cow paths were still there, although they were faint. A tractor-wide lane, lined by evergreens, was an easier way to walk to the house.

Jack and Arlie were already at Jesse's when they got there. The dining room table was set for six with what Libby said was her mother's favorite china. She said the silverware and glasses were unfamiliar, though. Tucker had been a bachelor long enough to think Jesse had probably broken the old glasses and lost the flatware. If a person used it with disposable dishes, he tended to throw away the forks along with the paper plates.

"Let's sit." Holly, always animated, fairly pulsated with energy. "I don't have enough faith in my cooking to chance letting it get cold."

"I helped," said Jesse mildly. "I got the dinner rolls and the pie at the Amish bakery."

"Good man." Tucker offered a fist bump.

"I got the wine." Jack puffed out his chest

a little, and his brother thumped it. "Well, I did."

Arlie was pouring ice water into glasses. "Settle down," she admonished. "You're among friends and relatives." She looked around, smiling at Jack. "And soon some of the friends will be relatives."

"Does this mean I have to be nice to him when he's my brother-in-law?" Holly elbowed Jack.

"I don't think so," said Tuck. "He might get used to it, and we can't have that. On the other hand, you should be really nice to me because I'll be your sister's brother-in-law."

Libby grinned at her brother. "I take it from this conversation that we don't have to be nice to anybody."

"Well." He snagged Holly's hand when she came to stand beside him. "About that."

It was as if the world stopped moving. Arlie stood stock-still. Jack put his arm around her, pulling her into his side. He took the water pitcher from her hand and set it on the corner of the table. Libby clasped her hands in front of her and Tucker stood behind her, draping his forearms over her shoulders. He felt her tremble against him and drew her closer.

"We talked to Mama this afternoon," said Holly. "You know how she always wants me to have a boyfriend, even when she doesn't come right out and say it. That's why Arlie's been her favorite ever since she and Jack got engaged."

"That's only one reason." Arlie looked smug even as laughter lit her golden-brown eyes. "There are lots of others."

Jack slipped a hand lightly over her mouth. "Go on, Holly. I'll control her. For a minute, anyway."

Holly sighed heavily. "Thank you, Jack. Anyway, Jess heard about me needing a boyfriend, and what do you know? He was looking for someone, too." She stopped and extended a hand toward Jesse, inviting him to continue.

"I wanted someone who would talk so I wouldn't have to." Jesse let go of Holly's hand and put his arm around her. "As you know, if you don't answer her, she just keeps right on talking. After a while, you kind of get used to it, and the house is too quiet when she's not in it." He reached past her to pick up one of the wineglasses that sat beside a plate. "Today, she brought glasses when she came. A few weeks ago, she brought spoons and forks and stuff and told me I couldn't take any of the knives out to the clinic anymore." Jesse did his best to look haunted. "I think she means to stay."

Arlie spoke into the waiting silence. "Mama won't go for it." She shook her head solemnly. "Jack and I don't really want to get married, but Charlie and Mama said we had to."

"See?" Holly gazed up at Jesse. "I told you."

"Okay, fine." Jesse laughed, something he didn't do nearly often enough. "We're getting married, too. We decided it even before we called Gianna." He reached to tug Arlie to him. "I love your sister," he promised, "more than anything, ever, and I always will."

Holly reached across the table to grasp Libby's hands. "And I love your brother. More than anything. I always will."

While the food cooled on the table, everyone hugged everyone else. Jack poured the wine, and each person toasted the happy couple with varying degrees of hilarity and sincerity. By the time they sat down, they agreed that in one way or another, they would all soon be related.

When Tucker and Libby left the farm, they rode as far as the golf course with Jack and Arlie, where they picked up Tucker's car. "You look happy," he said, looking over at her. "And yet you don't."

"I am," she assured him, "for Jesse and Holly both. But my brother was my last commitment, the only thing that really held me here. Whatever I want to do, wherever I want to go, there's nothing holding me." Her smile was wobbly. "I even forgive my dad. Jesse's happy, so I could do that. Have you forgiven yours?"

"Pretty much. I talked to Jack about it, and he said being happy was up to us. If we go on blaming our father, it'll hurt us, not him. So I think I've let it go."

"That's good. You and I will both be better for it."

"We will." He hoped. He wasn't sure how much faith he had in the power of forgiveness.

He pulled in beside the carriage house and they got out of the car, moving to the bench beside the lake. He wanted to ask her how she could think of leaving him, but he didn't.

As deep as it was, until the past year, he'd always been a part-time friend. Maybe it was her turn for that.

"I still don't know where to go or what to do," she said, "but I'll figure it out."

He tugged her close and pointed at the sky, at the stars that were appearing from between the clouds. "Look up there. Find Venus. Ask her."

LIBBY GAVE UP baking for the restaurants after the tornado and discovered she didn't miss it at all. After a couple of days, she asked Neely if she'd like to buy the business and wasn't surprised when the other woman agreed immediately. "But I'll lease the property from you. I don't have children to leave it to, so I'd rather not own it, but as soon as you find where you want to live, I'll sell my condo and move into the apartment."

"Do you want to rebuild the house?"

Neely shook her head. "The space in the carriage house is actually more convenient for the tearoom business, don't you think?"

Libby nodded agreement. "It is." She tilted her head. "Did you ever think when you came to work for me that you'd end up in business for yourself?"

The other woman laughed, looking years younger than the sixty-something Libby knew she was. "Never. I guess it's just one of those things that happen when you least expect it."

"That's it!" They said it in unison, then broke into a very unmusical version of Cole Porter's "Just One of Those Things."

"It couldn't be any better," said Libby. "Everything about it, including the tornado that changed everything, was just exactly that. You can even put some kind of explanation on a sign."

Libby sold Neely the stove, feeling a pang because she'd bought it with the winnings of the gambling adventure she'd had with Tucker.

She bought a little blue SUV, the first brand-new car she'd ever owned, and named it Venus. She drove it to the Dower House to show Tucker, stayed for dinner with him, Arlie, Jack and Charlie, and announced she was leaving the next day on a road trip.

Tucker exchanged a glance with his brother. "I'll go with you," he said. "I can work from the road."

"Sure," Jack agreed quickly.

"Better yet," said Charlie, "Uncle Tuck can stay here and *I'll* go with you."

Arlie tugged at his hair. "Not happening, big boy." She smiled at Libby, their eyes meeting. "Want us to watch Pretty Boy and Elijah for you?"

"If you would."

"You'll be back in time for the wedding rehearsal?" Arlie didn't look worried.

"Like I'd miss it. I have to practice up to catch the bouquet the next day."

"Where are you going?" Tucker *did* look worried.

"Up to see Alice and Dan first, then to North Carolina to see Nate and Mandy for a couple of days. They've been asking me to come down, and there's no better time." She met Tucker's concerned gaze. "Besides, I've heard Venus looks great from the beach."

He reached to cup her cheek. "You'll pocket dial me in the middle of the night if you need me?"

Tears flooded her eyes before she could stop them. "I will. I promise."

Tucker went with her when she left, to go for a ride in the new car. "I know you don't need me to kick your tires or set the right stations on the radio, but I'll do it anyway."

They drove for a while, parked at the carriage house and went to sit by the lake, where they watched the water and made desultory conversation.

"I won't get in the way of you taking your trip," he said when they got up to leave, tangling his fingers with hers, "but I need to tell you something before you go, so you can think about it. Or not."

"Okay." She pulled free and picked up a flat stone, tried skipping it on the lake's smooth surface, and shrugged when it sank without even a little hop.

"Like this." He side-armed a stone and it bounced three, no, four times over the dark, glassy water. "You try."

She shook her head. "It's not something I need to do. I'd rather watch you. So, what is it you want to tell me? You already kicked my tires and programmed my radio, including one station I'll never listen to even once because it's so bad."

"Let's do this first." He sounded nervous, which was unusual for Tucker. But when he pulled her into his arms and covered her lips

with his, she understood why. It wasn't a
buddy kiss, or a brotherly one. It wasn't even
one of the warm, yearning ones they'd done
some experimenting with since the night of
their birthday party.

No, this was a kiss of passion, of possession, of…she wasn't sure what, but she was
powerless to resist it. Her arms went around
his neck, and she stood on her toes to gain
more access. To get nearer, and nearer yet,
because nothing was close enough.

Her heartbeat—or was it his?—thundered
in her ears. He tasted of coffee and spear-
mint and all that was familiar and beloved.
And more. The sound of the lake calmed the
rush of need, yet left urgency unsated between them. They kissed again. And again.
And yet again.

Her breath came shattered and uneven, and
she didn't care. Her toes ached and burned
with the effort of standing on them, but she
would have let them break rather than disconnect from Tucker's touch.

This…oh, Lord, yes, this was why she'd
lived when she hadn't cared if she did or not.
Why the viper had never reached her.

She didn't know whether it had been twenty

seconds or twenty minutes when he raised his head, separating them before she wanted him to, and set his hands on her hips to put space between them. She relaxed enough for her heels to touch the ground. Although she couldn't feel the earth at all. It was still moving.

For a minute, neither of them spoke. He didn't let her go, and she didn't pull away. When he rested his forehead against hers, she reveled in the connection. Rejoiced in how he made her feel in every cell of her body.

It had been kisses. It had been, in the vernacular of high school days, making out. It had been...

"That, Llewellyn, was an adventure." Her voice sounded airy—no surprise, since she *felt* pretty airy from the top of her head to her aching toes.

"It goes with what I have to tell you." His voice was thready, too. They were standing near one of the old-fashioned post lamps that lit the lakeside walking path, so she could see his eyes. The warmth in them washed over her, and she waited.

"I love you," he said, and he didn't sound funny anymore.

She lost her breath, then gained it back almost as quickly. Of course he did. They loved each other. They always had. "I know," she said. "I—"

"No." He laid gentle fingertips over her lips, raising his index finger to tap the end of her nose. His voice was low and calm, and it strummed her senses like she was a stringed instrument. "No, I mean I'm *in* love with you. You're the one I want to be with forever, whose kids I want, who I want to share the four bedrooms and two baths with." His fingers left her mouth to tunnel through her hair. "Well, maybe just one bedroom."

She closed her eyes, and for a moment she was silent. She turned her head to press her lips to his palm. "Tuck." She could feel it. The panic was rising up to eclipse the joy, just as it always did. "I don't—"

"No." He interrupted her again. "I don't want you to say anything now. I just want you to think about it. We're best friends. There is no better basis for being in love than that one." He shrugged so that her hands slipped from his shoulders to his chest. "I know now that being in love—as over the moon as Jack and Arlie are—that's what I want." He smiled, and his eyes smiled, too. "It's what I feel, but if you don't feel the same way…well, we'll go on like we were before."

"You know I love you, too?" she said, unable to get her voice above a whisper. "I don't think I can be what you need, but I will always love you."

"I know."

At the door of the carriage house, he kissed her again. "Be careful driving. Let me know where you are. Okay?" He looked upward. "I'm counting on Venus."

She nodded and hugged him hard. "Stay safe, Tuck." She stepped inside before he could reply, then laid a hand on one of the panes in the French door. He placed his fingers against the glass on the other side, and she fancied she felt their warmth. She smiled and blew him a kiss.

It was time to go.

CHAPTER TWENTY-ONE

ALICE INVITED HER to spend the night with them when she visited the next day. "I'll even let you get up with Carson," she promised, moving around the kitchen. "There's plenty of milk for him in the freezer."

Libby looked down at the baby in her arms. He grinned gummily at her, and she grinned back. "You're giving me a new appreciation for bald men," she told him. "Tucker wouldn't stand a chance next to you."

"You need to have a few of your own." Alice set tea in front of her and slid into the chair across the table. "I know, I know." She held up a hand when Libby started to speak. "Not everyone should have children. Not everyone should be married. However—" she smiled at Libby and the baby she held, her expression tender "—you're not everyone, are you, Libby? You're dying to get married, dying to have kids. And when anyone mentions Tucker Llewellyn, you light up from the inside out. Did you know that?"

"I'm not surprised," Libby said drily.

"And he reacts to you the same way."

Carson whimpered, and Libby rocked from side to side, humming under her breath as she remembered the kisses beside the lake last night. Remembered what he'd said to her. What he'd asked her to think about.

As if there was a snowball's chance in Hades she could think about anything else.

"There's more to it." How could she explain the secret without telling it? It was all well and good that Tucker knew—sort of—but she wasn't ready to put it on a résumé. "I have baggage—"

"Do you know I've been taking antidepressants since I was twelve?" Alice's voice was pleasant and conversational when she interrupted. She stretched an arm across the table. The scars on her wrist were faint but easily distinguishable. "That was when I did that. My brother found me on my bedroom floor. I ended up in a psych unit because...well, because I was twelve years old and I tried to kill myself. When I was sixteen, I tried again, with pills—stomach pumping is not a process I recommend, by the way. I met Dan when I was in college. He was in grad school answering a suicide hotline. One night during finals, he talked me off the virtual ledge. He's been doing it ever since."

"How did you—" The baby whimpered again and Libby nuzzled his sweet-smelling neck and rocked once more. "Where did you find the courage to take a chance? Not just with your own life, but with Dan's. With the kids'?" It was a horrible question, but she needed to hear its answer.

"I don't know," Alice admitted. "To begin with, probably from Dan and from whatever fortitude of my own I had, because it *takes* strength just to get from day to day, Libby— you know that. I was terrified to have kids, just like you are, and as soon as Gavin and then Mari were old enough to understand what they needed to do if Mommy went off the deep end, we sat them down and explained. We'll do the same thing with Carson." Tears rolled down her cheeks, and she scrubbed at them with a napkin. "I hate that I've given Gavin the kind of responsibility he has—in the end, it's up to him to try to watch after the little ones if I have what we euphemistically call a visit from Uncle Petrie. Please don't ask me where that came from—I have no idea."

Libby laughed, although she had tears on her cheeks, too. She'd cried more in the past two weeks than she had in the eighteen years before them. "I call it the viper. I think I like Uncle Petrie better."

"Feel free to borrow him." Alice refilled their teacups. "It's not smart that we keep it to ourselves as much as we can, but that doesn't alter the fact that that's exactly what we do. I just want to be Alice, not Alice *with depression*. I don't want the kids having to explain 'Mom has a problem' their entire lives." She met Libby's eyes. "Know you can call me any time of day or night. And don't hang up before I answer. I will know the same thing about you. Okay?"

"How did you know that? That I hang up when I call?"

"Because I've done the same thing so often. But when I was sixteen, I stayed on the line when I called my sister at the last minute to ask her to tell our parents how sorry I was. It saved my life."

Libby sipped her tea, missing her tearoom

but glad she'd sold it at the same time. "What made you say something now?"

"Two reasons. One, we're by ourselves, so I knew I wasn't going to be letting any cats out of any secret bags—Carson won't say a word. Two, because something is different. I don't know what it is, but I imagine—and hope—it has to do with Tucker."

"It does," Libby admitted. "He knows now, and he says it's okay. But I don't want him to spend his life pulling me off that ledge you mentioned." She chuckled drily. "Remember that pact I told you about? I was the one who wanted adventure, not him. I'm just not ready to subject anyone else to the viper, especially someone I—" she hesitated "—love. Someone I love."

Carson got demanding then, and Libby handed him over to be fed.

"So, will you stay tonight?" asked Alice. "We could talk about what you just said."

"No. I'm going to the beach for a few days. I want to see Nate and Mandy's house, and I have some thinking to do. Including about what I just said." She needed to talk to Venus for a bit, too.

Libby smiled, feeling lighter somehow after what she'd just shared.

"YOU ARE ABSOLUTELY useless this week." Jack stood in his office, hands on his hips, and glared at Tucker. "You're better at meetings than I'll be if we live to be a hundred, and yet you completely blew that one for the simple reason that you weren't listening. Do you have anything even close to a viable explanation?"

Tucker would have responded in kind except that his brother was absolutely right, and, no, he didn't have an explanation, viable or otherwise.

"I'll tell you what—" Jack smiled his thanks when the office manager brought in a carafe of fresh coffee and two cups. "Patty, you probably just saved his life."

"That's what I was hoping for," she said, grinning at them both. "Even if he is useless, which the whole office staff heard you say, we like him."

"I like him, too," said Jack, "but don't let *that* get around."

When the door closed behind her, Tucker

reached for the cup of coffee Jack poured and said, "What were you about to tell me?"

"That if you're real nice to Patty, she'll probably get you a ticket to Wilmington and you'll get there in time to ride home with Libby."

When Tucker started to answer, Jack talked over him. "I'm not being completely unselfish when I say that. The truth is that Arlie's worried sick about Libby, although I'm not sure why, and since our wedding is coming in a little over a week, the last thing I want is for Arlie to be worried about *any*thing. The other truth is that I'm a little worried about you, too. You haven't exactly poured your heart out to me, for which I'm grateful, but you've been both grumpy and stupid ever since Libby left the other day. What that means is, if you make sure she's all right, we won't have to worry about either of you."

"She's all right." He hoped. His phone hadn't rung in the middle of the night, and their texts had been brief but reassuring. They'd shared jokes and early morning temperatures and messages from the Parsonses and Nate. Still, he kept hoping for a *Wish you were here*, which hadn't happened yet. "But I'll go."

He reached for the phone on Jack's desk and dialed the office manager. "Hey, Patty?" He listened for a few minutes and hung up laughing. "Not that my life is an open book or anything, but the plane leaves Indy at 4:35 and I should hurry. She's already printed out my boarding pass."

By nine o'clock that night, he was in a motel on Topsail Island—Patty had taken care of that, too. Since he hadn't let Nate know he was coming, he hadn't wanted to show up at his house, although he'd fed the address into the GPS and driven past it. No lights had been burning. He started to text Libby to let her know he was there but changed his mind. Saying he'd give her time to think and then reneging on it probably wasn't the best way to make a sweeping right turn in a relationship.

He fell asleep easily, which was unusual for him in a motel room, but the sound of the waves was a powerful lullaby.

He didn't know what time it was when the phone rang, but when he said, "Hello," she didn't answer.

SHE COULDN'T SLEEP even though she'd been in bed for at least a half hour. She was sweaty in her short cotton nightgown under the expensive pearl-gray sheets, even in the cool guest room of Nate and Mandy's house.

The last week had been…whoa, something. Libby had agreed to sell her business. She'd spent time on the farm where she grew up that had left her with a vague longing she couldn't quite identify. She'd taken a road trip by herself and spent hours sitting and staring at an ocean—something she'd never done before but had loved every minute of.

She'd thought about her future. And feared it. Although she'd always liked being single, it wasn't how she wanted to spend the rest of her life. She was done dating nice men like Jim Wilson who didn't want a committed relationship. Or men without jobs or cars or ambition to have either.

She was more tired than usual. That must have been what was disturbing her on this peaceful night in this beautiful place. It explained why she couldn't settle into the comfortable bed in the guest room. It certainly didn't have to do with the last evening she'd spent with Tucker. With the kisses and caresses that even now sent shivers of longing racing through her. It wasn't the memory of the words he'd spoken that were both a balm to her broken spirit and a whole bucket of hope that perhaps she could love a man without ruining his life. She wasn't used to buckets of hope. Too much of the time, she wasn't used to hope at all.

But she'd never fallen in love with her best friend before. She'd never heard him say he loved her, too—at least not the way he'd said it while he was holding her and kissing her until they were both light-headed.

With the bucketful of hope that was keeping her awake, she dared to consider something else: maybe she could even have children. Alice had done it. Ellen Curtis had done it. Most mothers weren't perfect, were they? Although Crystal and Gianna had come close.

She would marry Tucker if that was what he wanted. They'd have four bedrooms and two baths and a little boy with blue eyes and blond hair they would name Curtis to keep Tuck's mother's maiden name in the family. If they had a little girl, they could call her Crystal, or maybe Darby—Libby had always loved Tucker's middle name. Maybe they could adopt children, too. That had been what she'd wanted back in her slumber-party days—a houseful. Having one nice but very quiet brother had made her long for more siblings. She'd relished the noise of the Gallagher house. She'd love to have it in a home of her own.

The waves crashed below, soothing and ultimately cooling. She held tight to the hope as she fell asleep.

It had been weeks since she'd had the dream. The bad one when she knew she was dreaming but couldn't escape it. She'd been in England with Tucker the last time, and what a comfort it had been to be brought to wakefulness by her own real-life hero wearing flannel pajama pants.

She'd been vigilant about her medications since then, other than the blip when the tornado came through and left her life flat and shattered in its wake. Although she'd often felt close to that edge she'd talked about, her sleep had been largely undisturbed. The viper had indeed been more like a storm in a teacup for a while.

So why was it happening now, when she

could hear and even smell the sea? She could, and yet…and yet there was her mother, so silent and still there in the dining room of the farmhouse, where she'd slept in a rented hospital bed. She was smiling a little, but her hands were cold where they rested on the covers. Libby had tried to wake her then. She tried to wake her now. *Don't go, Mom. Please don't go.* When Jesse came into the house in the dream, he knew Libby had failed to take care of their mother. Her father stayed in the barn because he knew it, too.

Then it was the accident. The bright lights and the screaming and Libby trying to shout, *Dave, watch out, watch out.* But she was too late, always too late.

The barn appeared in the vision she knew was a dream but couldn't escape. Tall and painted white instead of the red it was now, it didn't look threatening at all that morning. The grass was green and the scent of spring was in the air, even stronger than that of the sea as she walked toward the big building to start the morning milking. She didn't like April, but it was a beautiful morning. She stopped to pick a few of the golden daffodils that lined the driveway, taking time to scratch the barn kittens under their fuzzy chins. They followed her to the big doors, tumbling about her feet.

Libby tried to stop the girl in the dream, screaming *Don't go in* at the top of her voice. Experience had taught her that her dream voice wasn't loud at all, but still she tried. Her throat hurt with the effort.

The dream always ended then, with her a trembling mess of quiet hysteria reaching for her phone, but this time was different. This night at the beach, the freight-train sound of a tornado drowned out the omnipresent music of the sea. She reached, trying to find Pretty Boy and Elijah, then remembered they weren't there because she was only dreaming. She would wake up soon, whether she wanted to or not.

And the bucket of hope would be empty.

She didn't mean to dial his number, but since she had, she'd wait for his voice mail to pick up so she could hear his voice. Even that helped; it was always a calm in her personal storm. She wondered, lying there with her head and her heart both thumping so loud they were physically painful, if this was how

Alice had felt when she called the suicide hotline the night Dan answered.

Tucker's line didn't go to voice mail. Instead, he answered, his voice low and sleepy. "Hello?"

She didn't say anything, just waited breathlessly for him to hang up.

"Hey," he said after a moment, sounding more wide-awake. "I'll be right there."

And he was, meeting her on the house's front porch and hugging her hard before they went down to the shore, their hands together.

An hour later, he'd seen her at her absolute worst, because now besides the agony of heart attack symptoms, panic and wishing death upon herself, she cried, too. Which was all his fault—he'd made her break her no-tears rule.

She had done it all in the presence of someone whose respect and affection she never wanted to lose. Not only was her secret out, but it was all the way out. It was dark and messy and scary, a trip through hell she'd never wanted anyone to travel with her.

When the attack was over, which didn't take as long as it felt, they sat silent and wrung out on the dark beach. The waves still crashed and sang merry tunes into the night.

She got up from the sand, moving to his other side and sitting back down. He wouldn't be able to hear her over the roar of the ocean if she sat on the side of his deaf ear.

"I'm sorry." Her voice was scarcely more than a whisper because her throat still hurt. She leaned close so that her mouth was near his ear. "I never wanted you to see me like that. It doesn't happen often, but I can't always foresee it. Sometimes the viper just sneaks in without warning and I become this crazy person." She hated admitting it, just as she'd hated telling him the secret in the first place. Her thought found voice. "I hate this. It's as if now that you know the worst about me, that's what I am. I'm not good old Lib anymore—I'm just a friend you have who's defined and controlled by clinical depression and its ugly stepbrother, anxiety."

He turned his head just enough to look at her from the corner of his eye. And wink.

She grinned back at him, although it shocked her. What could possibly be funny on this night?

He put his arm around her, tucking her head into the hollow of his shoulder. "Do you think less of me because I can't hear out of my left ear?" he asked. "You've been making allowances for it ever since it happened. My guess is you never even think about it. You just do it. Right?"

She nodded.

"Even though I'm somewhat controlled by this partial deafness? I'm not really your best friend after all, you know, just a guy with limited hearing and beautiful eyes." He hugged her closer and kissed the top of her head. "Not to mention probably the sexiest body on the lake."

She drew back to meet his eyes, rejoicing in the laughter she saw there. "Did you really just say that out loud?"

"I did." He grinned. "But we can keep it to ourselves." He brought her up close, his lips capturing hers. "I missed you."

"I missed you, too, Llewellyn." She threaded her hands through his hair. Thick and smooth and shaggy, it needed cutting. She loved it that way. "How did you know?" He would understand her question. She didn't need to spell it out any more than that.

He hesitated. "I'd love to say I had some kind of sixth sense about you or that I knew in my heart when you needed me, but it wouldn't be true. Arlie was worried and I was driving Jack crazy, so he sent me after you."

She gaped at him, widening her eyes in pseudo-shock. "You mean I was giving you credit for all kinds of intuitive powers you don't have? Why, I am so disappointed."

He laughed and pushed himself to his feet, pulling her up after him. "What a whopper. You've always known you were the intuitive half of the Worth-Llewellyn combination. You've even referred to me as a brick wall a few times, if I remember right."

"Oh, at least a few."

He took her into his arms, fitting her in close so that no empty spaces remained between them. "I'm an unintuitive class clown who can't cook unless you count stopping at the bakery or calling out for pizza. You skate better than I do, swim better—you even walk on ice better. Probably if we had a flat tire, you'd change it better than I would. You're the best friend anyone ever had." He let go with one hand long enough to point at the sky. "I can never find Venus, so I need you to show her to me every day for the rest of my life. In return—"

He stopped to kiss her, and she thought that

she mustn't ever again think about dying, because heaven was wherever he was.

"In return?" she whispered when the kiss ended. She opened her eyes and looked into his.

"In return, I'll always answer the phone. I'll always show up. Just like Jack and I are equal partners at work, I'll be equal partners with you in life. None of this fifty-fifty stuff. I want a hundred-hundred and I want it with you. I will love you every day, every minute of the rest of our lives, and I will always, always be your best friend."

"What about the days one of us doesn't have a hundred to give?" she asked. "Times like tonight when I had nothing. Times like when you slide right under the car on the ice."

"Then we'll help each other up, won't we? Every time. And we'll be back to a hundred-hundred in no time."

She had to force herself to breathe. Was this really happening? "There's one more thing."

"Let's hear it."

"Kids. At least two or three. Possibly four. What do you say about that?"

"Maybe one more bedroom and one more

bathroom when we build that house back there by the creek on your farm." His palms shaped her cheeks, his fingers finding her hairline and stroking gently. "What do you say, good old Lib? Want to extend the adventure pact into a lifetime plan?"

She slid her arms around his neck and rose to her bare toes in the sand. "I do."

And overhead, Venus beamed.

* * * * *

If you fell in love with Libby and Tucker, don't miss these stories from USA TODAY *bestselling author Liz Flaherty.*

BACK TO MCGUFFEY'S
EVERY TIME WE SAY GOODBYE

Available now from
Harlequin Heartwarming!

Get 2 Free Books,
Plus 2 Free Gifts—
just for trying the Reader Service!

Get 2 Free Books,
<u>Plus</u> 2 Free Gifts—
just for trying the Reader Service!

YES! Please send me **The Hometown Hearts Collection** in Larger Print. This collection begins with 3 FREE books and 2 FREE gifts in the first shipment. Along with my 3 free books, I'll also get the next 4 books from the Hometown Hearts Collection, in LARGER PRINT, which I may either return and owe nothing, or keep for the low price of $4.99 U.S./ $5.89 CDN each plus $2.99 for shipping and handling per shipment*. If I decide to continue, about once a month for 8 months I will get 6 or 7 more books, but will only need to pay for 4. That means 2 or 3 books in every shipment will be FREE! If I decide to keep the entire collection, I'll have paid for only 32 books because 19 books are FREE! I understand that accepting the 3 free books and gifts places me under no obligation to buy anything. I can always return a shipment and cancel at any time. My free books and gifts are mine to keep no matter what I decide.

262 HCN 3432 462 HCN 3432

Name _____ (PLEASE PRINT)

Address _____ Apt. #

City _____ State/Prov. _____ Zip/Postal Code

Signature (if under 18, a parent or guardian must sign)

Mail to the **Reader Service:**

IN U.S.A.: P.O. Box 1867, Buffalo, NY. 14240-1867
IN CANADA: P.O. Box 609, Fort Erie, Ontario L2A 5X3

* Terms and prices subject to change without notice. Prices do not include applicable taxes. Sales tax applicable in NY. Canadian residents will be charged applicable taxes. This offer is limited to one order per household. All orders subject to approval. Credit or debit balances in a customer's account(s) may be offset by any other outstanding balance owed by or to the customer. Please allow 4 to 6 weeks for delivery. Offer available while quantities last. Offer not available to Quebec residents.

Get 2 Free Books,
Plus 2 Free Gifts—
just for trying the Reader Service!

HARLEQUIN® *Romance*